# Antique Living

EarthCent books by the author in reading order:

Destiny: Union Station
Date Night on Union Station
Alien Night on Union Station
High Priest on Union Station
Spy Night on Union Station
Carnival on Union Station
Wanderers on Union Station
Vacation on Union Station
Guest Night on Union Station
Word Night on Union Station
Party Night on Union Station
Review Night on Union Station
Family Night on Union Station
Book Night on Union Station
LARP Night on Union Station
Career Night on Union Station
Last Night on Union Station
Independent Living
Soup Night on Union Station
Assisted Living
Freelance on the Galactic Tunnel Network
Con Living
Empire Night on Union Station
Space Living
Traders on the Galactic Tunnel Network
Orphans on the Galactic Tunnel Network
Swap Night on Union Station
Slow Living
Artists on the Galactic Tunnel Network
History Night on Union Station
Bits of Anarchy
Double Living
Bits of Flower
Synergy on the Galactic Tunnel Network
Substitutes on Union Station
Bits of Catalyst
Elder Living
Royals on the Galactic Tunnel Network
Deal Night on Union Station
Intellectual Property
Bits of Business

# Antique Living

Book Eight of EarthCent Universe

Foner Books

978-1-948691-97-0



Hardwick, Massachusetts.

# One

Bill squared his shoulders before entering the kitchen of the small cafeteria where he'd first learned how to bake under the tutelage of Harry, a member of Flower's independent living cooperative. "I will not let Flower put me off again," he repeated under his breath like a mantra and then pushed through the swinging door.

"Hey, Bill," Jake greeted him. "Can you help me out with lunch? Flower told me that it's Brynlan's birthday and I can never get the biscuits hard enough or salty enough for him."

"Harry isn't here? Flower said he wanted to meet me."

"His wife asked him to help with a field trip she organized for the students in the documentary production course she teaches for retirees. He should be back any time."

"All right," Bill said, taking an apron down from its hook and tying the strings. "But rather than biscuits, I'll make him some hard pretzels. Verlocks like baked goods that would break everybody else's teeth, with salt crystals so big that even Jorb would spit them out. When you make something special for him, don't worry about whether or not the other aliens can eat it. Besides, anything that hard and salty is going to have a shelf-life of years."

"Good point," Jake said. "I feel kind of guilty about asking for help when I turned you down the last time you needed a shift covered in your café, but Beth wanted me to babysit."

"It's not my café, I just manage it for the School of Government, and my contract with Flower is almost up." Bill located the canister of whole wheat flour and threw a few cups into a bowl without sifting. "Brynlan will like it even better if there are little bits of rock from the millstone in there."

"Somebody still uses stones to grind flour?"

"I'm using the organic flour from the Old Way movement," Bill explained. "Razood and Jorb helped build an old-fashioned mill on the ag deck where the groups we're transporting to Earth Two live while they're on board. Come to think of it, Brynlan sourced the millstones for them. Verlocks are big on stone in general."

"It's funny how the advanced species have more respect for low-tech occupations than we do," Jake said. He began slicing vegetables for the lunch platter since all the aliens enjoyed a good carrot spear or cucumber chip. "Do we have to make a separate dessert for Brynlan, or is there something he likes that everybody can try?"

"Didn't the peach harvest begin? Instead of pretzels, I'll do a couple of peach cobblers, one with white flour, one with the whole wheat, and we'll add the peach pits to the whole wheat one."

"Now you're just playing with me."

"I'm serious," Bill said. "And if we triple, no, quintuple the salt in the cobbler with the pits, it will have a good shelf life if he doesn't want to eat it all at once."

"Do you think Brynlan would eat a whole casserole dish full of peach cobbler?" Jake asked as Harry entered the kitchen.

"If he likes it," Harry said before realizing that his assistant had been talking to Bill. "Did you see the peaches on the back counter? Flower sent two bushels this morning."

Bill laughed. "I didn't see them, but my subconscious must have smelled them. I'm making dough for Brynlan's cobbler. Do you want to do the one for everybody else?"

Harry shook his head. "I'm already over my working limit for the day. Flower reminded me in the lift tube. You have another forty minutes before lunch, and if you save the dessert for the end, call it an hour. Why don't you handle the cobbler for the other aliens, Jake? Start by throwing a dozen or so peaches in boiling water for a minute to make them easy to peel."

"Do you think that will be enough peaches?" Jake asked.

"That's just for your guys," Bill said. "Brynlan wouldn't peel anything if he was doing the cooking."

Harry took a seat on the high stool out of the way and watched as the two much younger men made their cobblers. Bill would have finished first, but he had to wait on Jake for the extra peach pits, so they both put their cobblers in the oven at the same time.

"We need to talk," Harry said when Bill hung up his apron and Jake went back to the basic lunch prep.

"That's why I'm here," Bill told him. "But if Flower asked you to persuade me to extend my contract managing the School of Government café for another year, you're wasting your breath."

"I know better than to get between a man and his dreams, and you've given Flower two years. But she just made me an offer I can't refuse, providing you'll come along for the ride. Maybe I'm being selfish, but I think it's a fantastic opportunity for you."

"I thought you said when you turned seventy that you would never start another business."

"And I stand by that," Harry told him. "It will be your business, and in four months, you'll have a café to go with it since that's what you want."

"What kind of business has a café to go with it?" Bill asked.

"Specialty catering. Strictly desserts, not sandwiches and cafeteria food. And it will be an educational journey because Flower wants us to make desserts from Earth's history, as far back as we can find good recipes."

"Why does Flower want a catering service that does antique desserts?"

"You hit the nail on the head," Harry said. "I didn't stay for all the details, but your wife was in the meeting so you can ask her when you get home. Flower Entertainment is reviving—it's hard to describe exactly—but around the turn of the twenty-first century, there was a popular show on old-fashioned television that followed a group of antique appraisers around the world. People could bring in their family heirlooms and the experts would tell them about the history of the items and give an estimate of how much they might bring at an auction."

"Why would anybody buy antique anything?" Bill asked. "I thought that antiques were stuff that's so old that they're not good for anything anymore."

"The usual meaning of the word is old things that are worthy of being collected and preserved," Harry explained. "When we stop at Earth next month, Flower is going to hire specialists to do the appraisals. We'll produce a show at every stop until we get back to Union Station, and then it will move to the Empire Convention Center and start a circuit of Stryx stations."

"So I would work with you for the next four months reviving old desserts from Earth to cater the shows, and when we get to Union Station, I'm all square with Flower and I can open my own café." Bill thought for a moment. "I'll have to talk it over with Julie."

"That's fine. Remind her that I'm an old man and I need help. Speaking of which, we can run the catering out of this kitchen, and if Jake wants to start working full-time hours instead of just doing lunch, we can fill his time."

"I'm game for that," Jake said. "Working with old recipes sounds like fun, kind of like what I did at the Bits bakery when I was fooling around." He looked up from the cassava root he was chopping into thin chips for Jorb, the only one who ate it raw because he enjoyed the cyanide aftertaste. "But do you think we'll be able to produce authentic desserts from the Middle Ages if we bake them in a modern Dollnick kitchen?"

"Good point," Harry said. "We'll have to see what the recipes call for, and if necessary, I'm sure the members of the Old Way movement will let us use one of the wood-fired brick ovens that Razood built for them on the ag deck."

"And I'll ask him if he can bang out a wood stove in his blacksmith shop that we could install in the back of the kitchen to test small batches," Bill said. "He offered to make me one for when I open my café, so I could just take it with me."

"There was a wood stove in the basement of the old house we owned back on Earth and I'm sure it was cast rather than forged."

"Razood likes doing foundry work, but he doesn't get much excuse. I'll drop by Colonial Jeevesburg on the way home and tell him."

"What about the smoke?" Jake asked.

"I guess we can have a stove pipe, but I doubt it's needed," Bill said. "I've set enough accidental fires in this kitchen to know that the ventilation system can deal with anything."

"I appreciate your confidence," Flower joined the discussion via an overhead speaker grille, "but in this case, I believe a stove pipe would be the best approach. I'll see about buying firewood at our next stop."

"I've watched the Old Way bakers work that giant brick oven Razood built them, and they mainly burn twigs and old branches pruned from the orchards," Harry said.

"Iron stoves perform better with split hardwood," the Dollnick artificial intelligence informed him. "It's a renewable resource and there are trees on the majority of worlds where we stop, so it won't be a problem."

"And you're done asking me to manage the school café for another year?" Bill asked.

"I'm already scouting potential locations for you to open your new café."

Bill groaned inwardly, but he didn't have the heart to tell the pushy artificial intelligence that he'd rather do it himself.

"So we're all set," Harry said. "I'm going to spend the afternoon at the library going through the oldest cookbooks they have and see if I can come up with a couple of dessert ideas to get a running start." He peered through the transparent door of the oven and added, "Brynlan is going to love that cobbler. If there's any butane left in the brûlée torch, you might want to char a few of the pits where they're standing proud, just as an extra treat."

"Char the peach pits," Jake said. "Got it."

Around twenty minutes after Harry left, the alien intelligence agents who were hosted on board Flower as part of a deal with EarthCent began trickling into the cafeteria. Bill brought out the tray of vegetables and found himself pulled down into a chair by Jorb's tentacle.

"What's your hurry?" the Drazen asked. "You haven't eaten with us in a week and you're missing out on all the good gossip."

"The School of Government ran a lunch series with guest lecturers from the Conference of Sovereign Human Communities and Samuel asked me to be there to make sure nothing went wrong," Bill explained. "I was going to sit down after all of the food is on the table."

"Jake can bring the food out," Razood said from Bill's other side. "Today is a big deal."

"It's Brynlan's birthday," Bill confirmed. "We made him a special peach cobbler."

"Verlocks have birthdays every year, that's not what I'm talking about," Jorb said. "It's a new business opportunity for everybody, and it's going to be big."

"Here he comes now," Razood said, and to Bill's surprise, the Frunge and the Drazen both rose from the table when the Grenouthian hopped into the room. "Is it a sure thing? Did you make a paw print on the dotted line?"

"We're in business," the Grenouthian director told the younger aliens. "Pre-production starts immediately. Bill, I hope you aren't busy the next four months because we'll all be scrambling."

"I just agreed to cater some sort of show for Flower," Bill said, glad he had an excuse to opt out of whatever the intelligence agents had cooked up. Then the coincidence of the four-month timeline sank in, and he asked, "Is this related to the antiques thing?"

"The *Antiques Tunnelshow*. I came up with the title myself."

"I'm going to be the consulting Frunge expert on bladed weapons," Razood said. "And one of the broadcasts will start with a visit to my forge where I'll be training some blacksmiths from the Old Way movement."

"Rinka will be the Drazen expert on music boxes and any choral arrangements in manuscript form that turn up," Jorb said proudly of his girlfriend. "I'm going to be a unit director for the immersive recording."

"You're making a documentary about the show?" Bill asked the director.

"I'm responsible for the entire shooting match until we hand it off to the Empire Convention Center at Union Station," the Grenouthian said, brushing some imaginary dust off the brilliant white fur on his left arm. "I'll edit the recordings into a standard-length show while we're in the tunnel between stops, and the Grenouthian Network will broadcast them in primetime spots. We'll shoot a behind-the-scenes documentary at the same time, and I'll release that after the first season when everybody is hungry for more *Tunnelshow* content."

"You seem pretty confident that it's going to be a success," Bill said.

"How can it not be?" Yaem asked. The skeletal Sharf slid into the seat across from Bill and set a gift-wrapped package on the table. "It's got antiques and auction appraisals. I'm going to consult on animation cels."

"Is that for Brynlan?" Jorb asked, indicating the package.

"Just something I picked up for him on the Bazaar deck."

"We never bring presents for birthdays," Razood complained. "You're making us look bad."

"I could let you bring out the peach cobbler," Bill suggested.

"Avisia is buying a card," Yaem told them. "We'll all sign it."

Both Jorb and Razood relaxed visibly.

The Vergallian station chief whose cover job was running a finishing school for teenage girls entered the cafeteria with Forgath, the Horten spy who'd now been with Flower for a little over a year. "We passed Brynlan in the corridor," she said, opening an envelope and placing on the table a card featuring an erupting volcano. "He'll be here in two minutes."

"Where's Lume?" Bill asked, referring to the Dollnick station chief.

"He's still on Union Station," the Grenouthian director said. "Flower sent him with Dewey to finalize the details for the *Antiques Tunnelshow* handover with the manager of the Empire Convention Center there."

"I'll sign the card for him," the Horten said.

"No, let me do it," Yaem said. "I've got his signature down pat."

"We'll do it the usual way," Avisia said. She took a gold fountain pen out of her three-feather Baa's bag and scrawled Lume's signature on the back of the envelope. Then she handed the pen to Yaem, and the envelope quickly went around the table, with each of the intelligence agents contributing a forgery of the Dollnick station chief's signature. When the envelope got to Bill, he tried to pass it on, but Jorb insisted that he give it a go.

"Brynlan is going to walk in any second and see us practicing Lume's signature," Bill said, laboriously trying to copy one of the other forgeries, all of which looked identical to him. "And I'm useless at this."

"With gifts, it's the thought that counts," Avisia said, and gave Yaem the card. "This time we sign our own names."

Brynlan was just shuffling in the door as the Grenouthian director added his signature to the card, and Avisia put it back in the envelope and gave it to Yaem to stick to the gift wrapping.

"Surprise!" all the aliens shouted in English.

"I am surprised," Brynlan said, the quick pace of his usually ponderous speech testifying to his emotional state as he accepted the present offered by the Sharf. He held it near his ear and gave it a shake. "Radiobarite?"

"Bill, go in the kitchen," Avisia ordered. "Flower, how could you let a human get so close to Radiobarite? You know how sensitive they are to radiation."

"It's shielded in lead to keep all of the good stuff in," the twenty-thousand-year-old artificial intelligence responded promptly. "The gift-wrapping is to cover up the dull grey color."

Brynlan pulled off the card and examined all the forged signatures on the back of the envelope. "The first one is the best," he announced. "Avisia?"

"Yes!" the Vergallian declared and pumped her fist. "I took an elective course in forgery since so much royal business in the Empire of a Hundred Worlds is done on parchment."

"You could be the expert on the *Antiques Tunnelshow,*" Forgath suggested.

"That won't be necessary," a synthesized voice said from the doorway, and M793qK entered the room on his hindmost set of legs. The towering Farling, who resembled a beetle blown up to the size of a bull, continued rubbing out words on his speaking legs which were instantly translated into Humanese by the pendant he wore on the front of his carapace. "The core staff of technical experts will come from my ReproMan business, where they have been underemployed creating artworks for the replica market. Which reminds me, Bill. I'll have an errand for you when we arrive at Earth."

"I'm going to have to start coming to lunch every day again," Bill said. "I seem to be the last person on Flower to hear about anything."

"If you hadn't been avoiding me since that little accident in our *All Species Cookbook* testing lab last month, you could have been part of the planning for the *Antiques Tunnelshow,*" M793qK said. "It was my idea."

"You're interested in antiques from Earth?"

"I have a few in the vault, but more to the point, it's a chance to build a new entertainment franchise in cooperation with Flower, the Empire Convention Center, and the Grenouthian network. The publicity for ReproMan won't hurt, either." The Farling turned his enormous multifaceted eyes on the package that Brynlan was clutching to his chest. "Radiobarite?"

"It's warm," the Verlock said gleefully. "I'll use it instead of a hot water bottle."

Jake brought out the catering cart with entrees that suited the tastes of the aliens, which put all conversations on temporary hold. Then Jorb manned the bar and made drinks and Jake returned with both glass casserole dishes of peach cobbler on a tray. He placed the one with the blackened pits peeking out of the crust directly in front of Brynlan.

"This is the nicest birthday I've had in a century," the Verlock said. "But does this mean that everybody is going to expect presents from now on?"

"I noticed the Radiobarite in the bazaar and suggested to Flower that buying it for you would benefit the public health," the Farling doctor said. "It's a one-off."

"Win-win," Flower added through an overhead speaker grille.

The Grenouthian director nibbled a little of the regular peach cobbler to be polite and then cleared his throat. "While you're all enjoying your desserts, I'd like to sketch out my vision for the *Antiques Tunnelshow* and how it's an opportunity to get in on the docking deck of something really big. You should think of the three months that Flower hosts the show as a beta test for the real thing, which will start when we hand it off to the Empire Convention Center and the Grenouthian Network. Our primary job is to create a formula that can be repeated on a circuit of Stryx Stations, and eventually on location at worlds and orbitals around the tunnel network and beyond. If done correctly, I can see this show lasting for ten thousand years."

"Does that mean you'll be leaving Flower at Union Station?" Bill asked.

"Not if they offer me fifty points in the production. I had enough of living on the road doing regional theatre around the tunnel network, and I didn't even have a second income from Grenouthian Intelligence to make it lucrative. But if our assessment of the market is accurate, anybody who contributes significant intellectual property to the *Antiques Tunnelshow* can expect to be mentioned in the prayers of their distant descendants who will still be receiving royalties long after this fork I'm holding is worth five creds as an antique."

"What sorts of ideas are you open to?" Jorb asked. "The way Flower described it to me, people will bring in their antiques, and appraisers will give them inflated valuations for what the items might bring in a good auction. It sounded pretty straightforward."

The Grenouthian director shook his furry head in mock despair. "Use your imagination. If we do nothing but appraisals and reaction shots, the only people who watch will be antique collectors."

"How about a segment where you ask participants to try their hand at some craft involved in the arts, like forgery?" Avisia suggested. "They could win a prize by beating the show's expert, or even fooling an appraiser."

"Excellent idea," the Grenouthian said.

"And somebody needs to point out to Samuel what an opportunity this is for the Human Empire," M793qK said. "Unlike sponsoring the Elder Documentary Festival, which we all know was in name only, the *Antiques Tunnelshow* will provide ample opportunities for the imperial family and ministers to appear on the galactic stage."

"The Human Empire doesn't have an imperial family," Bill objected.

All the aliens let out groans or sighs, and the Farling rubbed out, "The most important thing that those of you who are friends with young Samuel McAllister can do is get him to drop that ridiculous First Administrator sobriquet and start using his proper title. How does he expect the rest of the imperial families to take the Human Empire seriously if he isn't willing to act as a figurehead?"

"I'll work on him, but it won't be easy," Jorb said. "Humans obsess about the literal meaning of words, probably because their vocabulary is so limited."

"You think we should convince Samuel to start calling himself the emperor?" Bill asked. "They'll kill him."

"No," Flower said through an overhead speaker. "They'll line up to get into a restaurant where he's eating, push their children to apply for the Human Empire's School of Government, and dress their little girls in whatever Rose is wearing. Trust me on this, I know Humans. The gap between what your species says you believe and what you really want is big enough for a Class Three Dollnick colony ship to pass through."

# Two

"It can't be that much," Rinka said, pushing the programmable cred back across the desk to Julie. "There's been some mistake."

"I double-checked the sales numbers and everything adds up," Julie said. "We told you that your lullabies guaranteed to put human babies asleep would be a goldmine. Flower says you have to do something with the money, or the value will start to decay because it exceeds the maximum you can keep in Stryx creds."

"But it's—" the Drazen let out a sob, and tears appeared in her eyes. "Jorb's family will have to accept me now. It's like waking up and finding out that I'm from a family who are stakeholders in a consortium instead of a poor choirmistress from the wrong side of the river."

Julie smiled at her friend's joy, but then she remembered the rest of Flower's message and her shoulders slumped. "Flower had a couple of suggestions about investments for your excess earnings. I mean, she makes it sound like different options, but they all amounted to the same thing."

"I can't walk around with enough on a programmable cred to buy a space yacht," Rinka said. "What does she suggest?"

"Buying points in the documentary about the *Antiques Tunnelshow* that the Grenouthian director has already started shooting at our preparatory meetings," Julie said. "I don't understand how the different financing levels work, but she says you have more than enough to be listed as a producer."

"How many points is that?"

"It depends on how much you decide to put in, but Flower said that a hundred thousand creds per point is a bargain."

"And does that gain me the option to invest in the show?" Rinka asked, suddenly all business. "A documentary is all well and good, but if the show is as successful as Jorb says it's going to be, that's generational wealth."

"Flower?" Julie asked.

"Points in the *Antiques Tunnelshow* are ten times as expensive as the documentary, and there are only a handful available due to all of the strategic partnerships," Flower said. "We've been using equity in the production to grease the wheels, and I'm not sure whether M793qK has already pledged what's left of our allocation."

"I thought it was a Flower Entertainment production," Julie said.

"It is, but getting the Empire Convention Center and the Grenouthian Network on board required giving up a majority stake," Flower said. "I checked with M793qK and there's a single point left."

"I'll take it," Rinka said.

"Are you sure?" Julie asked her. "It seems like a huge gamble, and that's more than half of your earnings from the lullabies."

"Half of her royalties as of four cycles ago less the standard reserve for returns, though I don't imagine there will be any," Flower said. "I project that she'll be receiving regular payments of only slightly diminished amounts for years to come."

"How about taking a break and we'll go to the Blue Tea Café to celebrate," Rinka suggested. "Then I'm going to go shopping and buy something to surprise Jorb."

"I wish I could, but I have a meeting with Yaem and the Grenouthian Director on the con deck to plan the layout for the show," Julie said. "Maybe you'd like to come along now that you're an owner."

"No, it's enough that I'll be making appearances as a Drazen music specialist. I'll leave the organizational work to the professionals."

Julie exited the lift tube on the con deck, which included ten theatres, each with a five thousand seat capacity, and an expanse of open deck space as large as the bazaar. She immediately felt lighter, as her weight was now about ninety percent of what it was on the residential deck where she and Bill lived. Yaem, who had been so busy since taking over as the executive producer for Flower Entertainment that the other aliens from Harry's cafeteria clubbed together to write his reports for Sharf Intelligence so he wouldn't be replaced by a new spy who might not fit in with their culture, waved as soon as he saw her. She started walking toward him, being careful not to scuff the chalk lines he'd been making on the deck.

"Where's the director?" Julie asked when she was within speaking distance.

"He's coming," Yaem said. "Dewey just returned from Union Station with Lume and a Human woman to audition as the show's host."

"I hadn't thought of that. We talked about a host in the last meeting, but for some reason, I thought we'd hire somebody from Earth."

"My understanding is that Lena is from Earth, but she left there over a year ago to join Flower with her boyfriend, who was employed by the Human Empire. Then they both decided to give Union Station a try."

"Oh, she'd be perfect," Julie said. "Lena is a couple of years younger than me, but she's been doing on-air interviews since she was twelve on the Children's News Network."

"We wanted to find somebody as young as possible due to your aging—difficulties," the Sharf concluded after a brief hesitation. "If the show looks like a success, the Grenouthian network will offer her a fifty-year contract. The first five decades are critical for establishing an audience, and none of the other species will understand if the hosting spot looks like a game of musical chairs."

"Fifty years is a long time to do anything. She'll be in her early seventies by then."

"Is that an issue? Flower told me that the median age of the Human females on the independent living deck is just under seventy-three, and most of them are still active. I know that the Grenouthian director will be entrusting one of the documentary camera units to Irene, who must be around that age since she qualifies for Independent Living. If Lena stays in the job that long, I'm sure she'll have the routine down to where it only takes her a few hours a week."

Julie thought for a moment. "If nobody has brought it up yet, you might want to postpone mentioning the fifty-year contract until you get her hooked on doing the show. It could be a bit off-putting otherwise."

Yaem's eye stalks lengthened like a cartoon character going over a cliff, and then they snapped back into their sockets. "Humans are strange," he said. "If I live another five hundred years, I'll never figure you out."

The lift tube door opened, and the first one out was Dewey, an artificial person who had been accidentally created by the community on Bits and had moved to an android body with immersive-star looks after working several years as a robot librarian on Flower. Then came Lume, walking backward in front of Lena and Scott, while gesturing with all four arms at once as he explained something about the layout of the con deck. The Grenouthian director came last, shepherding a pair of immersive cameras through which he was recording the moment for posterity.

"Be careful of the chalk lines," Julie called to them. "Yaem has been working on a layout."

"Not me," Yaem said. "The chalk lines were here when I arrived."

"Then who made them? Did Flower send a bot?"

"I think I see your answer flying under the horizon," Dewey said and pointed with his whole hand to where something had just appeared at the point where the curvature of the deck faded into the high ceiling. The shape grew larger at a speed that might have won an old aerodrome race in the early part of Earth's twentieth century, and then M793qK braked hard and dropped to the deck, his wings disappearing into his carapace.

"Triage," the Farling physician declared as if he was continuing a conversation rather than flying up and dropping into their presence. "When the ticket holders exit the lift tubes with their items, they'll be met by our production staff which will assess them and their treasures for broadcast suitability. I chalked in the outlines of barriers for crowd control."

"Do you expect violence?" Lena asked.

"Not until later, when they reach the appraisal tables and find out that they invested their life savings in fakes," the Grenouthian director said. "I'm planning three camera units, plus the documentary crew, and we don't want them wasting their time on subjects who are too camera shy to answer a few questions about how they came to own the item and what it means to them."

"Will I be expected to interview all of the people chosen to have their antiques appraised?"

"Our appraisers will draw out the Humans about the stories behind their items," Yaem assured her. "We hope to attract a minimum of a few hundred visitors for the initial show, rising to over a thousand a day by the time we reach Union Station. But ninety percent of the show will focus on the most valuable items and the most compelling stories. In addition to the introduction and the wrap-up, it's the human-interest stories where you can add the most value."

"We have three months to experiment with the format before handing the show over to the Grenouthian Network and the Empire Convention Center," the director said. "At that point, you'll be the face of the *Antiques Tunnelshow*."

Lena frowned. "I agreed to come and talk to you because I thought it was an opportunity to interview aliens about their lives and family histories, but this is starting to sound more like one of those horrible gameshows that are so popular on Earth."

"Our goal is the galactic audience, not Humans. As soon as the show moves to the circuit of Empire Convention Centers on Stryx stations, you'll be interviewing sentients from all over the tunnel network and beyond. While you'll be working live, the show will be created in the editing room, and we plan to split the time evenly between valuable objects and those that say something about the cultures that produced them."

"And every show will include a cautionary tale about counterfeiting and greed," M793qK rubbed out on his speaking legs. "We also promised the Stryx to do a segment on Galactic Historical Sites and the illegal trade in protected artifacts once a cycle."

"The Stryx are involved?" Lena asked, obviously impressed.

"I negotiated with them for discounted Stryxnet access for Flower Entertainment," Lume said. "While we're all convinced that the show will be a great success, startup costs for any production are high, and including a public service announcement seemed like a small price to pay to save fifty percent on bandwidth charges."

"Why did you become a journalist?" Yaem asked Lena.

"Because I wanted to make the world a better place, and I thought that if people were accurately informed about what was going on they could reach better decisions."

"Better decisions about what? Where to live, what to eat, what kind of career to pursue?"

"I'm not sure I understand what you're getting at," Lena said slowly. "I guess my ultimate goal was to help people live their best lives, but at the Children's News Network, we were also pushing back against all the stupid stories on the 24-hour news channels whose only purpose was to make people angry about something. If a tree fell in the forest, you could be sure that the media supporting the government would blame it on the opposition, and the media supporting the opposition would blame it on the government. Everything was about politics and special interest groups."

"If they wanted the real news, they'd read the Galactic Free Press," Dewey observed.

Yaem's eyestalks swiveled toward the artificial person and then refocused on Lena. "My point is that by hosting the *Antiques Tunnelshow* you'll be helping people live their best lives, and other sentients as well. Don't forget that entertainment is the biggest trade category on the tunnel network, and that means it also draws the greatest interest from investors and criminals alike. I'm not sure if we can work investigative journalism into the show on a regular basis without bringing everybody down, but you'll be building up an expertise in the field that you can use for independent journalism."

"If you're saying that I can continue freelancing for the Galactic Free Press, I want to see it written in my contract," Lena said.

"Then it's settled," M793qK rubbed out on his speaking legs. "Flower has informed me that her bots are bringing a patient to my clinic who is suffering from a thoracic aortic dissection, so I have to rush to surgery. I should have him back on his feet in ten minutes if you need me." The Farling took a couple of steps on his hindmost legs, and then dropped parallel to the deck so he could employ more limbs as he skittered rapidly to the lift tube, where a capsule was waiting with open doors.

"Why is the Farling doctor involved with the show?" Scott asked as soon as the lift tube doors closed. "I thought he was busy with galactic politics and trying to maneuver his way back into the Hierarchy."

"M793qK brought us the idea for the show and he's providing employees from his art reproduction business to help with authentication," Yaem said. "Will you be returning to work for the Human Empire? I read a report that I supposedly wrote detailing your efforts to establish a recordkeeping system for their personnel last year, but if you and Lena are a couple, you'd be a great fit as our personnel manager while the show is on Flower. If everything works out, I'm sure you could continue in that role for the Grenouthian Network or the Empire Convention Center after the first three months."

"Do you mean that after the first three months, I won't be working for Flower Entertainment?" Lena asked. "What happens to that quarter-point in the production that Lume promised me."

"Technically, the show will still belong to Flower Entertainment, but the rights will be licensed to the Grenouthians and Dollnicks," Lume explained. "If you sign a long-term contract before we transfer the rights, we could lock in your terms for the next century."

"I won't live that long."

"Then the next fifty years," Lume said, and Julie couldn't help marveling at how the Dollnick station chief had turned what she thought would be a hard sale into an attractive proposition. She also couldn't help wondering how much equity Lume had received in the show for negotiating the deals on Union Station.

"I'm not saying I'll do it, but let's pretend that I did and walk through the basics," Lena said. "Right now, all I have are some chalk lines on the floor and the assurance that I'll be making the galaxy a better place by interviewing people about their prized possessions."

"I think we'll get a much greater variety of people than you might expect," Yaem said. "Some of them will bring family heirlooms, but others will be bargain hunters who think that they scored the deal of the century at an estate sale or a thrift store. We're also open to inviting museum curators willing to exchange a little publicity for bringing in a priceless artifact, and our contract with the Stryx to educate viewers about protected historical sites and items will allow you to interview government representatives from the tunnel network species, and perhaps beyond."

"I didn't realize that the Stryx enforced any rules away from the tunnel network."

"A limited subset," Dewey told her. "The Stryx protect Galactic Historical Sites throughout the galaxy, sometimes by simply hiding them, and they police artificial intelligence everywhere to prevent rogues from setting up robotic factories creating war bots and attempting to exterminate the biological species again. Stryx science ships also keep an eye on the research carried out by the most advanced species to prevent them from accidentally rupturing the space-time continuum in a way that could prove destructive to their neighbors."

Julie noticed that the Grenouthian director was still capturing the conversation with his floating immersive cameras, and despite his insistence that documentaries be unscripted, she suspected that some of the speeches she was hearing had at least been penciled in.

"Now, where were we?" Yaem asked himself, studying chalk lines on the deck. "Yes. During triage, the attendees will be assigned to different areas of the show floor, such as furniture, tools, jewelry, ceramics, and items of general historical interest. We'll want to have a group of people waiting with their items as background scenery for our featured appraisals, and every show will include a few reaction shots from the crowd, especially if they're more lively than the owners of the item."

"But I won't be participating in those appraisals," Lena interjected.

"We'll save you for when there's an interesting background story or something in question beyond the mere authenticity or value of the antique," Yaem told her. "In the meantime, you can circulate and use your interviewing skills to prospect for anybody with a good story to tell, even if their item is nothing special. We plan on starting with two days on the Human weekend to get enough content for one show, though we may expand to three days if there's enough demand for appraisals. All scheduling issues are subject to change after the handover to the Grenouthian Network."

"But they may be willing to stick with what suits you," the Grenouthian director told Lena. "You're fortunate to be standing on the shoulders of a giant, and I imagine Aisha was right around your age when she started with *Let's Make Friends*."

"I grew up watching that show," Lena said. "I was hoping to interview Aisha when we visited Union Station, but she prefers to let her show speak for itself."

"Julie is Flower's representative for all issues involving the show, so feel free to contact her any time of day or night if you have any questions," Yaem continued. "The Grenouthian director will always be on-site, supervising the camera crews. As the producer, I'll be at the meetings, but I'm afraid my schedule is too busy for me to be on set."

"Will the specialists from Earth be able to appraise the alien antiques that the people living on open worlds will bring in?" Lena asked.

"Excellent question," the director said. "For the initial shows, we'll be encouraging guests to bring antiques from Earth, primarily family heirlooms that they chose to take with them when moving to alien worlds. Members of the advanced species living on Flower have agreed to fill in as specialists in areas where they have knowledge. If you need an alien's opinion in a hurry, in addition to myself, Jorb and Razood will be operating cameras and always available."

"Why isn't the show starting with alien specialists?" Lena asked. "It seems like an odd omission."

"I'll be honest with you," Yaem said, crossing his bony fingers behind his back in keeping with his understanding of humanity's legal code. "When M793qK approached us with the idea for the show, my first thought was to sell the rights to the Grenouthian network as a packager and never get involved with the production. I'm sure they would have gone for the idea, especially with the Empire Convention Center stepping up as a sponsor in exchange for the publicity of hosting the first season in their facilities. But M793qK and Flower insisted we do a pilot season on board and start with the emphasis on Humans."

"Have you ever stayed at an Empire Convention Center?" Lume asked Lena. "They pride themselves on providing the premiere home-away-from-home for travelers of all the tunnel network species and beyond. You can be assured that once the show moves to their facilities, the Humans will make up such a small percentage of the guests that you'll wonder why you ever thought aliens are interesting."

Lena glanced up at Scott, who didn't look any more impressed by the Dollnick's argument than she was. "If I'm going to have a role in managing personnel," he said, "I would want to start advertising for alien specialists now, so I'd have a chance to review their backgrounds and make offers long before we get to Union Station. I can't imagine that top-level appraisers will be able to leave their current positions without giving notice."

"There's always a buyout," the Grenouthian director told him. "Business is business, and nobody expects to keep a star employee if a once-in-a-lifetime opportunity comes along. Where were you working before you jumped to the Human Empire?"

"Uh, I had just been fired and Larry, Phil's son, hired me and my buddy on the spot," Scott said.

"Tell her that the *Antiques Tunnelshow* is more than an entertainment property, it's a diplomatic effort that has already won the backing of EarthCent," Flower said over Julie's implant.

"I'm told that EarthCent is backing the show as a showcase for humanity," Julie improvised. "Why don't I bring you by Human Empire headquarters and we can sit down and talk with Samuel and Vivian about ways you can leverage the hosting role to benefit mankind."

"You're laying it on thick," Lena said. "Leverage?"

"Sorry. I spend most of my day talking with Flower and she uses a lot of marketing-speak."

# Three

"You're sure you don't want to come up to the president's office?" Samuel asked his wife.

"You'll get more done if I'm not there, and I promised Rose I'd take her to see the Statue of Liberty," Vivian said. "She's been obsessed about it ever since Dwight brought her that souvenir."

"It is a pretty cool statue," Samuel said. "My dad took me to see it when we were on Earth for the first conference EarthCent held for ambassadors. I wonder why they never had another one."

"Probably too expensive to rent out a hotel with all the alien tourists Earth gets these days. It would be cheaper to do it on a Stryx station or Flower."

"Don't even think that too loud, or we could find ourselves hosting. There were almost a hundred active EarthCent ambassadors at the last count, and all the consuls would probably come as well."

"They're all going to be your ambassadors at some point, Samuel, so you may as well get used to it," Vivian said, keeping a hand on the stroller so their daughter wouldn't push it into the street. "I know you think you're too old for the stroller now, Rose, but we're going to do a lot of walking, and Mommy doesn't want to carry you all afternoon if you get tired."

"Krey carries me," Rose asserted with all the confidence of a two-and-a-half-year-old who had the universe three-quarters figured out.

"Yes, Krey would carry you if she was here, but Krey is on Flower." Vivian pointed up at the sky, and Rose tilted her head so far back that Samuel thought she would lose her balance.

"Flower," Rose called. "Send Krey."

"I've got to go up or I'll be late," Samuel said. He gave Vivian a quick kiss and then went to one knee and kissed his daughter on the cheek. "Be a good girl for mommy."

Vivian hailed a self-driving floater cab and Samuel entered the lobby of the skyscraper and took the elevator up to the floor where the EarthCent president's office sublet space from QuickU, one of the most successful human-owned high-tech firms on Earth, which created recreational personality upgrades for artificial people. The receptionist brought him directly into the conference room, where the president was helping Hildy Grueun set up a giant pad of paper on an easel.

"Welcome to Earth, Samuel," President Beyer greeted the young First Administrator of the Human Empire. "When can I expect to be put out to pasture?"

"Not for a few years yet," Samuel told him. "After accidentally triggering an early milestone review last year, we were given a three-year respite until the next one, or a thousand days, which is close enough."

"Take your time," Hildy said, flipping the cover of the pad over the easel to get it out of the way. "I'm not ready to retire yet."

Samuel studied the list of bullet points that had been printed on the pad with colored markers. "Forward EarthCent mail to Human Empire, care of Flower. Throw phones in the ocean from the ferry. Send fake obituaries to Galactic Free Press?" He shook his head in mock despair. "If that's not a retirement plan, what is it?"

"Oops," Hildy said, flipping to a blank sheet. "I thought I tore that page out. We were just fooling around."

"When I'm making plans, she says I'm fooling around," the president said. "When I want to fool around, she has plans."

"Stephen," Hildy scolded the president. "Not at work."

"If I've come at a bad time…" Samuel said.

"Not at all. We both want to talk to you. The *Antiques Tunnelshow* is a great promotional opportunity for humanity, and we want to make sure that you take advantage."

"She wants to make sure," President Beyer mouthed from behind Hildy.

"Two of our School of Government students who graduated last year are going to make working with the show their priority," Samuel told her. "One of them is setting up our Ministry of Antiquities, which is required by the tunnel network treaty and will be responsible, among other things, for policing any trafficking in artifacts from Galactic Historical and Heritage sites. The other student is responsible for our Ministry of Entertainment."

"Do all empires have a Ministry of Entertainment?" Hildy asked as she uncapped a marker that Samuel could smell from the other side of the conference room table. She printed on the pad in block letters, 'Minister of Antiquities' and 'Minister of Entertainment'.

"The research conducted by the minister showed that while the younger empires, such as the Drazens and Hortens, include 'Culture' in the ministry's titles, the older species all drop it in favor of 'Entertainment', so we thought we'd get ahead of the game."

"Smart," the president said. "Changing the name of a government ministry costs a fortune when you take into account all the signs and stationery."

The marker continued producing wet-felt-on-paper noises, and when Hildy stepped back, Samuel saw that she had added 'Cultural ambassadors' to the list.

"I can bring it up with Flower, but it's her show," Samuel told Hildy, who was responsible for EarthCent's public relations. "If you want to come up to orbit and talk with the aliens in charge, I'm sure I can get you a meeting."

"It will be more persuasive coming from you," Hildy said. "I know I can come on a little strong, but this is all about the soft-selling approach. We want you—" beside her, the president was again mouthing something and pointing at Hildy with his hand held close to his chest where she wouldn't see it in her peripheral vision, "—to tell them that you have an idea for a short segment to go with every show featuring something about the human history of each stop. I've visited Flower's Paradise, and I'm sure you'll be able to find well-spoken seniors on the independent living deck who are willing to speak about their first impressions when arriving at the world in question, that sort of thing."

Samuel scratched the back of his head. "Well, Flower loves doing cross promotions, so she might go for it based on the attention it will bring to the independent living deck."

"I'm sure they'll be able to find something interesting to talk about, and they may even have a keepsake from that time that would dovetail into the antiques theme. The important thing is to make sure that the show includes real people talking about their lives and their experiences on the tunnel network. It all counts toward humanizing us, if I can repurpose a word, in the eyes of the aliens."

"I'll bring it up with Flower as soon as I return," Samuel said, and then he noticed that Hildy had turned back to the giant pad on the easel and the squeaking noise had started again. "Canned footage from Grenouthian theme parks?" he read when she finished printing and stepped to the side.

"Their ambassador approached me with the idea," Hildy said. "He suggested that for each type of craft that's represented in one of the historical theme parks they're running on Earth, they could provide high-quality immersive recordings of human craftsmen creating similar pieces using traditional methods." She pointed at a large metal box on the conference table that Samuel had been wondering about. "Being Grenouthians, they're always recording immersive quality holograms for potential use in documentaries, and the ambassador told us that there are tens of thousands of hours of previously unseen footage in that box. He gave me to understand that their network will be taking over responsibility for the show after Flower arrives at Union Station, so it's all in the family, so to speak."

"I don't know if our Grenouthian director will be willing to use reenactment footage," Samuel said. "I've heard he's very strict about that sort of thing in documentaries."

"But this won't be for a documentary, it will be for the regular show," Hildy said. "I've visited quite a few of the theme parks, and it's fascinating to watch how people around the world manufactured fine furniture, textiles, and metal tools, all long before the invention of electricity. If your director will use just a couple minutes in each show and include a reference to the Grenouthian theme park on

Earth where it was recorded, I'm sure it can only help the tourist industry."

"Which is the biggest employment sector on Earth," the president added. "I'm negotiating with the Dollnicks to grant them extraterritorial status for a convention center complex in the Rockies."

"Is that a city-state?" Samuel asked.

"A mountain chain, the biggest one in North America. It's impossible to beat Stryx stations when it comes to convenience for interstellar travelers, but the Rockies have one thing that they don't."

Samuel realized that the president was waiting for him to guess and did a quick mental review of what Bathsheba, the young woman who was setting up the Human Empire's Ministry of the Environment, had presented about the large fauna of North America. "Grizzly bears?" he guessed. "Or is it Bighorn sheep?"

"Ski slopes," President Beyer told him. "The Dollnicks are fanatical skiers. Their extra pair of arms let them carry a second set of poles."

The receptionist appeared in the doorway of the conference room. "Governor-General Mayhew called," she announced. "He said the floater limo is waiting out front."

Hildy sighed and looked guilty. "I was going to bring that up next. Do you have time to go see him, Samuel? In the floater limo, it's only ten minutes to his mansion, and he'll have it bring you back to the city."

"Vivian took Rose to see the Statue of Liberty, so I have a few hours free, but why does the governor-general want to see me?" Samuel asked. "I thought none of Earth's governments were interested in even acknowledging the existence of the Human Empire."

"Mayhew is an interesting man, as far as career politicians go, and he's focused like a laser on the future," President Beyer said. "Either he wants to get a jump on the other city-states and start planning for when you take over from EarthCent, or his Vergallian princess twisted his arm."

Samuel nodded. "If we're finished here, I suppose there's no harm in meeting him. Was there anything else you needed?"

Hildy looked at the easel and said, "No, that was everything. Don't take the holo memories," she added as Samuel moved to pick up the metal box on the table. "It doesn't make sense to carry them around when I can have the box sent up to Flower for you."

"All right," Samuel said and shook hands with them both. "If Vivian should call the office, tell her where I am."

"You don't have a phone?" the president asked in astonishment.

"I have a diplomatic implant. If it's really important, Flower can relay any messages to me."

After what seemed like an interminable ride down to the lobby in the elevator which stopped at every other floor, Samuel pushed through the revolving door. He was surprised to see a familiar face next to the open rear door of the limo in a chauffeur's uniform.

"Thomas," Samuel greeted the artificial person who was second-in-command at EarthCent Intelligence. "What are you doing here?"

The artificial person looked puzzled for a fraction of a second, and then he said, "I understand your confusion. My name is Wooster, and I recently purchased this android body from a catalog. Your friend must have made the same choice."

Samuel blinked at the strange voice coming from the mouth of the handsome artificial person. "It's just that Thomas was always around when I was growing up," he said. "I'll get used to it."

The floater limo rose to the level reserved for emergency vehicles in Manhattan, and good to the president's word, ten minutes later it set down inside the courtyard of a mansion. A young teen ran up as Samuel emerged from the back seat and regarded him with a tragic look of disappointment. "You're not Semmi," she said.

"No, I'm not," Samuel admitted, and the girl ran off again before he could even introduce himself.

"The governor-general's granddaughter," the chauffeur explained. "She has him wrapped around her little finger. Ah, here comes Bertie. He'll take you in to see Governor-General Mayhew."

Samuel did a doubletake as Dewey, or an artificial person who looked exactly like him, approached the limo.

"How many of you are there?" he asked the chauffeur, before realizing how insensitive his question must have sounded. "I mean—"

"It's alright," the artificial person told him. "There are four of us, plus Darlene. You'll meet her."

Bertie introduced himself to Samuel, who was now prepared to find himself face-to-face with an artificial person wearing the same android body as Chance, but instead, he was met at the door by an alien princess. "That will do, Bertie," the Vergallian said. "Tell Wooster not to go anywhere because he'll be needed to run First Administrator McAllister back into the city."

"Will do, Darlene," Bertie said.

"You're an artificial person?" Samuel asked Darlene, unable to keep the astonishment from his voice. "I didn't know that Vergallian androids were available."

"They aren't cheap, but with a Stryx mortgage, I didn't see the reason to economize on a Human model," Darlene said in a posh accent that Samuel couldn't quite place. "Please come with me. Governor-General Mayhew and his special advisor are waiting."

It wasn't until Samuel was shaking hands with Aazil, the first princess assigned to Earth by the Council of Queens in response to the Ladies in Waiting petition, that he was able to accept that Darlene was an artificial person. The real Vergallian princess had a presence that went beyond simple beauty, and while she was too young to gland pheromones to control males, he sensed that she might be a truthsayer.

"Sam," Mayhew greeted him as if they were old friends. "Welcome to my humble abode. I hope all of the artificial people I'm mentoring didn't throw you, but they were a package deal, and the Stryx picked up their salaries."

"That's great," Samuel said, unsure what to make of the confession. "And how are you settling in, Aazil?"

"She's doing great," the governor-general said before the Vergallian could respond. "I wish I had a hundred more like her. In the four months that Aaz has been here, she's completely revamped our court system and cleared the backlog. And complaints about public utilities have already fallen by sixty percent."

"Aazil," the princess corrected Mayhew, but Samuel could tell that her words fell on deaf ears.

"Did Stevie tell you why I wanted to meet?" the governor-general continued.

"President Beyer," Aazil explained.

"He had a few guesses, but he didn't seem certain," Samuel said.

"Always keep them guessing," Mayhew said with a chuckle. "First, can I offer you something to drink? There's a full bar behind the bookcase, and what happens in the mansion stays in the mansion—unless my granddaughter is planting spy cams again."

"I'm all set, thank you."

"Don't trust us, do you? I guess I'd be careful about accepting drinks from strangers after the incident last year where the Vergallians drugged you with a chocolate bar—no offense, Aaz."

"None taken," the princess murmured in a long-suffering tone.

"I had lunch with my wife and daughter before seeing the president, and it was a short meeting," Samuel said, hoping that his host would take the hint.

"I see you get right to the point," Mayhew said and winked at Darlene. "Take a note," he told the artificial person. "Sam is the human equivalent of royalty, and he knows how to use words. Shall we, Aaz?" The Vergallian princess made a subtle motion with her hand and a hologram of the globe seemingly covered in polka dots appeared above the conference table. "Earth is a mess, geographically speaking," the governor-general continued. "Before the Stryx arrived, there were fewer than two hundred countries in the world, and most of them went broke as their populations headed for the exits, leaving a patchwork of local governments and areas with no public services."

"What do all of the polka dots represent?" Samuel asked.

"City-states. I'm not sure why the mapmakers settled on little circles rather than borders, maybe to make them stand out, but the point is, there are over a thousand city-states and small countries operating on Earth today, though half of them do little more than run a power plant and a sewer system."

"Clean water?"

"You can get that from a cheap Horten filter as long as there's pressure in the pipe," Mayhew said. "The first time I showed the globe to Aaz, I was afraid she was going to pack her bags and take the next passenger liner home, but the next day, she already had a plan to begin consolidating the world by region. Aazy?"

The Vergallian winced at this latest liberty with her given name, but she made another small gesture, and the polka dots flowed together, leaving a dozen splotches of color covering all of the land masses in the hologram, except Antarctica, which was now labeled Penguinland.

"How did the existing governments react?" Samuel asked.

"We haven't told them yet," Mayhew said. "The other eleven princesses are just getting settled in, and then they'll begin breaking the news to governments in their region. Aazy thinks that three years will be enough time to get to the new map."

"What if some of the city-states don't want to be folded into regional entities?"

"The plan has the backing of the Ladies in Waiting Delegates Council, and they have more political muscle than any group in Earth's history." The governor-general glanced at Princess Aazil, as if seeking her approval, and added, "It's all to put our house in order for your takeover." A shadow suddenly swept across the room as if something had passed between the sun and windows, and Mayhew swore. "That would be my granddaughter jumping off the roof with her homemade gryphon wings again. Excuse me a moment. Darlene?"

"Is he serious?" Samuel asked the Vergallian as the older man ran out of the room followed by Darlene.

"The governor-general's daughter is quite the gryphon enthusiast, but he is wrong about the wings being homemade. I bought the girl a beginner's Frunge wing set and she decorated it with feathers. The harness is a Dollnick weight reduction belt, and its perimeter is restricted to keep her within the fence, so the worst thing that could happen is she might get stuck in a tree."

"You must have taken to the girl to go to so much trouble."

"Give me ten years to train her and she'll be ready to take over the continent after Earth gets folded into the Human Empire," Aazil said. "I've put the governor-general on an exercise and diet regimen to try to keep him going that long. He's very useful in his own inimitable way."

"Was he serious about all of the artificial people?" Samuel asked.

"Entirely, which turned out to be a blessing in disguise. They're highly competent and I enjoy training them more than I would have imagined. Don't let the fact that the governor-general treats them like household domestics fool you. They're my action team for troubleshooting, and Humans are surprisingly susceptible to the aesthetics of their android bodies."

"And the governor-general doesn't get in your way too much?"

Aazil gave an elegant shrug. "I have to make allowances for his ego, but so far he's made an excellent frontman for the changes I've put through, and he's quite good at predicting the reactions of the local population to our actions. At first, I thought he had a detailed simulation of the New York city-state running on a computer for testing, but it turns out that he has a genuine feel for the populace. I suppose it comes of having to run for reelection from time to time."

Samuel nodded. "I'd offer my help if the Human Empire had any resources here, but until we take over for EarthCent, I'm strictly a tourist."

"There is one thing you could do," the Vergallian princess said, and a slight blush gave away her relative youth, even though she must have been twice as old as Samuel to have finished her schooling. "The governor-general is going to ask you to take a box of documents and things that he chose from around the mansion to the *Antiques Tunnelshow* for him. He's less interested in the appraisals than in generating name recognition for the city-state."

"Sounds like a politician," Samuel said. "I'd be happy to do it. The Human Empire's mentor has been pushing me to appear on the show, but I didn't have any antiques to bring."

"That wasn't the favor," Aazil said, and reaching into her fashionable purse that was emblazoned with four feathers and the Baa's Bags logo, she brought out a sizeable package. "I've been indulging in shopping therapy as an antidote to life in the mansion, and I'm fascinated by how quickly your civilization adopts and then discards fashions in jewelry. These are all costume jewelry, of course, the most I paid for any piece was five creds, but I'd love to learn more about the fashions they're imitating. Perhaps your daughter would enjoy them after they've been on the show. Due to my position…"

"I understand. My wife or one of our students will be happy to present them on the show. I'm sure you have exquisite taste."

"Thank you."

Samuel had just tucked the surprisingly heavy package in his jacket pocket when the governor-general returned with Darlene, who was carrying a large set of feathered wings. "My granddaughter took down a security drone after asking Wooster to record it on her phone so she could show Semmi," Mayhew informed them. "She's grounded for the week."

"My daughter carries around a stuffed bear and wants to be Cayl when she grows up," Samuel said.

The governor-general appeared to be seriously considering something, and then he shook his head. "No, it won't work. My granddaughter is all in on Gryphons, she and Semmi share a social networking channel." He took a framed document off the wall and added it to the box on the table. "Did you ask him about bringing the collection on the show, Aaz?"

"Samuel said he'd be happy to do it," the Vergallian princess replied.

"Good. But wait until Flower gets to Union Station," Mayhew added. "The real premiere will come when the Grenouthian Network takes over the *Antiques Tunnelshow*, and there's no point in squandering the opportunity for maximum publicity by rushing. I may not know much about galactic politics, but if you have a chance to make a splash in public, you want to do it in front of the biggest possible audience."

# Four

Bill filled the black medical bag with jewels from the chest in M793qK's vault on the bottom level of the parking garage below the ReproMan building in Manhattan. Then he brought out his smartphone and ticked off the checkbox next to 'jewels' on the list the Farling had texted him. He scanned the whole list once more to make sure he hadn't forgotten anything.

"Stained-glass lampshade, silver pitcher number sixteen oh-eight, baseball that's been written all over, urn with Greek guys chasing each other, bear with a button in its ear, enamel and gold egg that opens, plate with ugly queen, painting of dogs playing poker. That's everything, Dewey. I can carry the painting and the medical bag if you carry the box with the rest of the junk."

The artificial person slipped the comic book he'd been reading back into its plastic sleeve, added it to the box, and then removed his cotton gloves. "You forgot about Spidey One," Dewey said. "M793qK is a fan of pictographic literature in which the heroes become more than humans by incorporating superpowers from the insect world."

"If he's a fan, why would he want to sell it at auction?" Bill asked. "It's not like he needs the money."

"The *Antiques Tunnelshow* isn't an auction," the artificial person reminded Bill. "The job of the appraisers is to tell the people what their items might bring *if* they came to auction. M793qK asked us to pick up these things as insurance, to make sure that there will be a high-value item for the show's opening and finale if it turns out that the attendees only bring old junk."

"We're going to be auction shills?"

"I told you, it's not an auction." Dewey lifted the box full of antique collectibles that would be priced at millions of eBucks if sold through Manhattan specialist shops, and added, "I believe the correct term would be ringers."

Bill sighed as he undid his belt, ran it through the handles of the medical bag to make a loop, and then hung it over a shoulder before picking up the painting with both hands. "I'm going to tell him to get somebody else to do it. I had enough of acting when I was a scaffolding stand-in for Flower's first anime production."

"I'm sure M793qK won't have any problem finding people who want to appear on a show that we project will be seen by trillions of sentients around the tunnel network. If not, he can always hypnotize somebody."

Bill froze. "Has he been hypnotizing me?"

"I meant it as a joke," the artificial person said, and set a flag for himself to think twice before mentioning the Farling doctor's hypnotic skills again. "Let me go first when we leave, just in case."

The lowest level of the garage was still empty when they emerged from the vault, and Bill put down the painting and pressed the call button. The vault door descended as the outer doors closed, disguising the vault as an elevator. "It should have an out-of-order sign on it so people don't get suspicious that it never works for them," he said.

"If there was always an out-of-order sign, people would notice. Instead, anybody who calls an elevator will take the one on the left and never think twice about it."

"I think I'd notice if the same thing happened every day I came to work."

"Look around," Dewey commanded as they left the glassed-in elevator lobby. "There's nobody else here. The lowest level of the garage is reserved parking only, and M793qK owns the building and reserved all the spots."

"Right," Bill said as they approached the self-driving limo that had been waiting at the spaceport when they landed in Dewey's freighter. "Do you think we should put this stuff on the back seat or in the trunk?"

"Didn't you get the last text?"

"I pinned the list to the top of the message queue so I wouldn't forget any of this stuff." Bill set down the painting again, put the bag of jewels in the trunk that Dewey had opened remotely, and slid the painting in beside it, longways. Then he got his phone back out and scrolled past the list. "We're picking up passengers? Is that safe?"

The artificial person set the box in the trunk next to the painting. "They aren't random passengers," he said. "Carlos and Evette are former art forgers who have been working at ReproMan for years."

"Why would a business that produces reproduction art need experts in—I don't want to know."

Dewey got into the driver's seat, even though there wasn't a steering wheel or any other controls for manual operation, and Bill climbed into the passenger side. "You're too suspicious, Bill," the artificial person said. "Who better to create reproduction art than expert forgers? By giving them gainful employment, M793qK was keeping them out of trouble, and now they're leading experts in detecting fakes because they know the business from the inside out."

"But who would gamble on bringing a forgery to be appraised on a show that everybody can see?" Bill asked.

The limo floated up off the concrete floor and began navigating the serpentine path back to the higher levels of the garage. "The forgers won't be the ones bringing in forgeries," Dewey explained patiently. "It will be people who bought them through private transactions thinking they were getting a bargain, or worse, families who treasured the works for generations without knowing that an ancestor had been taken in. The Grenouthian director told me that forgeries will add educational and dramatic value to the show."

"And give all of the aliens a chance to laugh at the silly humans, like in all those Grenouthian documentaries."

"Maybe in obvious cases, but for the main part, the advanced species take all types of fraud seriously, even those that don't value provenance over quality."

"What does that mean?" Bill asked.

"You know that Verlocks like furniture sculpted out of stone, right?" Dewey asked. "If you put two tables side by side, one by a famous sculptor from a million years ago, and another a recent copy made by a young art school student who was studying the master's technique, the important thing to the Verlocks would be the quality of the table, not who made it. If the new copy was identical to the original, but the original was cracked, the new copy would command a higher price."

"I guess that makes sense for a table if you're going to put things on it, especially since cracks can grow over time."

"But that's exactly the opposite of how humans see things," Dewey said. "You don't have any million-year-old antiques because modern humans haven't been around that long, but if you did, the original would be a priceless museum piece, and the price of the copy wouldn't pay the student a fair wage for the time that went into making it."

"Oh," Bill thought for a moment as the limo pulled out of the seemingly endless spiral ramp and began threading its way through rows of parked floaters. "Then I guess there won't be many Verlocks watching the show."

"I wouldn't say that, though they're less likely to be impressed by appraisals than the other species. The Verlocks have great respect for antiques and collect them avidly. They don't see why a cracked old table should be worth more than an otherwise identical new table. But when it comes to historical documents, it's a different matter entirely. If anybody was caught forging one, I imagine they would be cast out of Verlock society."

A man and a woman, both in their early fifties, were waiting near the ground floor exit. They walked toward the back of the limo, expecting to stow their rolling luggage in the trunk, but Bill hopped out and opened the rear door for them. "Plenty of room in here," he said. "The trunk is full."

"You're the boss," the woman said. "I'm Evette and he's Carlos. We've been told that the aliens only use one name and we've decided to go with the flow."

"I'm Bill, and he's Dewey. Are the two bags all you have?"

"These are just our overnight things in case our luggage is misplaced," Carlos said. "A service came to our home two days ago to take our trunks to the space elevator."

"He looks puzzled," Evette said to Carlos, then turned back to Bill. "Don't worry, young man. We aren't living in sin. I can show you our marriage license if you're concerned. Just give me a minute."

"Little forger's joke," Carlos said to Bill as he put both bags on the floor between the opposing seats. "I hope you're going to ride with us rather than sitting up front. We have so many questions about Flower."

"You've never been?" Bill asked, getting into the limo across from the couple. "Put down the window, Dewey. You should be part of this."

The limo began to move, but the window dividing the front seat from the passenger compartment remained up.

"It's soundproof," Evette said. "These floater limos have such good acoustic insulation that they don't need to use suppression fields."

Bill got out the smartphone M793qK insisted that he carry and texted Dewey.

"Sorry," the artificial person said a few seconds later once the window was down. "Did I miss anything?"

"Evette and Carlos have never been on Flower, and they have questions," Bill said without looking over his shoulder.

"Such as?"

"We hadn't started asking yet," Evette said. "The *Antiques Tunnelshow* sent us a handbook to living on Flower, but we didn't know what to make of the morning exercises and the required team sport. Is that for crew members as opposed to normal people?"

"As an artificial person, I'm exempt," Dewey said, "and Flower lets the aliens slide because they know how to take care of themselves. But all of the rules for residents will apply to you and the rest of the show's staff."

"Then you better stop the limo and let me out because I'm not a morning person," Carlos said.

"You don't have to do the calisthenics at any particular time," Bill said. "People who work regular hours tend to do the stretching in the corridor together as a social thing because misery loves company, but you can do it in your cabin at any time of day or night and Flower will give you credit."

"So the exercise requirement is based on self-reporting," Evette surmised.

Bill shook his head. "Flower keeps track and she'll start pestering you if you skip without a good excuse. Dollnick colony ships have high-resolution thermal imaging built into all of the interior spaces to watch for technical problems and Flower can use it to make sure you're exercising."

"It's a surveillance society?"

"As are Stryx stations and every alien city I've visited," Dewey said. "If you were putting them on a scale from one to ten, Stryx stations would be ten, and Flower might come in around eight. Alien cities only have cameras surveilling everything in public spaces, so they're about a five."

"What's a one?" Carlos asked.

"Earth Two, they don't have any cameras on the planet unless a documentary crew is visiting. I haven't spent much time in Manhattan, but I would put it around a five."

"Really?" Bill asked. "I know there are a lot of cameras on the streets, but half of them are probably broken, or nobody checks the video until after there's been a crime or an accident."

"That's true, but unlike alien cities, people on Earth fill their homes with devices that spy on them," Dewey said. "Did you have a smart speaker growing up?"

"The Sun Cult didn't approve of them," Bill said.

"You were in the Sun Cult?" Evette asked. "I used to buy pens and paper from the cult's pushcarts because I felt sorry for the people being out in all weather trying to sell such low-value merchandise."

"My mom and I mainly sold cheap toys."

"There's one now," she said, pointing out the window at a pushcart on the sidewalk where a young couple were hawking little stuffed animals that were piled up like apples.

"That could have been me if I hadn't gotten tricked into running away to join an illegal picking crew eight years ago," Bill said. "Sometimes I wake up feeling guilty that I have it so good these days."

"I'm sure it would be an interesting story, but right now I'm more worried about having to play a team sport," Carlos said. "I wasn't that athletic when I was young, and these days, walking two blocks to work is my idea of exercise."

"You can meet your team sport requirement with dance lessons, swimming pool aerobics, yoga, whatever works for you as long as it's physical activity and there are other people involved," Dewey told him. "Flower even counts crafting as a team sport, if you're interested in quilt-making, pottery, or spinning wool. It's also a chance to get to know Alts and people from the Old Way movement who we transport to Earth Two."

"What about the volunteering requirement?" Evette asked.

"That's separate, but the two of you might enjoy working as guides in the bazaar. There's a constant turnover of traders who have interesting merchandise from all over the tunnel network, and it would be a way to start learning about other cultures before the show moves to the Stryx station circuit."

Carlos and Evette took turns asking questions for the rest of the ride to the spaceport, and by the time they arrived, Bill realized that after seven years of living on board Flower, he had a pretty good idea of how most things worked.

"We're not taking the shuttle?" Evette asked as the limo rolled by the queue of people waiting to board.

"I brought my ship because I had some last-minute cargo to pick up and Flower will be leaving before the next space elevator car reaches orbit," Dewey explained. "The shuttle has more cargo capacity than my freighter, but it's spoken for months ahead of time."

The freighter beat the shuttle back to Flower, and after pointing Carlos and Evette in the direction of the lift tube, Bill and Dewey delivered M793qK's art and collectibles to the clinic.

"Splendid," the Farling rubbed out on his speaking legs. "And the rest of my cargo?"

"In my hold," Dewey said. "Do you want me to unload anything?"

"No. The containers are going to the Miklat for delivery to Farling Four and I don't need anything from them. Talk to me before you leave because I may have something to add."

"I need to get back to the kitchen to help Harry," Bill said. "If there's nothing else…"

"Hold on," M793qK said, and went over to the counter where a scalpel lay on a block of white material that looked like fine clay surrounded by crumbly bits of the same substance that might have been gouged out. He put the scalpel to one side, shook off the excess, and said,

"Watch your eyes." Then he reached up to the cluster of instruments that were hanging from the ceiling above the operating table and pulled down something that looked like a wand. He played the light from the wand over the surface for around thirty seconds.

"What are you doing?" Bill asked.

"Performing a medical miracle. I developed this ceramic for bonding teeth, and it cures in fifteen seconds using ultraviolet light. All done."

"That was thirty seconds," Dewey observed.

"It's a thick piece. I cranked the power up as well."

"But the skin depth of ultraviolet—"

"Trust me," M793qK cut him off. "As long as the carved surface is hard, the rest will dry when Bill puts it in the oven."

"You want me to bake this for you?" Bill asked. "A backward sculpture?"

"I believe the term you're looking for is a counter-relief, though I'm sure the specialists on the *Antiques Tunnelshow* would refer to it as intaglio or cavo-rilievo," the Farling said. "But in this particular instance, let's just call it a cookie mold. I see it as a virtuous circle, since the more cookies you bake, the more dental business I'll get."

Bill left Dewey and the Farling to discuss their plans for the artificial person's next trip and brought the semi-cured cookie mold to Harry's cafeteria. He wasn't at all surprised to find Jake stirring a bowl of stiff dough under the direction of the old baker.

"Just in time," Harry said, accepting the proffered mold from Bill. "Did M793qK say where he got this?"

"He carved it out of tooth repair putty, unless the scalpel and the bits on the counter were there to trick me," Bill said. He looked at the stack of ceramic molds on the counter and asked, "Where did all of those come from?"

"My old bakery. Irene and I went down to Earth earlier this week to stop in and see how the family we sold it to is doing. I saw that these ceramic molds were in exactly the same spot where I left them when we joined Flower, so I ended up bringing them back."

"If soft clay was the target consistency, I think this shortbread dough is ready," Jake said. "Do you always make it this way?"

"One, two, three," Harry said. "One part sugar, two parts butter, three parts flour."

"I've been doing four parts flour," Bill said. "Three sounds awfully rich."

"Mary, Queen of Scotts liked it rich," Harry said. "And you don't want it too crumbly or it won't pick up some of the finer lines from the mold. The important thing is that the dough shouldn't be too sticky."

"Good," Jake said. "I tried molding some chocolate-chip cookies once on Bits, but they kept sticking in the plastic mold and coming apart, even after dusting with flour."

"I've got some metal cookie molds I bought for the School of Government café that work with chocolate-chip cookie dough, but they're much deeper than these, and the carvings are less complicated," Bill said as he tied on his apron. "How many of these are we going to make?"

"We'll use up all of the dough," Harry said. "Most of these shortbread molds give you six or eight wedges with the same design. I've already preheated the big oven and added the spare racks, so we'll fit them all without a problem."

Jake split the giant clump of dough in the mixing bowl roughly in half, quickly shaped two balls, and plopped one of them down on the counter where Bill was set up. "Do we dust the molds with flour first?" he asked.

"Give them a quick spray with that easy release, and then dust them with flour and leave what sticks," Harry said. "Today we're baking an assortment for the Grenouthian director to choose from."

Jake sprayed and dusted a couple of the older ceramic molds as Bill did the same with the new one made by M793qK.

"I've never done one this big before," Bill confessed as he misjudged the amount of dough needed to fill the mold and had to add more around the edges. He pressed it in with his fingers in hopes of getting the full impression. "The whole thing goes into the oven?"

"Yes, but let's get them all prepped first so they can go in and come out at the same time," Harry said.

"Even though there are different thicknesses of dough in each mold, and the molds aren't the same sizes either?" Jake asked.

"Thirty-two or thirty-three minutes should do it. The dough turns golden brown around the edges, so it's pretty hard to overbake shortbread if you're paying attention."

"That's it?" Bill asked, showing Harry the smooth rectangular surface that was left after he filled the mold up to the raised edges of the ceramic.

"Take a fork and poke in some shallow lines of holes," Harry said. "It will let the moisture from the butter escape more quickly so the cookies bake evenly and come out crisper."

When the shortbread dough was finished and the molds were all filled, Harry opened the oven and the men formed a bucket brigade, passing the molds forward as Harry slid them onto the racks.

"This isn't going to work to get them all out at the same time when they're hot," Jake said.

"That's where the Dollnick oven comes in handy," Harry said. "Haven't you noticed how quickly it returns to room temperature when the heat's off and the door is opened?"

"Right, I wasn't thinking. What are we going to do while this batch is baking?"

"Drink coffee," Bill said. "I got up early to go down to Earth with Dewey and I'm dragging."

Forty-two minutes later, the men all donned oven mitts and removed the already cooling molds from the oven. "A tap on the bottom should be enough to release the cookie," Harry said.

"It's funny calling something the size of a pie a cookie," Jake observed.

"As soon as you cut those big ones into wedges on the indent lines, they'll be biscuits. I do it as soon as they come out of the molds. If you wait until the cookies are cold, they're more likely to crumble."

As soon as Jake and Bill started freeing the cookies from the molds, a theme soon emerged. "All the molds you brought from Earth show steps from pottery or glassblowing."

"I wouldn't have recognized any of these scenes if I hadn't watched potters and glassblowers from the Alts and the Old Way working," Jake added.

"There used to be a cooperative in our town that was focused on ceramics, though they had some glassworkers too," Harry explained. "They made these molds for me in exchange for free bread, but that was when Irene and I were starting out. Eventually, they all signed up for alien labor contracts and left Earth."

"I like the hands shaping the pot," Bill said.

"And the glass blower, though the pipe looks dangerously short," Jake said. "Or maybe they exaggerated so it would fit on a wedge. What did M793qK's mold make?"

Bill tapped the bottom of the mold and lifted it off, revealing the Farling's coat of arms, complete with his alien retainers.

# Five

"Try to ignore us," Irene told Julie, Lena, and two dozen specialists gathered in the conference room. "We'll be moving around and recording, but it's unlikely that more than a few seconds of anything we shoot today will end up in the finished documentary."

"How come you're all controlling two cameras each?" somebody asked.

"A straight shot with a reverse angle view is sufficient for the Grenouthians to create a three-dimensional holographic image with post-processing," Irene explained. "The second camera is slaved to the first to maintain the proper perspective. June will be primarily focused on framing shots for context, Dave will be handling close-ups for that side of the room, and I'll handle this side."

"The Grenouthian director couldn't be here this morning because of another obligation, but he asked me to say a few words in his absence," Julie said. "He personally selected all of you from your demo reels so he's confident in your on-camera ability when reading from a script. The director is hoping that the parallel documentary production will help some of you learn to relax a little bit more."

"Are you saying there won't be any script?" asked a nervous-looking man in his thirties wearing an old-fashioned suit with a bowtie. "Nobody told me."

"There won't be a script, but there will be editing," Julie said. "We're targeting a one-hour show from two days of shooting with three camera crews. If you do the math, that means that when you see cameras capturing an appraisal that you're making, there's less than a five percent chance it will end up in the final cut."

"The whole show is going to be us appraising the antiques people bring?" asked a woman who had her tab out to take notes.

"That's what today's meeting is for, and I'm just here to facilitate," Julie said. "The director and executive producer have hashed out a rough framework for how each show will proceed, which I'll be putting up on the holographic display in a minute. Neither of them are human, so they wanted to give us a chance to talk things through ourselves."

"Are you the assistant director?" Evette asked.

"I'm Julie, and I'm Flower's executive assistant. The *Antiques Tunnelshow* is a Flower Entertainment production, and I'll be your main point of contact for any questions you have, or issues that you're not comfortable bringing up with the aliens. Before I turn on the hologram and we begin, I'd like to ask the show's host, Lena, to say a few words. Some of you may know Lena from her reporting for the Children's News Network or the Galactic Free Press. This is her first time hosting a regular show, and the Grenouthian director asks that you all give her your support. Lena?"

Dave used a gentle hand movement to shift his pair of floating immersive cameras from focusing on Julie to Lena, while Irene, who had the most experience of the three camera operators, took the more difficult job of remaining on alert to rapidly zoom in on anybody who asked questions. Both of them were working from the inside of the large square created by folding tables with all of the meeting participants sitting around the outside.

"Thank you, Julie," Lena began. "My broadcasting background is in news, but I've always had a strong interest in history, and every show will have a historical theme that's tied to the human community where Flower is stopping. If the show is a success and we continue on to the Stryx station circuit, we'll start seeing more aliens and alien artifacts."

"Excuse me," said an older man who looked like he already had tunnel lag even though Flower hadn't left Earth's orbit. "Will the guests have to get some sort of pre-approval to bring their antiques to be appraised?"

"Not while the show remains on Flower," Lena said. "Our main worry for the next three months will be getting enough interesting antiques from Earth for you to demonstrate your expertise. But if the show survives to move on to Empire Convention Centers where the vast majority of the guests and items will be alien, there's no way that we could cover the last seven million years of tunnel network history with even ten times as many specialists as we have in this room right now. The current plan is to bring in local specialists for each show, in addition to the regular team of a dozen each of aliens specialists and yourselves."

"There are a lot more than a dozen of us here," the man observed dryly.

"Think of the next three months as an extended audition for all of us," Lena said. "For the show itself, for whether it's a good fit for you, and whether you are a good fit for us."

"For me, it's the extended spa vacation that I couldn't afford on Earth," the woman next to the man said. "I'm looking forward to three months with an artificial intelligence as my dietician and personal trainer, and whatever happens after that can take care of itself."

Julie glanced at Lena, who gave her the nod. Then she activated the holographic system using her implant as the remote control. In keeping with the arrangement of tables, the same holographic projection was repeated twelve times in the center of the square so that the people sitting at each table could easily read the display by looking up a little, while retaining direct lines of sight to everyone present.

"Canned introduction," Julie began. "The Grenouthian director is currently working on that in the studio, and it will feature people carrying various antiques walking through Flower's corridors, getting out of the lift tube, and queuing up for triage, where you'll all take turns assigning the incoming traffic to the specialist of the day. They're shooting it all with actors to save time."

"Will there be music?" asked a woman wearing a gold violin broach.

"Flower is running a contest for theme music, but the lead time is so short that they may end up licensing something or using a piece of classical music from Earth's public domain." Julie looked back at the hologram and continued, "Immediately following the canned introduction will be Lena's opening, where she'll talk a little about the history of the location where Flower is stopping. That will be recorded after the live appraisals to take advantage of any themes that might appear."

"It's easier to appear prescient with hindsight," Lena contributed. "The magic of editing."

"From there we'll move directly on to scenes of people gathering around the specialist tables with their items, and then zoom in on a particular guest and the antique they've brought in. The director's current intention is to open each show with a bang, ideally a high-value item that the owner thought was a keepsake worth a few creds, or the opposite."

"Denise Thornsby, Ceramics and Glass," a serious-looking woman interjected. "Are you asking us to make fun of people who have been taken in by scammers? What if they bring in what they believe to be the most important relic of their family history only to discover that great-great-grandfather was playing a prank?"

"This won't be a gotcha show," Julie said. "We'll ask people to authorize the use of the recording after each shoot. If they aren't comfortable with the way they appear, it goes straight to the trash."

Lena cleared her throat and said, "My experience interviewing people who have been victims of scams is that most of them are eager to share their stories. I like to believe that they are hoping to prevent other people from being taken in, but I do remember one person telling me that it was worth losing a few hundred eBucks to appear on the news."

"And if any of you have suggestions, the Grenouthian director is open to input," Julie added.

"Why don't we start the show with the least valuable appraisal and work our way up?" asked a man who looked too young to be an expert in anything. "That would give viewers a reason to stick out the whole hour."

"Fakes will have the lowest appraisals," said the man sitting next to him.

"Not necessarily," a woman on the other side of the square put in. "Anne Stewart, furniture and lamps. People have been collecting valuable objects since the dawn of civilization, and I frequently see three-century-old copies of five-century-old furniture that still bring tens of thousands of eBucks at auction. The originals are all in museums, but in some cases, the craftsmanship of the copies is just as good."

"Funny you should bring that up," Carlos said. "I'm a specialist in fine art forgeries, and depending on the age and the name of the forger, they can bring appreciably more than perfect reproductions."

"But no documents," Evette said. "Forged documents are worth less than their frames."

"Archie Morris, clocks and watches. Are you targeting getting all of the appraisals done in a fixed time, like thirty seconds or a minute, or will we have the flexibility to go several minutes for an exceptional piece or background story?"

Julie nodded. "Thank you for asking that question. The director will be doing the final edit for every show, and he wanted me to tell you that more is better than less, so long as you don't turn every appraisal into a lecture. In some cases, an otherwise uninteresting appraisal may make the final cut based on the reaction shot of the owner, so it's best to treat every item as if it may be featured on the show."

"If the cameras are on us," somebody else spoke up.

"That's another good point that I was coming to. If you hear a story or see an item that you're passionate about, ping Lena, and she'll come over and take a look. If it makes sense to repeat the appraisal with the cameras, that's what we'll do."

"How do we ping Lena?" Carlos asked.

Lena took out her smartphone and held it up. "Group chat. Flower supports phones from Earth, so I hope you all brought yours, but if not, the show will provide them. While what Julie said is true, the director would prefer not to reshoot whole appraisals because the owner's reaction will be different the second time around. If you think you have a winner and there isn't a camera crew at your table, ping me and ask the owner to wait while you go to the next person in line."

"If there are three camera crews and a dozen appraisal tables set up, how will you decide which ones to shoot?" Anne asked, looking directly at Irene.

"Me?" Irene shook her head. "I'm documentary crew, I'll be floating around. The director will decide how to rotate the show's camera crews, but I did hear him say something about making preliminary choices based on triage as the people arrive."

"That's right," Julie said. "Those of you working triage will get the first impression of the items and their owners. When you sense a good opportunity, take a photo of the people and ping the director who will have his own group chat set up. While most aliens may have trouble differentiating between humans, the director can pick a face out of a crowd as easily as you'd spot a giraffe surrounded by zebras."

"Deborah, no last name," an older woman said. "Dolls and stuffed animals. I was thinking it would be fun if there was a segment where Lena could compete with the audience in picking out the most valuable teddy bear from all the ones people bring in."

"Do you expect that many teddy bears?" Lena asked.

Deborah nodded so enthusiastically that if her head had only been sewn onto her neck it might have fallen off. "Oh, yes. I've worked as an appraiser at antique fairs, and teddy bears are huge."

"If you'll all look back at the hologram, Host's Challenge is the next line item," Julie said. "The Grenouthian director had an idea to have Lena try to choose the genuine article from a selection of fakes, or maybe assign values to three outwardly similar items."

"And then the specialist will make fun of me because I don't know anything about antiques," Lena said.

"You'll catch on in no time," an appraiser told her. "It's all about seeing things in volume, which is why most of us come from an auction house background. If the show is a success, you'll get a year's worth of experience every month."

"Mark. I'm a specialist in tools and technology," a middle-aged man spoke up. "I think it would be fun and educational if I picked out a tool or a kitchen gadget every show and challenged Lena to figure out what it does."

"I know a hammer from a saw, but I can't find the faucet in the kitchen," Lena said. "Maybe it would be fun trying to guess."

"Anat, and I appraise textiles and dresses," a slender woman wearing what looked like a designer gown introduced herself. "How about Lena tries on some of the old styles of clothing people bring in? It will make more of an impression than a random model because the viewers will already know her face."

"People bring second-hand clothes to antique shows?"

"Heirlooms," the specialist corrected her. "My favorite thing is when somebody brings in a well-preserved garment along with a photograph of a famous person from history wearing it. I regularly see gowns and dresses that were worn a single time by a queen or a princess and then given to somebody who worked in the palace as a gift. People tend to hang on to things like that because a story goes with them."

"Oscar Simon, sports memorabilia," said a giant of a man whose legs stuck well out from under the table with the ankles crossed. "Team uniforms worn by famous players are some of the most valuable items I see, though I doubt the owners would be willing to let Lena try them on. Everybody started sealing their valuable memorabilia in those Horten inert gas storage bags that are guaranteed for a thousand years if you keep them out of the sun."

"I refuse to appraise anything in a Horten bag," Anat said. "But it's a good point because we should have a station set up where people can reseal bags and recharge the inert gas."

"I could see putting on a queen's kimono, maybe, but not a sports uniform," Lena said. "Or shoes, but I would try fancy hats."

"These are all good ideas," Julie said. "Anybody else?"

"Are aliens going to be watching?" Carlos asked.

"We certainly hope so," Julie said. "If aliens don't watch, Flower Entertainment might continue producing the *Antiques Tunnelshow* as space in the con deck schedule allows, but the deal with the Grenouthian network and the Empire Convention Center would be off."

"Then shouldn't we put something in that the aliens would enjoy?" Carlos asked. "Lena's challenge would be the ideal place to do it because it's not dependent on the guests or what they happen to bring that day."

There was a general murmur of consent, and a few people started to speak and then stopped as they thought better of it. Julie was surprised by Flower's silence and wondered if the Dollnick artificial intelligence was treating the meeting as a new sort of brainstorming experiment where only the humans get to talk.

"Sophie Keach, jewelry," a woman introduced herself. "How about we present Lena with three pieces and challenge her to pick the one that a particular species of aliens would find desirable? It would work with any type of antique and any species of alien since it's all just opinion."

"I like it," Lena said. "I'd like it even better if we could have an alien present to say whether I'm right, and why."

"That could be easily arranged," Julie said, making a note on her tab. "The next bullet point on the list is the grand finale. The Grenouthian director will get the final say, and part of that is making sure that we do appeal to alien viewers, but every specialist who works the floor will be allowed to nominate one of their own appraisals."

"And the director will do whatever he wants," somebody grumbled.

"I see you have experience in show business," Julie said.

Irene motioned her cameras up into a parked position to get them out of the way, and then said, "I've found the Grenouthian director to be open to input as long as it has some thought behind it. And he's entirely approachable when he isn't operating a camera, or on his way somewhere, or eating, or directing. It's safest to approach him when he's already talking to somebody else and wait for them to finish."

"We get the picture," Evette said.

"And speaking of finishing, we'll close the show with guest testimonials," Julie continued with the second-to-last bullet point on the hologram. "The director envisions ending every show with three or four guests talking positively about their experience on the *Antiques Tunnelshow,* even if their items weren't as valuable as they hoped."

"Do you mean something like—" Lena paused for a moment, and then started in a peppy voice, "—It turned out that the earrings my grandmother always kidded us she found in a cereal box really were from a cereal box, but I had a great time on the *Antiques Tunnelshow*."

"The later twentieth-century painting that we thought was worth a fortune even though it looked like it was done by a cranky ten-year-old really was done by a cranky ten-year-old," somebody else said as soon as the laughter died out. "But I'm still glad I brought it to the *Antiques Tunnelshow*."

"That's the spirit," Julie said. "If we don't have any willing guests, we could use you as a ringer."

"What's that final bullet point?" Oscar asked. "Eating proud?"

"It's a Grenouthian expression that doesn't have a good translation," Julie said. "All of the staff, from the specialists to the camera crews, get together for breakfast a few days after the show and discuss what went right and what went wrong. It's a chance to praise your colleagues and point out areas where you need help or have a plan to improve."

"The implication is that we shouldn't criticize each other," Lena said. "Is it intended as a social event, or have the Grenouthians determined that it's an effective way to improve the quality of their shows?"

"I think I can answer that," Dave said, waving his cameras up to the ceiling to get them out of the way. "I've been part of eating proud as both a cast member and a cameraman while working with the Grenouthian director and it's very much a serious meeting. The Grenouthians believe that there's always room for improvement and that individuals can train themselves to be their own best critic, in both the positive and the negative sense."

"But what if somebody is doing a really bad job and doesn't know it?" Carlos asked. "Everybody who worked at ReproMan had to take a training course in criticizing their own work, because that's the only way to produce quality reproductions without constant supervision. For most of us, it was the first time anybody had asked us to critically analyze our technical ability. Art schools on Earth tend to value exploration and free expression over draftsmanship."

"If you think you're doing a great job and you notice that you aren't getting any time on the broadcast, that means that the director and the rest of the production crew don't agree with you," Dave said. "And the Grenouthians also practice live peer check, which means if you see anybody screwing up, you should tell them in the moment rather than waiting until it's too late for them to fix what they're doing."

"Even if the cameras are rolling?" somebody asked.

"Especially if *our* cameras are rolling," Irene said. "We're counting on live peer check to add interest to the documentary and create a story arc as everybody improves at their jobs."

A woman who wore a large gold pocket watch as a necklace perked up and said, "So if I see Archie appraising a nineteenth-century night watchman's station as a grandfather clock, I should jump right in and tell him he's wrong."

"That happened once," Archie said with an exasperated sigh. "I was twenty years old and I'd never seen a night watchman's clock before. Aren't you ever going to let me live that down?"

## Six

Samuel slapped the mat as loudly as he could and the Drazen martial arts instructor rolled off him. The aliens watching from the edges of the mat began stomping their feet, drumming on their bellies, and otherwise expressing their appreciation in the manner of their species.

"Good job," Jorb said, offering his tentacle to help Samuel back to his feet. "You almost lasted the full round."

The Grenouthian director hopped over, clapped a paw on Samuel's shoulder, and said, "Don't give up your day job." Then he turned to Jorb. "Hit the showers and I'll meet you on the con deck. And wear something professional."

"You're working a camera crew for the dress rehearsal?" Samuel asked after the director left the dojo. "What about your classes when the show starts tomorrow?"

"Avisia and Forgath are covering my private lessons this weekend, and after that, I've rescheduled all of my classes to weekdays until we get to Union Station," Jorb said.

"Why does the director care what you wear to work camera crew?" Avisia asked.

"I'm also rehearsing to be the alien specialist for the first show. The director is concerned that guests from Break Rock will bring mining collectibles, and the Human appraisers won't know what they're looking at."

"Call me if anybody brings lava," Brynlan said as he shuffled by on the way to the door. "And break a leg."

"Did the Grenouthian director ask all of you to take turns as alien specialists?" Samuel asked.

"I'm on call to do glass if they get anything really good," Forgath said. "Hortens are known throughout the galactic arm for our glassworks."

"Dresses and tapestries, though I'm far from being an expert," Avisia said. "Making tapestries is so popular on our tech-ban worlds that they've turned into the empire's second biggest export category after dramas. I hope people bring in some interesting ones that will give me a chance to explain the symbolism."

"How about you, Razood?" Samuel asked the Frunge who was packing up his gym bag.

"Weapons and metalwork in general," Razood said. "I'll be featured twice, once as a silversmith and once as a blacksmith. I'm also on call if any interesting mechanical pieces come up, especially clocks, but that will be a short walk since I'm handling a camera unit for all the shows."

"What about your smithy in Colonial Jeevesburg?"

"I'll still be open in the evenings on the weekend, the show only runs for eight hours each day. It's amazing that Humans manage to get anything accomplished with all the sleeping you do."

"Will you make a guest appearance this weekend, Samuel?" Lume asked after working his fourth arm through his dress shirt. "It's a chance to show the flag for the Human Empire."

"I don't want to be a distraction," Samuel said. "The Grenouthian director has already set aside a guest spot for our Minister of Antiquities—"

"Who's barely old enough to drive on Earth," Jorb put in.

"—and I want to wait a few shows for Lena to get established."

"It would be a shame not to take full advantage of the opportunity for publicity for the Human Empire while the *Antiques Tunnelshow* is hosted on Flower," Lume told him. "A chance to appear on an unscripted show with the audience numbers Flower is projecting only comes up once in a lifetime if you're lucky."

"I'm surprised how enthusiastic you all are about it," Samuel said as he looked around for where he'd left his gym bag. "When it was the New Worlds Fair last year, that made sense because it gave you a place to meet with your human agents from all over the world, but..." He trailed off, looking from one grinning alien to the next. "You're going to use the show to try to recruit new agents from the people who come to have their items appraised rather than going down to the planet at every stop?"

"Should we tell him?" Avisia asked.

"Now we have to," Jorb said. "It's better than that, Samuel. It's a chance to practice sending hidden messages in plain sight."

Samuel groaned. "I wish you hadn't told me. Does that mean you'll be making secret hand signs at the camera while you're giving your expert opinions?"

"Give us more credit than that," Razood protested. "Besides, if the Grenouthian director notices, he'll either cut the scene in editing or point it out and say we owe him one."

"The trick with secret communications is to do it in such a way that it only means something to the intended recipient," Avisia said. "The classic example is Queen Aberid passing on the command code for Fleet's flagship in her last words before she was executed by the Empire after the Council of Queens tricked her into delivering herself into their hands on the pretense of negotiating an end to the schism."

"How did she do that?" Samuel asked.

"If I told you, it would never work again," the Vergallian said, and then laughed at his disappointed expression. "I was kidding. It happened hundreds of thousands of years ago and everybody already knows the story. She demanded the right to recite her lineage on the execution scaffold and intentionally got the order wrong in eight instances. The command code consisted of the fifth letter of each of the names she misplaced in reverse order."

"How many of her ancestors did she name?"

"Oh, a hundred or so."

"Queen Aberid could have come right out and said, 'Here's the command code,' by the end because she'd bored everybody into a state of stupefaction," Jorb said, dancing back just in time to avoid Avisia's roundhouse kick.

"Try not to do anything that gets the Human Empire in trouble," Samuel told them. "I'd appreciate it if you don't send secret messages while any of our official representatives are on camera with you."

"It's a deal," Forgath said without hesitation, causing the First Administrator of the Human Empire to believe he'd been tricked into something.

"Is Vivian going to have a role on the show?" Jorb asked Samuel while they were in the shower. "Rinka is a silent producer now, so let me know if you need any strings pulled."

"Rinka is going to work for Flower Entertainment?" Samuel asked in surprise. "I thought she loved her job as a choirmistress."

"She's not working *for* Flower," Jorb said proudly. "Rinka bought a point in the production with her lullaby royalties so she's a partner. Being added to the credits as a silent producer is a perk."

"That's great. Vivian has a couple of pieces of old jewelry that she might take on the show, but I don't think she'd want to be on just to promote the Human Empire. Is that soap safe? I forgot to put a new bar in my travel soap box."

"Hold on a second," Jorb said and finished lathering up his tentacle. "It's safe, but I stole it out of Brynlan's locker."

"And you think I'm too much of a square to use stolen soap?" Samuel asked, extending his hand.

"No, but the pumice might be hard on your skin."

"My dad used to buy Verlock soap with pumice to clean up after doing mechanical work. I only used it on my hands and arms, but it won't hurt me."

Samuel arrived at Human Empire headquarters at the same time as his wife who had just come from dropping Rose off at Flower's crèche. "Why is your face so red?" she asked.

"I probably shouldn't have scrubbed so hard with the pumice soap, but I guess I was showing off to Jorb," Samuel said. "Either that or the water was too hot."

"Why would you take a shower with water that was too hot?"

"Showing off to Jorb," Samuel admitted. "I know, you don't have to tell me."

"You've been friends since the Open University on Union Station," Vivian said. "It's just that I thought you'd grow out of it by now."

"Jorb offered to ask Rinka to put you on the *Antiques Tunnelshow* if you want," Samuel said to change the subject. "She owns a point in the production."

"Julie mentioned it. I'm meeting them both at the Blue Tea Café on Thursday for our girls-night-out so remember that you're watching Rose."

"I'll ask Flower to remind me. How do the new students look?"

"Exactly like the old students," Vivian said with a sigh. "Some of them are older than I am, but something about their being first-years makes them look younger to me. And we promised to meet with Bertrand this morning."

"When?" Samuel asked. "I was going to finish the fruit salad in the breakroom fridge for breakfast."

Vivian checked her implant. "You have time. I'll be in the conference room going over the tunnel network treaty. I seem to remember that the Minister of Antiquities for every empire has a sort of fiduciary duty to the Stryx."

Samuel stopped at the door of the breakroom and turned around. "Fiduciary duty? Like they have a financial liability if we don't do our part to protect Galactic Historical Sites?"

"I mean it in the sense that unlike all the other ministers, who only answer to the empire that employs them, the Minister of Antiquities is responsible for enforcing rules that come directly from the Stryx. Nobody else in the empire has that direct obligation, not even the emperor."

"Or First Administrator."

"Suit yourself," Vivian said, then continued to the conference room. Samuel ducked into the breakroom and was surprised to see Krey eating something with chopsticks.

"Good morning, Samuel," the Cayl emperor's granddaughter greeted him. "You look like you have sunburn, but you smell like a Verlock, so I would wager that you borrowed Brynlan's soap after your sparring."

"No bet," Samuel said. "Is that Chinese takeout?"

"Brown rice. The new place in the food court makes it so the grains don't stick together, and I find that eating them one at a time with the chopsticks is as good as meditation."

"Won't the leftovers dry out and harden in the fridge before you get a chance to finish the carton?"

Krey changed her grip slightly, raised the carton to the level of her snout, and used the two chopsticks together as a shovel to dump most of the rice onto her cupped tongue.

"Nice," Samuel said. He opened the fridge and took out the sealed container of fruit salad and an individual yogurt serving from Flower Dairy. After peeling the foil off the yogurt, he dumped the contents over the fruit salad and sat down with a tablespoon for his breakfast.

"Did you get in a good sparring session?" Krey asked between picking out the remaining grains of rice.

"I almost lasted a whole round with Jorb, but I know he wasn't going full out. Everybody was taking it easy this morning because most of them were saving their energy for the dress rehearsal." Samuel loaded another spoonful, then added, "They're going to compete on sending secret communications in plain sight when they get camera time as alien experts."

"That sounds reasonable." Krey chose another grain of rice with her chopsticks before asking, "Do you want me to stop attending your morning meetings with the ministers-in-training? I've noticed that they sometimes look at me when they ask questions as if they believe that I'm your boss rather than your mentor."

Samuel swallowed and stirred the mixture of fruit and yogurt while he thought. "I'd prefer if you continue participating in all of our meetings," he said finally. "You don't say much, but when you do, it's always valuable.

And I think the students sometimes watch you when they ask me questions because they want to see your reaction."

"I doubt they can tell what I'm thinking behind the fur, and I've been told that I have a perfect poker face."

Rather than telling the Cayl emperor's granddaughter that she had the most expressive eyes he'd ever seen, Samuel asked, "Are you going to bring any of those samplers you've been collecting to the *Antiques Tunnelshow*?"

Krey closed an eye and picked one of the last grains of rice out of the bottom of the carton with her chopsticks. "I'll wait until they have done a few shows to get the bugs out first. I want to make sure that the works I've collected are treated with proper dignity."

"It seems funny that needlework done by schoolgirls hundreds of years ago could become so collectible. Was learning to stitch the alphabet such an important skill in the days before electricity?"

A young man with a goatee stuck his head in the breakroom, muttered, "Sorry," and disappeared again.

"Wait, Bertrand," Samuel called after him. "You're always welcome in the breakroom, and if you need a coffee before our meeting, I'd rather you get it now."

The young minister reappeared, looking slightly sheepish. "I saw you talking with Krey and thought it might be private."

"Good morning, Bertrand," Krey said. A few years of speaking Humanese had removed the growly undertones from her voice unless she wanted them there. "Are you interested in needlework?"

"I could learn," Bertrand said. "Is it important?"

"It's foundational, but not for your job."

"She's teasing," Samuel said, scraping the bottom of the container for the last of the yogurt after the fruit was all gone. "Are you going to brew a pot?"

"Do you want me to?" Bertrand asked. "I was going to make a cup of Instant Inca. Can I make you one?"

"I'm trying to cut back." Samuel got up and brought the container to the sink where he rinsed it out and put it in the drying rack. "Do you have any off-the-record questions before we go into the conference room?"

"Are you saying that our meetings there are recorded?"

"Since Dwight joined us," Samuel said. "You know that creating a transparent and trackable system for decision-making is one of the milestone requirements for the Human Empire. When Dwight came from Earth to replace Scott as our documentation specialist, he suggested recording all our official meetings."

"Do all empires record everything?" Bertrand asked.

"I don't know the answer to that," Samuel said. "Krey?"

"Recording all but the most confidential meetings is common, but so is erasing the recordings after a few centuries if nobody accesses them," the Cayl mentor replied. "Even though storage is cheap, data has a way of piling up over millions of years to the point that it takes an artificial intelligence to locate anything."

"Is that a problem?"

"Finding an artificial intelligence willing to do the job is the problem," Krey said. "I've heard of species that wasted a lot of time and money trying to create non-sentient artificial intelligence to do archival work, but those systems have a way of becoming self-aware when you least expect it. Have you met Dewey?"

"Yes," Bertrand said. "The artificial person who owns the freighter that runs back and forth between Flower and the Miklat. He gave me a ride when I was sent to intern at Void Station."

"Dewey was accidentally created by the programmers on Bits who were trying to create a limited artificial intelligence to index their archived version of Earth's internet," Krey explained.

"It's a Stryx rule," Samuel said. "Nobody can hold a sentient artificial intelligence against its will."

Vivian came into the breakroom and used the instant hot water dispenser to make herself a pot of blue tea. "It's time," she said.

Krey folded up the takeout carton from her rice and dropped it in the recycling chute before joining the three humans as they moved to the conference room. A large hologram with language from the tunnel network treaty related to Galactic Historical Sites and Preserves was projected at one end of the conference table.

"I've got it all down by heart," Bertram said as soon as he saw the hologram. "It hasn't changed since I did my second-year project where I created a plan for the Ministry of Antiquities."

"So you know about being directly accountable to the Stryx," Vivian said.

"Yes. It's a reporting requirement if you read everything in context. As long as I submit any violation reports involving humans to the Emp-First Administrator," he corrected himself, looking toward Samuel, "and to any Stryx librarian, I'm fulfilling my duty."

"Is there anything in there about what happens if you notify me that humans are looting a Galactic Historical Site, and I can't make them stop?" Samuel asked.

"The text is all focused on what constitutes violations," Bertram said. "I got the impression that the Stryx will take care of enforcement if we don't move fast enough to suit them." He took a sip from his coffee, and asked, "Has something come up that I need to know about?"

"We want to make sure that you're prepared to answer Lena's questions on the show tomorrow," Vivian said. "Flower put together a reel of the interviews Lena's done in the last few years and I watched it last night so I could help you get ready."

"That's cool. I was getting a little nervous since I'm going to be representing the Human Empire without having done anything other than a couple of internships and a lot of reading."

"So, what got you interested in antiquities?"

"What?" Bertram asked, and then said, "Oh, you're being Lena now. Uh, I studied geology at university and I was thinking of going into mining, but then the opportunity to join the first class of the Human Empire's School of Government came up, so I jumped at that. I started thinking about getting involved in antiquities and xenoarchaeology after we had a Verlock as the guest speaker for our seminar. Even though the math went over my head, there was something about the passion he brought to the subject that made me want to learn more about it."

Vivian nodded. "And who's your favorite band?"

"What?"

"You know, music."

"But what does that have to do with the Human Empire?"

"Lena's interview style is to mix on-topic questions with lifestyle questions, as a way to get subjects talking about themselves," Vivian explained.

Bertram frowned. "I don't want to talk about myself in front of millions of strange people and aliens. What business is it of theirs what band I like?"

"You're new to being interviewed, but soon enough you'll be an old pro, and then you'll realize that you're basically reading from an internal script. Lena came out of the Children's News Network which independently developed a philosophy very similar to that of the Galactic Free Press and the alien news services. They don't see the point of subjecting their readers and viewers to repetitive talking points. Nobody wants to interview a talking press release."

"Look, when I was living on Earth, the Children's News Network was the only news I watched, other than the Grenouthian Network, I mean. Maybe I didn't pay enough attention to the interviews, but I still don't get how my personal life comes into it."

Vivian decided that her Frunge blue tea had steeped long enough and poured herself a cup before replying. "The reason for the personal questions is to put all your answers in context for the audience. If viewers know where you're coming from as a person, they'll be able to make better sense of your answers to professional questions. It's not a trick to get you off balance."

Bertram seemed to be struggling with the concept, and then he said, "I listen to Bad Excuses a lot."

Krey perked up. "The Apologist band?" she asked.

"I guess some people would call it Apologist music, but I think of it as more like common sense. I mean, I'm sure that I've insulted aliens without intending to because I don't know enough about them. I hope I don't do that by saying the wrong thing in the interview."

"What's your favorite Bad Excuses song?" Vivian asked.

"Plastic Soldiers," Bertram said. "Do you know it?"

Vivian and Samuel both shook their heads, but Krey said, "The lyrics make up for the music."

"Does it have something to do with toys?" Samuel asked.

"No," Bertram said. "It's about all the plastic that people dumped in the oceans back before the Stryx opened Earth. In the song, the whales get together with that species from the Farling empire who look like sharks, and they fashion the plastic into an army that marches onto land and destroys all the factories producing single-use plastic bottles and utensils. I saw the lead singer of Bad Excuses interviewed a few years ago, and she said that everybody on Earth knew that plastic was getting into the food chain, but it was just too convenient to—" He paused, a strange look on his face. "It might have been Lena who did that interview. You know, I think it was, but I was paying attention to Pauli."

"The lead singer's name is Pauli?"

"Pauli Mer. Get it?"

"Apologist bands aren't known for their subtlety," Krey said. "It's one of the reasons they can bridge the species gap. When I listen to traditional Earth bands going on about their vices and anti-social behavior, I can't figure out whether there's a point to it all or if they're simply unaware of how it reflects on them."

"You see?" Vivian said to Bertrand. "It's not about whether you're telling the truth, the assumption is that no reputable network would air your interview if you're simply lying. Your taste in music tells people that you aren't embarrassed to admit that humanity makes mistakes on a planetary scale. I think that's an important piece of information when it comes to somebody whose job includes protecting Galactic Historical sites that can span entire planets."

Bertrand bobbed his head. "I guess I'll just answer Lena's questions and try not to think about it too much. What should I say if she asks about the two of you?"

"What do you mean?"

"You must know that everybody refers to you as the imperial couple when you're not around. Do I have to stick with that First Administrator business?"

"I know it's an uphill battle, but I'm trying to make the First Administrator title stick," Samuel said. "I don't want to believe that everybody is calling me Emperor McAllister behind my back."

"It's what I call you when talking with non-Humans," Krey said. "So do my hounds."

## Seven

"Homemade sweets from Roman times," Bill answered Jake's question. "They have a Latin name, but I already forgot it."

"Dulcia Domestica," Flower contributed through an overhead speaker grille. "But it's a general description for sweets that could be made by any cook, as opposed to a specialty baker. They're described by Cato and many of the other Roman writers."

"They're simple, but we have to make enough for hundreds of people, which is why Harry chose them for the first show," Bill continued.

"Harry isn't coming in today at all?" Jake asked.

"He's working as a backup camera operator for the documentary crew his wife is running. And he's not a big fan of frying anything in olive oil or frying in general. He has a saying about bakers that—"

"If bakers were meant to fry, they wouldn't be called bakers," Flower interrupted. "Your whole milk delivery fresh from the dairy is about to arrive at the back entrance."

Jake went and opened the door to admit a floating robot carrying a large stainless-steel milk can that looked to contain around twenty liters with each of its four arms. The bot carefully navigated around the men, placed the cans one at a time on the counter, and then departed the way it came without a word.

"Why don't they ever say anything?" Jake asked. "I've given up thanking bots, but it feels awkward."

"They don't say anything because they're machines," Flower told him. "They have just enough programming to stay out of the way and not hurt anybody if I'm not controlling them directly."

"That's a lot of milk," Bill observed. "I'll be surprised if we use up one can in two days."

"We'll see how popular the desserts are," Flower said. "If guests like them and keep arriving through the day, I have a half dozen cooks from the Old Way movement on standby to come and help you."

"Durum flour, right?" Jake asked.

"Yup," Bill said. "We cook it on low heat with the milk to make a sort of porridge, add a little black pepper, cut it into small squares, and fry it in extra virgin olive oil."

"For frying? I thought the extra virgin was for salads."

"The ancient sources are very specific on this point," Flower said. "Fried desserts use the very best oil from the first pressing."

"We better get four pots of milk going and stir two at a time each," Bill said. "Low heat, around fifteen minutes."

Jake hesitated. "I don't want to sound like the guy who doubles the oven temperature to bake the cookies twice as fast, but why not use a bigger pot and double the amount of milk?"

"You have to stir pretty constantly to keep it from getting lumpy, and if you try too much in the same pot, it's almost impossible without a mechanical stirrer."

"Which I offered to provide," Flower said.

"I don't know much about Roman history, but I don't think they had Dollnick paddle mixers," Bill said as he poured around a liter of milk into a pot, passed it to Jake, and repeated the operation with three more of the medium pots. Then he opened a sack of Durum flour and dumped half out into a large stainless-steel tub from a steam table. He added a couple of measuring cups on top and moved the container to the cold part of the large cooking range. "It will take a little more than a cup and a quarter of flour per liter of milk, but I like to start porridge wet and add flour rather than starting dry and adding liquid."

"Same here," Jake said, bringing up the heat on his two pots. "Almost forgot." He opened one of the utensil drawers and brought out four long-handled wooden spoons. "Pick two, any two."

The bakers spent the next fifteen minutes stirring their pots, and when the porridge was well cooked and stiffening, turned off the heat to let it cool a bit.

"I'm going to grind some fresh black pepper," Bill said, getting out the mortar and pestle. "The extra virgin olive oil imported from Earth is in those cans on the back counter."

"Should I set up four pans with it?" Jake asked.

"Two large pans would probably be safer in this case. I can stir with both hands, but I wouldn't want to work with hot oil that way because you have to watch what you're doing."

"Seems weird making a dessert where the only spice is pepper."

"It adds bite and a complex bouquet for the nose," Flower told them.

"Where are you getting all of this from?" Jake asked the Dollnick artificial intelligence. "I know you were already around for eighteen thousand years or so when the Roman Empire was at its height, but I thought you never visited Earth."

"I do my research on the archival copy of the Internet that the residents brought from Bits."

Bill placed a bowl with the ground pepper on the counter and retrieved a couple of wood cutting boards from their rack. "Here," he said, passing one to Jake. "Spread the dough on there to an even thickness, something like a cookie, then cut it into small squares and fry it."

"I thought you were calling it porridge," Jake said.

"That felt right while it was cooking, but now it seems more like a dough."

"Whether it's fried porridge or fried dough, it doesn't seem like much of a sweet, all due respect to Flower's research."

"You're forgetting the honey," Flower said as each of the men started frying a half dozen pieces of dough. "They didn't have sugar, so sweetness came from honey or fruits. There are versions of this dessert that use diced dates or figs instead of dribbling honey on top."

Bill and Jake exchanged a look, and then Bill asked, "Do you recommend dusting them with pepper before or after dribbling with honey?"

"After," the Dollnick AI said decisively.

Jake tasted one of the soft sweets from the first batch, and said, "Wow. That's a lot better than I thought it would be. Do we need to rush them up to the con deck while they're still warm?"

"They're also good when they've cooled to room temperature," Flower answered before Bill could get a word in. "But I recommend that one of you brings up the first batch when you finish making them, and the other starts on the next batch. Why don't you bring them up, Bill? You might start with offering them to people waiting in line, and don't forget to tell them that they're eating Dulcia Domestica from a two-thousand-year-old recipe."

"Your wish is my command," Bill said with a laugh as he dribbled honey over a plate filled with the sweets, which looked almost golden from frying in olive oil. "I'm going to need one of those double-decker trays to carry them all up."

"Bring a stack of napkins," Jake said. "We'll get grief from the appraisers if everybody's antiques have honey on them from handling after eating our sweets."

When Bill arrived on the con deck with the double-decker tray and a package of two hundred paper napkins slung over his shoulder, the first guests were starting to queue up, even though the show wasn't scheduled to open for another fifteen minutes. He cautioned everybody who wanted a sweet about the honey and insisted that they each take two napkins. To his surprise, the top tray was used up by the time he got to the front of the line. Bill took a minute to restack, swapping the top tray to the bottom and removing the duplex spacers that were no longer necessary, and then he stepped over the velvet rope and headed for the tables where the appraisers were setting up.

Behind him, the Grenouthian director left the lift tube and cast a doleful eye over the crowd of people eating sweets from napkins while waiting in the area marked off by velvet-covered ropes and hollow brass stanchions. He hopped over the rope in a single bound, just to prove that he could, and drew Scott away from where he was talking with the specialists who would be working triage for the first day.

"Why hasn't triage started?" the Grenouthian director demanded. "Didn't you offer to be the floor manager on show days?"

"I thought the doors didn't open until 09:00," Scott said. "Do you want me to start letting people in as soon as they arrive next time?"

"No, they'll be showing up hours early if we do that. From now on, let's start triage fifteen minutes before the show opens and not tell anybody."

"Director," Irene called from where she was expertly manipulating a pair of floating immersive cameras. "I've been focused on the gathering crowd while Dave and June have their cameras on the specialists setting up. Should I stay on the queue, or shift to triage?"

"Wait until the rope comes down to capture the initial crowd surge and then switch to triage," the Grenouthian told her. "We'll do the same tomorrow, and that should give us enough entry scenes for the whole documentary." He turned back to Scott and pointed to a row of baby carriages with Flower Perambulators branding. "I don't remember those from the final production meeting."

"It was a last-minute thing," Scott said apologetically. "When I was working the Human Empire pavilion at the New Worlds Fair, I saw how many people who showed up carrying small children ended up wilting by the end of the day, so we bought a few dozen carriages for use in the tent."

"Excellent idea. Do you know why I agreed to hire you?"

"I assumed it was because of my experience with the New Worlds Fair, my background in the New York Guard, and my girlfriend being the show's host."

"Those are all good reasons," the Grenouthian director said, "but I hired you because you were the tallest Human in the room so it's easy to find you in a crowd. Keep up the good work."

Lena spotted the director talking to Scott and wondered what they were discussing, but according to the antique wristwatch Julie had delivered to her that morning, a last-minute gift from Flower, it was thirty seconds to opening time. Lena waved to Irene, who now had both of her cameras positioned to capture the grand opening, and she rehearsed the movements to unhook the velvet rope in her head. After counting down the final seconds, Lena thumbed back the slide to open the connector. People began surging through the gap as soon as she began walking the end of the velvet rope over to the stanchion on the other side, which was equipped with a second eye ring to secure the loose end.

"Where should I bring my vase?" asked a woman holding a large ceramic funeral urn clutched to her chest.

"Any of the specialists at these tables will be able to help you," Lena told her. "This is the triage area where they'll give you an idea of what you might have and direct you to the most suitable appraiser."

As the woman merged back into the stream of people flowing between the double row of tables, Lena slipped around the back of the tables on the left, so she could observe some of the evaluations.

"Documents and Photographs," a specialist told a man who had presented a sheet of paper with print, calligraphy, and some kind of raised seal.

"How will I find them?" the man asked.

"Hologram above the table," the specialist said, pointing in the direction of the show floor, where glowing blurbs of text could be seen above each of the appraisal stations, high enough to be out of the way and low enough so people wouldn't have to crane their necks.

"But is my treaty genuine?"

"I'll put it this way. If it's a fake, it's good enough to fool me at first glance. Next?"

"My family voted on what I should bring, and they chose this because nobody knows what it is and we want to find out," the next person said. She laid a well-worn leather roll on the table, a metal tool of some sort in each of the pockets. "Is it a carpenter's kit?"

"Surgical tools, eighteenth-century ship's surgeon from the Royal Navy if they're genuine," the specialist said. "Take them to Weapons and Militaria."

Lena moved on to the next table where a woman was trying to persuade her five-year-old son to let the specialist look at the large stuffed animal he held wrapped in both arms. "But you said you wanted to learn more about Brown Cow."

"Brown Cow doesn't want the strange man touching him," the boy said stubbornly.

"Can you take a look at this while they're deciding?" a young man asked, setting a small silver box with a gold embossed hunting scene on the table without waiting for an answer. "It was my grandfather's, and then my father's, and he left it to me."

"Cigarette case, twentieth century. Did your father and grandfather smoke?"

"I remember my dad always smelled like tobacco."

"That explains why you inherited so early."

Lena shook her head and moved on to the next table where a man had presented a long-barreled firearm that was almost as tall as Scott.

"Mid-eighteenth-century Pennsylvania rifle, .40 caliber, could be a twentieth-century replica," the woman working behind the table said. "Is it loaded?"

"Of course not," the man said. "I doubt it's been fired in the last two centuries."

"That doesn't mean it's not loaded," she said. "Did you ever prime the pan and pull the trigger?"

"I don't even know how a flintlock works."

A four-armed bot carrying a long rod arrived, with Irene trailing behind it guiding her floating immersive cameras. The bot took the gun in two padded pincers and then inserted the business end of the rod, which terminated in a twist like a corkscrew, into the rifle's barrel. The bot spun the rod a few times and then drew it out again with a lead ball impaled on the end. Then the bot pulled a length of flexible transparent tubing out of its own chassis, ran that down the barrel, and there was a sucking sound. What looked like a scrap of cloth followed by a stream of black powder shot through the tube before it ran clean. Finally, the bot handed the rifle back to the astonished owner.

"Now it's unloaded," said the woman working the table. "Weapons and Militaria. Next?"

Lena felt a large paw on her shoulder and turned around to see the Grenouthian director looking at her through his big black eyes. "It's not working out," he said.

"You're firing me? I haven't even recorded the introduction yet."

"Not you, the whole concept," the director said, and Lena noticed that his large furry foot was tapping like a machine gun. "It's the antiques the people are bringing. I have yet to see anything older than me, and I'm not even middle-aged."

"But the show is for humans," Lena pointed out. "Antiques to us are anything more than, oh, twenty-five years old or so."

"It's still not working. There's no narrative thread."

"You instructed the specialists working triage to move people through as quickly as possible. They aren't supposed to get the whole story."

The Grenouthian blinked. "I'm not cut out for reality programming. It's all so—random."

"Are you feeling okay?" Lena asked. "I've never seen a nervous Grenouthian before, but I'm beginning to think that there's a first time for everything."

"It's not a complete disaster, the parallel documentary is going fine, but look at these guests milling around," the director continued, waving a paw in the direction of the people who had cleared triage and were looking for the assigned appraisal table. "Something is wrong."

Lena sighed and looked where the giant bunny was pointing, and then her eyes narrowed. "That's not the holographic font I remember from the dress rehearsal. I can barely puzzle out the letters, and what are Effigies and Vestigial?"

"Portraits and Prints," the Grenouthian said. "It seems obvious."

"It seems obvious because you either know Latin or your implant is translating for you," Lena said. "All of these people speak English."

"I know they speak Humanese, but I thought they read Latin," the Grenouthian said. "I've visited many notable buildings on Earth, and most of them had Latin inscriptions. And *E Pluribus Unum* was on all the coins I saw at the New Worlds Fair."

Lena sighed and pointed at her ear to indicate she was activating her implant but continued to speak out loud. "Flower?"

"I'm monitoring your conversation, and I suspect I made a mistake," the Dollnick artificial intelligence replied immediately. "When Bill began passing out ancient Roman sweets, I thought it would help everybody get in the spirit to change the holograms to Latin. I was sure that everybody knew a little."

"Like *alibi* and *vice versa,*" Lena said in exasperation. "Not categories of antiques."

"The idiot with the loaded gun found the right table," Flower countered.

"What's Militaria in Latin?"

"*Militaris,*" the Grenouthian director and the artificial intelligence replied at the same time.

"Change the holograms back to English, Flower," Lena said. "Everybody is going to get frustrated trying to figure out the Latin. And no calligraphy."

"Roman cookie?" Bill offered.

The Grenouthian director sniffed at the tray and then hopped away, but Lena tried one and smiled.

"These are good. Can I take the last one?"

"Please," Bill said. "I don't usually play waiter, so I hadn't realized that the speed with which people take what's on offer is inversely proportional to the fullness of the tray. I've been wandering around with those last two sweets for five minutes and I was getting ready to eat them myself."

"Could you bring some sort of folding stand and leave full trays near the line where people are waiting to get in?" Lena asked after finishing the first sweet.

"Flower said it won't work because of the napkins," Bill said. "People need them because of the honey, but then they don't want to walk around with a napkin, so they'll throw it back on the tray. Nobody will want to eat the cookies that have used napkins on them."

"No, I guess I wouldn't either. Hey, are you in a hurry?"

"Jake will have another double tray ready by now so I should go pick them up."

"That's even better," Lena said. "This show has a weird feel, like nobody is quite sure what they're doing, and I want to do a warm-up interview to get things rolling. I've tried approaching a couple of people but they turn away as soon as I smile at them. How about I round up a camera crew and meet you at the lift tube when you get back?"

"Why near the lift tube?" Bill asked.

"So you can give out sweets while we're talking and put everyone at ease. I know from your wife that you have some experience on camera, but most of our guests don't. I want them to see that I don't bite and that an interview is just a friendly chat."

"Okay, but it could take me ten or twenty minutes with all the people using that lift tube bank. It might even be faster for me to walk to the next spoke."

"I dispatched a bot to pick up the next two trays and it will take a maintenance shaft rather than a lift tube," Flower told them both. "Estimated arrival time is two minutes. It will meet you outside the rope line, and you can give it the empty trays."

Lena checked her implant for the channel that showed the camera crew assignments and discovered that they were all scheduled for the next fifteen minutes due to a series of promising appraisals. She was about to tell Bill that the idea would have to wait when Harry walked up, shepherding a single floating immersive camera.

"Irene assigned me to shoot some random scenes that she and the director can look at later to get ideas for future shows," Harry said. "I've never heard either of them mention it before, so I suspect I was just in the way."

"Want to shoot us?" Lena asked. "I'm going to interview Bill while he's handing out Roman sweets."

Harry accompanied Bill and the show's host over to the rope-line queue before the triage area, and a bot floated up with a full duplex tray held by its top two arms. It took the empties from Bill with its lower arms and then handed over the fully laden trays before moving off. Harry positioned the camera parallel to the rope line so he could frame Bill and Lena, as the former began handing out sweets.

"Tell us about these cookies you made," Lena began.

"They're based on an ancient Roman recipe from two thousand years ago," Bill said, and added, "Take two napkins," to the first woman who tried one. "The Romans liked sweets, but they didn't have sugar. These are made from durum flour and milk, fried in extra virgin olive oil, and then topped with honey and a dusting of black pepper."

"Do you like living on Flower?"

Bill blinked at the unexpected question. "My whole life is here now. I have a wife and a son who's just starting to talk, and I'll be opening my own café in three months."

"Will you be serving ancient desserts at your café?"

"I hadn't thought about it. Maybe?"

Rather than asking another question, Lena smiled and bobbed her head, inviting Bill to continue. Harry took a quick glance over his shoulder to make sure there was nothing behind him, and then took a step back with the camera so the other two could advance along the rope line.

"They have milk in them," Bill responded to a question a woman asked related to food allergies, and then he expanded on his earlier answer. "I have a sort of dream menu I've been working on the last three years, and I've learned a lot managing the student café for the Human Empire's School of Government."

"Excuse me," a man on the other side of the rope line said. "I heard you mention black pepper before, and somebody told me this is a pepper grinder." He held up an iron device mounted on a wood backing plate and gave the handle a spin. "I thought it must be from a restaurant kitchen because nobody would want to grind this much pepper at home."

Bill leaned over the rope line for a closer look, and a few arms snaked around the man with the grinder to take sweets and napkins while the tray was closer.

"I've been looking for one of those for my café," Bill said. "It's an antique coffee grinder."

"Are you sure?"

"I had one in my kitchen back on Earth," Harry said. "They work great."

"We had one at home in Switzerland," Lena added. "I think it was older than our house."

"So they aren't rare," the man said, sounding disappointed. "When I tried to research wall-mounted pepper grinders, I didn't find many. None of the ones I turned up looked like mine, so now I know why. What do you think it's worth?"

"We aren't appraisers," Lena said. "You're about to go through triage where they'll assign you to a specialist table, and they'll give you an estimate."

The man looked at the line, and then out at the growing knots of people around the specialist tables. "I'm meeting friends in the LARPing studio in twenty minutes, I don't think I have time. And since it's not rare, I don't want to wait. What would you give me for it?"

"I don't know if I'm allowed, but," Bill took a second look, "I'd go five creds."

"Deal."

# Eight

Julie delivered Basil to Flower's crèche where the one-and-a-half-year-old toddled off at top speed as soon as his mother set him down. "Maybe I should learn baby massage," she said to Flower over her implant. "When I let you talk me into signing Basil up for your crèche, it never occurred to me that he would prefer it over going to work with me."

"I think we've reached a fair compromise," Flower said. "You keep him when you're going to spend most of the day in your office, and the crèche gets him when you're going to be running around. You'll need all of your wits about you for the first post-mortem meeting today."

"I wish you wouldn't call it that. Nobody died."

"Only thanks to some aggressive editing and ringers. The Grenouthian director thinks he can salvage forty minutes of appraisals from the over forty hours recorded. He still hasn't shot Lena's introduction, and with the canned opening and closing sequences and the interview she did with the Human Empire's Minister of Antiquities, that will fill out the running time for an hour."

"A third of the hour will be filler?" Julie asked as she exited the crèche.

"It's not filler and it's not twenty minutes," Flower said. "You're forgetting about commercials."

"Right." Julie entered the lift tube and paused. "Where am I going again?"

"The small conference room at Flower Entertainment," the Dollnick artificial intelligence replied as the capsule began to move. "Yaem is officially the host, so he'll take care of the catering, but I want you to run the meeting."

"Why not Yaem?"

"Because you're better. Yaem knows the production business but barely pays attention to the worlds where we stop because the other alien intelligence agents cover for him. One of the problems with the first show should have been obvious to everybody due to the location."

"You mean that hard-rock asteroid miners don't bring a wealth of antiques with them to live in a cramped habitat," Julie surmised.

"Yes, and since the Frunge leased the habitat to the human cooperative, the miners have paid for their own transportation from Earth or wherever they're coming from, so we should have expected that they would travel light," Flower said. "It's a good thing that so many of the people who moved here from Bits brought along their possessions."

"Rafferty, the guy who appraises obsolete technology, certainly got a workout," Julie said. "And I thought Zick was going to faint when he heard that old hard drive he was using for a bookend might sell for two hundred creds at auction. We're going to have to make a rule going forward or we'll be flooded with point matrix printers."

"Dot matrix," Flower corrected her executive assistant. "And I think a rule is a good idea."

"That painting with the dogs playing poker will make a great closer. Do you think it would really bring two hundred thousand creds at auction? Carlos said over a million eBucks."

"Yes, but didn't Bill tell you?"

"Tell me what?" Julie asked.

"He picked that painting up from Earth," Flower explained. "It was in M793qK's collection."

"But the woman who brought it in said it belonged to her daughter's godfather, who's a doctor, and she had it because he—never mind."

Julie took a glass of fresh-squeezed orange juice from the tray on the stand next to the conference room table where most of the seats were already filled. Yaem was standing in the corner, talking in hushed tones to somebody over his much-maligned smartphone, and the Grenouthian director was gesticulating as he explained something to Lena. The surprise was John, an EarthCent Intelligence agent she'd met during his previous visits to Flower. Then M793qK arrived, and Flower said over Julie's implant, "That's everybody for today, we wanted to start small. Ask John to speak first so he can leave."

"No, no, no," Yaem shouted at his phone, holding it at arm's distance, and then brought it back to his ear and listened for a few seconds. "Yes. No. Yes. I have to go." He jabbed at the screen a few times, probably turning off the ringer, and then took his place at the table. "Sorry," he said. "Problems with the new production—not this one."

"Thank you all for coming," Julie began, remaining standing with the orange juice in one hand. "Flower told me that we're starting small for the first post-production meeting, but that we'll be adding unit directors and talent as makes sense in the future. Before we begin, does anybody—"

"Tell Bill that buying antiques from the guests is out," the Grenouthian director interrupted.

"He overpaid," M793qK rubbed out on his speaking legs.

"I told him it was okay," Lena said. "He was helping me out, and I think he said that he's an independent contractor rather than a *Tunnelshow* employee."

"I wasn't worried about the rules," the director said. "It undercuts the variety on the show if anybody buys the antiques from the guests before they even have them appraised."

"It was a one-time thing," Julie said. "Bill isn't interested in antiques, he's just vacillating about which direction to go for café décor. But we're getting sidetracked, and I understand that John has something to say to us."

The EarthCent Intelligence agent cleared his throat self-consciously and rose to his feet. "My wife came to cover the first show for the Galactic Free Press, so I was assigned to talk to you about establishing a policy for looted items. Before anybody asks, I've traded in antique tools, and I took a load of M793qK's art from ReproMan to the fair on Aarden, but I don't pretend to know much about the business. What I do know something about is working with ISPOA, the Inter Species Police Operations Agency."

"Are you suggesting that we're already in trouble?" Lena asked.

"I was dispatched to talk to you last week, before the show took place," John said. "But EarthCent is concerned that once the show picks up steam, you'll start seeing a lot of important cultural works from Earth that were looted from museum collections, even if the looters had a veneer of legal authority thanks to local politics."

"It could make good theatre," the Grenouthian director mused. "We could have actors dressed as law enforcement seize the works after the appraiser gives a value and then points out that they were obtained illegally."

"I could send a bot," Flower offered through an overhead speaker grille.

"It might be worth a special segment every show," Yaem said. "Maybe we could seize the work and then give the people a chance to flee. Everybody likes a good chase scene."

"EarthCent wasn't thinking about it in terms of production values," John said patiently. "Thanks to all of the retirees moving back to Earth, plus the steady growth of alien tourism, the president and several of the ambassadors are trying to repatriate important works to the museums from which they were, uh, liberated."

"Do you have any intelligence about which works you expect to see on the show?" M793qK rubbed out on his speaking legs.

"We have an incomplete list compiled by museum curators and academics of works that are known to be missing, though it's not clear how many of them were sold to aliens or smuggled off Earth by humans who kept them. People have short memories compared to the advanced species, and some of the works were taken almost a hundred years ago, which is longer than the vast majority of us live. That means people who inherited those works may not be aware that they weren't acquired in a legitimate manner."

"How many items are on the list."

John sighed. "It's in the hundreds of thousands, though a double-digit percentage may be misplaced in storage. It seems that all museums go through a period of hoarding where they acquire whatever they can get their hands on rather than what they need. But there's also a hot list of a few thousand pieces that are considered priceless, and that's spread across all of the disciplines, from oil paintings and sculptures to pottery and fossils."

"It's too many for my idea," the Farling rubbed out. "I was going to suggest that I have my ReproMan business prepare replicas that we could pre-position and then pull a swap when the originals are brought in."

"That's even better," Yaem said excitedly. "Conning the con. We'll hire some beautiful people to act as specialists so they can distract the marks while we pull the switcheroo."

"Excuse me," Julie said. "I don't want to be a party pooper, but isn't the goal to develop a show to hand off to the Grenouthian Network and the Empire Convention Center? Aren't they expecting something with regular people bringing in family treasures and specialists talking about what makes those items of value?"

"Sorry," the Sharf said. "I forgot myself for a moment there."

John waited a few seconds to make sure everybody had said their piece and then launched into his pitch. "What the EarthCent Intelligence analysts came up with, after consultation with their counterparts in other intelligence services and ISPOA, is that you need to put a policy in place and talk about it from time to time when a case comes up. I have a draft you can start from that I'll ask Flower to distribute after the meeting, but in summary, it suggests that your appraisers say whatever they would say about any important work, and then add that it's included in a list of objects missing from Earth's museums. Then the appraiser would say that the *Antiques Tunnelshow* has a policy not to place values on pieces where there's a question of ownership. You could also suggest the current owners contact the Human Empire about programs for repatriating pieces that are an important part of human heritage."

"It's not nearly as interesting as seizing the piece or pulling a swap," the Grenouthian director said. "But maybe the looks on the faces of the people bringing the items in will make up for it."

"Which ministry in the Human Empire would they contact?" Julie asked. "The Ministry of Antiquities?"

"That's up to Samuel and the government they're trying to put in place," John said. "I haven't talked to him. Like I said, I'm mainly here because Ellen was coming, and our ship can't be in two places at the same time."

"I'd heard it has a popper," the Grenouthian director said.

"Yes, a one-shot jump drive." John felt a sudden prickling at the back of his neck and asked, "Does it work by making a copy of the ship in a new place and then destroying the old one?"

"Never mind what I said. I was just thinking out loud."

"I think having a policy in place and publicizing it is a good idea," Lena said. "It might be interesting if I could interview a museum curator or somebody from law enforcement about the problem so we have it in the can ready to run the first time somebody brings in a piece from the list."

"Technically," John said, trying not to look in the direction of M793qK, "the painting of the dogs playing poker was on the list."

"You're mistaken," the Farling rubbed out on his speaking legs. "Coolidge painted a whole series of them for a cigar advertising campaign, and they're some of the most popular reproductions purchased through ReproMan. I bought the original painting in question through a gallery in SoHo many years ago, and the full provenance is on the back."

"Oh. I thought there could only be one painting like that."

"Lena should interview you about your investigation on Aarden," the Grenouthian director said. "The exploding spaceship adds to the story."

"I'll have to check with the home office," John said. "I'm hardly undercover, but appearing on the *Antiques Tunnelshow* might be a bit much."

"Thank John and get the meeting moving again before Yaem implodes," Flower said over Julie's implant. "He's been staring at his smartphone for the last five minutes."

"Thank you, John," Julie said. "That's a lot to digest, and I'll let you know as soon as we have a policy in place. Is there a good way to reach you?"

"Any of these guys know how to get in touch with me," John said, gesturing at the aliens. "Or Lena can message Ellen directly over her Galactic Free Press reporter's tab."

"A word," M793qK rubbed out on his speaking legs. He got up and escorted John out of the room and didn't return for almost a minute.

Yaem grabbed his smartphone, swiped it to life, and retreated to a corner of the room where he engaged in his usual monosyllabic conversation. "Yes? No. Yes. No. No. Maybe."

"Other than adding drama to the show, do you have any input about a policy for looted art and artifacts from Earth?" Lena asked the director.

"I see it as an intra-Human issue," the Grenouthian replied. "Work something out among yourselves and stick to it. You should probably get that Minister of Antiquities involved, and we'll get an interview out of it."

"Maybe we should have people preregister the items they're bringing for appraisal, so we'll know ahead of time," Julie suggested.

Lena grimaced. "I think we'd lose a lot of the last-minute crowd that way, and it would force the appraisers to become actors if they knew ahead of time what they'd be seeing."

"I could sneak a peek at what everybody is carrying when they enter the lift tubes and check the items against the list," Flower offered. "But I'd miss some of the things in boxes or paintings that have been wrapped for protection."

"No, Lena is right," the Grenouthian said as Yaem returned to the table. "Spontaneity is one of the key ingredients of the formula we're trying to follow."

M793qK slipped back into the conference room and leaned forward to rest his carapace on a chair back he'd tilted against the table. "Did I miss anything?" he rubbed out on his speaking legs.

"Flower offered to pre-screen what the guests are carrying, but the director thinks it would be counterproductive," Julie told him.

"Agreed. Now on to the serious business. Break Rock was a disaster. If I hadn't sent a few of my patients in with items from my personal collection the show would have been a dud."

"It wasn't just the dogs playing poker?" the Grenouthian asked.

"All the good stuff was mine," M793qK asserted. "We can get away with that once, but I believe the entertainment section tunnel network treaty includes a clause about the difference between reality shows and scripted drama."

"He's right," Yaem said. "We can script up to twenty percent of the show, though that includes the introduction, closing, and any educational inserts. But the Stryx added a paragraph about fake finds after a production group from the Free Republic made a killing with *Derelict Treasures* a few millennia ago. I had the case study in school."

Julie glanced up, expecting Flower to jump into her head with an explanation, but Lena asked, "Can you explain? I've never heard of the show."

"Some Horten pirates stumbled on a derelict vessel from a civilization that went extinct so long ago only the Stryx knew who they were, but the important thing is that it had been a luxury liner. The pirates got ahold of some immersive cameras and went through the cabins one at a time, and they had a former play-by-play commentator from the gaming tournament circuit who made it all sound exciting even though they mainly found junk. It was the top show on the tunnel network for two seasons, and then it turned out that it was all fake."

"There wasn't any derelict luxury liner?" Julie asked.

"The liner was real, but it had already been scavenged a dozen times over," Yaem explained. "All of the treasures the pirates discovered were planted, and they might have gotten away with it for a third season if somebody hadn't slipped up and included some gold coins with the profile of a Cayl emperor who was still serving."

"Goes to show why you can't trust pirates," the Grenouthian director said. "The bottom line is that if you're doing a reality treasure hunt show, no more than five percent of discovered objects can be planted throughout the season."

"But we aren't a treasure hunt show," Julie protested.

"Close enough that we have to be careful. Fortunately, the format of the show means that we can get away with appraising a lot of low-value items without any particular historical value, especially in the early episodes when it's all new to the audience."

"Flower seemed to think that Break Rock wasn't the ideal place to start because it's the smallest habitat on her circuit and the people working there don't bring a lot with them," Lena said.

"We keep Break Rock in the circuit because it was one of the first places she stopped and we supplied the police force," Julie explained. "Our next stop is Chianga, a heavily industrialized Dollnick open world that hosts some of the oldest sovereign human communities. And the people living there are more likely than most to have brought furniture and household goods from Earth because the locally manufactured goods didn't translate well."

"You mean because the Dollnicks are a four-armed species that's also much taller than we are."

"We should send a specialist down to offer free transportation on Flower's shuttle for interesting furniture," the Grenouthian director said. "I want to get some big pieces in the show, and we'll have to wait another two stops if nothing turns up."

"What's wrong with the stop after Chianga?" Lena asked. "My calendar shows that it's another open world where the sovereign human community makes high-end textiles under Frunge license, including the tent the Human Empire put up for its pavilion at the New Worlds Fair."

"Frunge," Yaem said, his eyes stalks protruding slightly as he swiveled to Lena. "They don't allow importation of wood products."

Lena face-palmed. "I should have made the connection."

The director rose to his feet and struck a formal speaker's pose with the thumbs of his paws hooked over the lip of his belly pouch, indicating that he had something important to relate. "I received a communication from the viewing statistics department of the Grenouthian network last night. As part of the marketing for the *Antiques Tunnelshow,* they've been rerunning commercials in low-demand slots with excerpts from an old Earth show of similar name and content. The response has been even better than we expected, with viewers contacting the network and requesting more commercials, something that hasn't happened since the launch of the Professional LARPing League."

"So Grenouthians are interested in human antiques after all," Julie said. "You mentioned that might be a problem."

"The network ran the commercials across the tunnel network, so we're talking about a wide variety of species, not just Grenouthians. The feedback showed that viewers loved the format, regular folk bringing in family heirlooms and tag sale bargains for appraisal. But the feedback also included two complaints, namely the lack of aliens in the snippets and the emphasis on art that they couldn't take seriously. They wanted to see more kitchen gadgets, representative artworks, and furniture."

"Where did the Grenouthian network get old episodes of a show from Earth?" Lena asked.

"I sent them along," M793qK said. "The copyrights had expired in some cases, and I was able to buy the rights to the remainder for a song since the broadcasting corporation that owned them has gone into receivership."

"I'd like to see the raw numbers," Yaem said. "Not now, but if you can send them to me later."

"It's too late to make changes for the first show," the director said, "but going forward, I want a minimum of one non-Human with antique items from their species on every episode, and one or more appearances by a non-Human specialist in the appraisal process. My target is having a non-Human in the frame for at least a third of the time in the final cut for Chianga, and depending on the reaction, we may go up from there."

"Will they come?" Julie asked. "I know there are a few thousand aliens on board—"

"More," Flower said over her implant.

"—but that doesn't mean they all want to be in a show, or that they brought their family heirlooms with them."

"Have you forgotten that the open worlds are primarily populated by non-Humans?" M793qK rubbed out in amusement. "There may be tens of millions of Humans on Chianga, but there are at least a billion Dollnicks and millions of members of other species doing business there."

"All of our advance advertising on Chianga has been aimed at the Human population, so we'll have to get something in front of the Dollnicks and the others," Yaem said and swiveled his eyes to the director. "Can you get Lume and shoot something today that we can send ahead?"

"I was going to spend the day editing," the Grenouthian director said with a sigh. "All right, but last-minute ad buy is expensive."

# Nine

"How's my favorite daughter's sister-in-law?" the mayor of Floaters greeted Vivian. "I hope you don't mind my dropping by unannounced, but my old friend Nule gave me a ride up to orbit and he was hoping to meet Samuel before continuing on his trip." Bob lowered his voice conspiratorially and added, "He's on his way to attend a Princely Convocation as the representative from Chianga."

Vivian, who was barefoot and still wearing her nightgown, stared at the towering Dollnick accompanying Bob, her eyes about level with the alien's lower set of shoulders. "Uh..."

"I thought Sam was an early riser," Bob continued, brushing past Vivian into the cabin. "Is that our little Rose looking all grown up?"

"Dollnick," the girl said, pointing past her mother.

"Yes, Nule is a Dollnick, and an important one. Is your father awake?"

"I'll be out in a minute, Bob," Samuel called from the bathroom. "I was just shaving."

"How about you let us take you to breakfast?" Bob offered. "I promised your mother to feed you if we met up."

"I have to finish getting dressed," Vivian said to her brother's wife's father. "Can you watch Rose?"

"I watching Dollnick," Rose said before Bob could reply. "Dollnick tall."

Nule crouched so he could reach the girl with his upper set of arms and then lifted her until her head was just shy of the ceiling. "Now you're taller," he said in a whistly English.

"I taller than Daddy," Rose said, twisting her head as Samuel came out of the bathroom. "Look at me, Daddy."

"Nice of you to stop by, Bob," Samuel greeted the mayor, who had been instrumental in providing political support in the Conference of Sovereign Human Communities for the founding of the Human Empire. "Was it Nule?" he followed up, offering the Dollnick a handshake.

Nule solemnly reached out with his lower right arm to return the handshake and then placed his lower left hand over the top in imitation of human politicians he'd studied from Earth's archival footage. "Thank you for meeting us in your home. I hope we aren't intruding, but time is tight."

"I'm always glad to meet with anybody Bob thinks well of," Samuel said diplomatically. "My daughter seems to have taken a shine to you. She doesn't let just anybody pick her up."

"Four arms," Rose asserted, holding out four fingers. "Flower says four is best."

"Vivian looked a little annoyed with me," Bob said in a low voice. "Is there somewhere we can talk?"

"She was just surprised," Samuel said. "Here is fine if you don't mind Rose climbing on you. Krey has banned me from Human Empire headquarters two weekends a month because she thinks I don't take enough time off. We were going to visit the *Antiques Tunnelshow* later, but there's nothing on the schedule before then."

"Breakfast," Rose reminded him.

"I'll give Rose breakfast," Vivian said, returning to the living room in a high-necked dress that had a Victorian look, despite the lack of a bustle. "Can I get you anything, Bob? Nule? Flower gave us a case of Harry's Fruitcakes last year and—"

"Yes," Nule whistled. "I'd better put Rose down first."

Samuel waved Bob toward the couch and detoured past the easy chair, where he gave the chrome pedal just visible under the skirt a few pumps to raise the seat to a comfortable height for taller alien species. Then he joined Bob on the couch and assumed a listening attitude.

"Have you heard anything from your family lately?" Bob inquired politely.

"Everybody is fine, the kids are growing like the gravity is too low, and my father is finally starting to take it a bit easy," Samuel said. "My mom's attempt to switch to part-time seems to be a failure, but I think it's because she's bored at home."

"I'd be surprised if EarthCent had a busier embassy than Union Station," Bob said. "It's the only one with a co-ambassador. I haven't seen Daniel since the last CoSHC convention."

"We have a visor conference every week to make sure the Human Empire and CoSHC are on the same track," Samuel said. "You're welcome to join in."

Bob made the sign of the cross with his forefingers. "Get thee behind me, Satan. The last thing I need in my life is more meetings."

Vivian reappeared with a brandy-soaked Harry's Fruitcake on a tray, along with a cake knife and three smaller plates. She cut the Dollnick a generous slice in her role as the hostess, then cut a sliver each for her husband and Bob before disappearing back into the kitchen.

Nule ignored the fork, picked up his slice, and took a large bite. In keeping with Chiangan tradition, all three of them ate the first piece silently, and then Samuel cut a large second piece for the alien and settled back again to listen.

"I've heard great things about you from Bob and Lume," Nule began. "They both say that you're a Human who can get things done."

"Thank you," Samuel said, resisting the urge to help himself to a real slice of cake and the equivalent of a stiff drink that it would deliver. "I rely on Lume and Flower for all matters touching on the Dollnick Empire."

"Yes, Flower too," Nule said, though without his earlier enthusiasm. "I wish I had the time to explain in more detail, but if my ship isn't in the tunnel an hour from now, I'll be late to the Princely Convocation."

"You can cut to the chase with Samuel," Bob said. "If he has any questions after you leave that I can't answer, I know where to find Lume."

"Excellent. You see, Your High—Samuel," the Dollnick corrected himself at the last second, recalling that the human didn't like being addressed as an emperor. "One of the topics on the table at the meeting I'm rushing to is the *Antiques Tunnelshow,* which is expected to deliver a windfall to our Empire Convention Center chain. But some of us are concerned that we'll be underrepresented as specialists and that our finest art will go unremarked because the critics working for some of the tunnel network species dismiss it as technology."

"I see," Samuel said, which was only a white lie since he had a pretty good idea where the conversation was heading.

"So I brought two standard-size containers of artifacts from the Chiangan Museum of Fine Arts and Mechanisms, which I'm sure Flower has unloaded by now, and I hope that you will use your influence to see that the pieces and Curator Shint are given a fair hearing by the show's management team."

"Shint?" Samuel asked. "That's a strange name for a Dollnick."

"It's a female name," Bob explained. "You don't run into many of them out and about on the tunnel network."

"My niece," Nule said as soon as he swallowed the bite of cake he'd taken when Samuel began his question. "Lume kindly offered to stand Protector, but her family worries that she will be hurting her future chance at happiness if it appears that she's here because of—" he concluded with a whistle that Samuel's implant failed to translate.

"He's hoping that the Human Empire will extend an official invitation to give Shint a reason to be here on her own," Bob explained. "Perhaps she could give a guest lecture at your school?"

"Of course," Samuel said, still feeling that he was missing something. "But where is Curator Shint?"

"Waiting with the containers," Nule said as he rose to his feet. "Not that we didn't trust Flower to store them, you understand, but without the Human Empire's invitation, Shint would have returned to the surface on the next shuttle. I'm sorry to eat and run, but I have to get my ship in the tunnel."

"Wait a second," Vivian said, appearing from the kitchen where she'd been listening at the door. She scooped the remaining three-quarters of the brandy-soaked fruitcake into a large plastic container and pressed it on the Dollnick. "Please."

"If you insist, Empress," Nule said, accepting the box with a bow. Then he was out the door in two strides, and something told Samuel that if he ran to look, the corridor would already be empty.

"I think that went very well," Bob said, rubbing his hands together. "Shint is a fine young Dollnick if you can get her to talk. You know how shy the females can be when they're approaching marriage age."

"What was the word Nule whistled that my implant failed to translate at the end of his request?" Samuel asked.

"Ah, it didn't translate for me either, but I'm familiar enough with Shint's story to tell you what it means. She's skipping out on an arranged marriage."

"What? Who was the suitor? Did you put us in the middle of a diplomatic crisis?"

"Of course we're happy to extend any protection we can, even if it's only for the sake of her reputation," Vivian said, shooting her husband an annoyed look. "I'd heard that some Dollnicks practiced arranged marriages, even for females who aren't part of a prince's family, but—"

"Shint is," Bob interrupted. "She's the youngest daughter of Prince Drume. Nule is married to one of the prince's sisters."

"Who was she promised to?" Samuel asked in a hollow voice.

"Prince Kuerda's second son, who has a bit of a reputation as an idiot. They say he couldn't engineer his way out of a paper bag."

"But you're not worried about the prince."

"Which one?" Bob asked. "Oh, you mean Kuerda? If anything, he'll think better of you for helping them out of a sticky situation. I'll be the last one to criticize the way Dollnicks do things—"

"I should hope so," Flower interjected through one of the room's speakers.

"—but promising children to each other in marriage before they're even hatched is just asking for trouble."

"Is that what this was?" Vivian asked. "An egg betrothal? I remember the Drazens I worked with joking about egg betrothals, but I didn't take it seriously."

"You did the right thing," Bob said. "I wouldn't have brought Nule here otherwise. And I know that Flower keeps the cabin adjoining yours open for guests, so hosting Shint as part of your family won't be a problem."

"What?"

"Well, you didn't think that Prince Drume's daughter could move into a cabin on her own. Lume will escort her in public, but she can hardly live with him. Can you have a nest moved into the cabin next door, Flower?"

"Already on the way," the Dollnick artificial intelligence said. "I'll have a bot stock her refrigerator as well."

Vivian started to say something, then she just laughed and went to make sure that Rose had finished her blintz.

"I would have warned you if I'd known ahead of time, but Nule sort of ambushed me at the spaceport," Bob apologized. "He's our prince's chief administrator on Chianga, and about as philo-human as Dollnicks come. My son interned in his office."

"As long as we aren't in the middle of some sort of fight between princely houses, I suppose it can only boost the

Human Empire's diplomatic profile," Samuel said. "When are we going to meet the young princess?"

"Oh, she's older than I am, but getting near marrying age. Shint spent a few decades studying the history of science and technology at one of their top universities, so you won't have to worry about her qualifications as a specialist."

"I just have to figure out how to break it to the Grenouthian director and Lena that we need to parachute a Dollnick princess into their show."

"The director will be thrilled, and Lena won't mind," Flower said. "All we need now is a runaway Vergallian princess who knows something about tapestries, and I think I know where we can find one."

"She's joking, right?" Bob asked.

"I don't think so," Samuel said. "Flower takes her entertainment division very seriously."

"Entertainment is the biggest trade category on the tunnel network," Bob said philosophically. "Well, I should get back to the docking deck and grab the old family silver that I brought to take on the show. It's just a few mismatched pieces, not a real set, but my grandmother told me that some of it might date back to the nineteenth century, around the time of the American Civil War. I'm hoping the experts can fill in the blanks so when it's time to divide the silver between our children we can do it fairly."

After the Mayor of Floaters left, Samuel went into the kitchen where he found his wife was still giggling uncontrollably, much to the amusement of their daughter.

"I can't help it," Vivian said when she caught her breath. "Is he gone?"

"Yes," Samuel said. "He went back to the docking deck to pick up some family heirlooms he brought for the *Tunnelshow*."

"I'm an idiot," Vivian said. "I never took Bob seriously, even though he's been running a major industrial city on a Dollnick open world longer than I've been alive. It's the way he's so jolly all the time like he's trying to sell something. Ever since his daughter married my brother, I've had the feeling he was taking advantage of our family connection, so I've tried to avoid him when we stop at Chianga."

"Bob was always one of the leading voices in CoSHC," Samuel said. "Technically, he's still the Human Empire's Minister of Industry, though he has the sense to keep a low profile."

"That's what I mean," Vivian said. "Here I've been making excuses not to go down and visit when all he wants to do is help. I'll bet he knows more about dealing with Dollnicks than the analysts at EarthCent Intelligence."

"Intelligence," Rose repeated, enjoying the sound of the word.

"Yes, intelligence, something Mommy is sadly lacking."

"Don't be so hard on yourself, Viv," Samuel said. "I didn't see any of this coming, but now I'm thinking that Flower is right."

"Flower *is* right," Rose pronounced with surprising vehemence.

"Why do I suspect that she's been practicing that with someone?"

"Can you tell me when Bob gets to the con deck, Flower?" Vivian asked without even glancing up at the ceiling. "I want to bring him a coffee and a breakfast croissant."

"The coffee is a good idea, but skip the croissant," Flower advised. "Harry, Bill, and Jake have been up for hours making *Libum*, an ancient Roman cheesecake. It was a ritual food that was offered to their gods."

Samuel ended up carrying Rose, because she brought her favorite bear, Kreytoo, to meet the other stuffed animals, but couldn't see where she was going with it clutched to her chest. Vivian cheated and agreed to let Flower send a bot with a takeout coffee for Bob, and the family hurried to the con deck. The bot met them as they stepped out of the lift tube and presented Vivian with a recyclable cup holder with a coffee and two large glasses of green liquid. "For Lume and Shint," Flower explained through the bot's speaker.

Vivian stepped over the rope line to catch up with Bob, who had exited the triage area, and then she returned. "He said that the screeners thought that a couple of the pieces were interesting and sent him to the silver specialist," Vivian reported. "I asked him to take his time getting there so we could catch up and watch. They'll be easy to find because he's with Lume and Shint."

"This shouldn't take long," Samuel said. "The line is moving faster than I would have guessed."

"They have as many specialists doing the pre-screening as the final appraisals," Vivian said. "Julie told me that it's an adjustment they made after the first show. They're also thinking of adding local antiques experts everywhere the show stops."

"For the appraisals or the screening?"

"I think she said both."

Two volunteers from the independent living deck wearing *Antiques Tunnelshow* T-shirts greeted Samuel and

Vivian by name when they reached the beginning of the triage area.

"And what have you brought?" Nancy asked. "Is Mister Bear here to be appraised?"

"Kreytoo," Rose said, having understood that much of the question. "Not Mister."

Nancy's late-in-life husband, Jack, who was the president of the original Flower's Paradise independent living cooperative, pointed down the left row of tables. "Third from the end, he's putting the model trains back in the box. And just in case you didn't know, there's a Dollnick female from a prince's family wandering around with Lume."

"How can you tell she's from a prince's family?" Samuel asked.

"The way she carries herself," Jack said. "I worked two full contracts on Dollnick ag worlds, and after twenty or thirty years, I developed an eye for aristocrats. The princes were always stopping by with their families to show the flag and let everybody know they cared."

"What a lovely Steiff bear," the specialist said as Rose presented Kreytoo. "And it still has the ear button. Take her to Dolls and Toys."

After emerging from the gauntlet, Samuel easily spotted Lume towering over the crowd, and they headed in that direction.

"Would you believe that I'm nervous?" Bob said. "The appraiser got excited by a couple of the pieces and took them to see another specialist at the other silver table. They called for a camera crew, so I'm going to be on the show."

"Sife," Rose told him proudly, brandishing her polar bear.

"We'll go to the Dolls and Toys table next," Samuel promised, and offered the slender Dollnick female an apologetic smile that his hands were full. "Samuel McAllister, my wife, Vivian, our daughter, Rose."

"Shint," the graceful alien whistled, and then turned on the translation pendant she was wearing. "I've just started learning Humanese and I find the words difficult to pronounce."

"Vivian and I have implants so you can speak Dollnick," Samuel said. "Flower is preparing the cabin next to ours for you, and we look forward to hosting you—" he glanced at Lume, who was making a subtle rolling motion with one of his forefingers, encouraging Samuel to continue, "—as a member of our family."

"Thank you, Emperor," Shint said, and surprised them both by dropping a sort of curtsey. "I hope it's not an imposition."

"We're happy to have you," Vivian said. "If you ever need anything or want to talk, we're right next door."

The Grenouthian director stepped up, offered Shint a deep bow, and then began barking orders at Jorb and Razood, each of whom was manipulating two cameras. "We have a live one," he said. "Jorb, you focus on the items and the appraiser, Razood, you get the Human and pick a good angle to get the Dollnicks in the shot. Is that okay with you, Lume?"

"Shint?" Lume asked.

"I think appearing in public with the emperor and his family will help quiet any rumors," she replied after a moment's thought.

"Right," the director said, and then addressed Rose. "Can you tilt your bear a little to the side so the camera can see your pretty face? Good, hold that pose. Appraisers ready? Action."

"What can you tell us about these pieces?" the silver specialist asked Bob.

"I know that they're silver and they've been in my family for generations," Bob said. "The story is that they were manufactured around the time of the American Civil War, which would make them around three hundred years old, but I'm not sure I ever believed that."

"These pieces," the appraiser said, pointing at the plates and a partial tea service that were now displayed on the velvet stand, "do date to that era, though you have the wrong country, as they were made in England. They're stamped on the bottom with hallmarks," she picked up a piece and pointed at the indented symbols, "which give both the date, 1862, and the maker. As a partial set, I would give them an auction estimate of between twelve hundred and fifteen hundred creds. But your tankards are something else entirely."

"Fake?" Bob guessed.

"You had the right idea but the wrong war. These were made shortly after the American Revolution by the son of a silversmith whose father is best known for riding his horse through the countryside shouting, 'The British are coming. The British are coming.'"

"The who?"

"The country that the Americans were revolting against," the appraiser said. "The tankards are in excellent condition, though I can see a little restoration work was done there and there. Have you ever had them appraised?"

"No," Bob said. "A visitor to our home who collected silver once offered me five hundred creds for the pair, but I already promised my children that we would split the family silver between them."

"Possibly the best promise you ever made. At auction, I expect these tankards would make fifty thousand creds, and if the right collectors or a museum got involved in bidding them up, the sky is the limit."

"But we drink beer out of them on my birthday," Bob protested. "They sit on the shelf in the kitchen."

"You may want to upgrade your security system."

# Ten

"Isn't this exciting?" June said to Harry. "Your wife thinks we could end up with credits on the *Antiques Tunnelshow.*"

"I already get a credit for the desserts," Harry said. "Besides, they roll by so fast that only the aliens can read them."

"But my granddaughter will be impressed. She worries that old people who stop working just curl up and die."

"We saw a couple of our grandchildren at that Frunge world where our daughter and her husband moved the family. They couldn't believe that their grandmother had directed a documentary."

"I wonder what's taking everybody so long," June said. "Dave stopped to pick up snacks, but he's usually the last one on the bookmobile. And why don't we wait for Flower's shuttle?"

"Because we have to be on the ground to shoot the shuttle landing," Jorb said as he climbed in through the back. "We're running a few minutes late because somebody forgot to recharge the camera power packs after we used them at the show last Sunday."

"Who?" Harry asked out of curiosity.

"I thought that 'somebody' always meant your closest coworker when you use it in that context," the Drazen said. "In this case, I was talking about—"

"Me," Razood said as he climbed into the back of the bookmobile and turned around just in time to catch the first camera case that the Grenouthian director had hurled at him a little harder than necessary. "I remembered recharging them the day before and got confused."

"You were confused because Bill and Julie were waiting to chaperone your date with a certain café owner," Jorb said.

"Who's that?" June asked.

"There must be something wrong with my Humanese today," Jorb said, scratching behind his ear with his tentacle. "I thought I was being obvious."

"The owner of the Blue Tea Café," Harry explained to June. "Fandaz."

"Oof," Razood grunted when the next immersive camera case slammed into his belly. "I get it already. From now on I'll put my cameras on the chargers after every show."

"Where's Irene?" Dave asked as he climbed through the side door after handing up two large takeout bags from his favorite diner in the food court.

"She's over there shooting the *Tunnelshow* staff getting on the shuttle," Harry said, pointing out the porthole. "It looks like she's got enough because she's herding her cameras in this direction."

The Grenouthian director reached an empty case in the stack he'd been tossing to Razood, so he popped it open and hit the recall button. One of the cameras Irene was shepherding with hand movements broke away and made a beeline for the empty case. Then the director slammed it shut and threw it at Razood's head.

"Temper," the Frunge said as he latched the case into the holding rack. "What would you do if you accidentally knocked me unconscious?"

"Replace you with somebody who remembers to charge the cameras," the director replied as he repeated the recall trick with the second empty case.

Irene climbed through the side door and then slipped into what would have been the pilot's seat if Flower wasn't flying the bookmobile remotely. "Come up front, June?" she invited the other woman. "It's a completely different view."

The bookmobile set down in a clearing near the meeting house on the border between the Alt and human halves of the continent. The Grenouthian and the Frunge repeated their camera sport in reverse, this time with Razood hurling the cases at the director. Irene and Jorb unpacked cameras as quickly as they became available, and Harry, June, and Dave each claimed one. By the time Flower's first shuttle set down, the two camera units, one consisting of the three aliens, and the other of four humans, were in position.

"Aren't there any Old Way or Alt colonists coming down today?" Harry asked as the staff of the *Antiques Tunnelshow* and a group of people carrying bundles and packages exited the shuttle.

"Both groups are landing near their respective coastlines," the Grenouthian director said. "I have enough of that footage to last for another season of the Earth Two documentary series, so we're focused entirely on the *Tunnelshow* today."

"I thought that Razood and Jorb were working on the show rather than the documentary," Irene said. "Will they be with us all day?"

"Until the other set of cameras are unloaded, and the operators disembark. Jorb and Razood wanted to come down with the bookmobile and catch the shuttle landing, but once the show is set up, each of you will take one of the cameras they're currently controlling. I'll go with them, of course, and you'll direct the documentary effort here. How many hours is Flower willing to let you work?"

"Four," Irene said, holding up four fingers. "But she agreed that we could go a full day if only two of us work at a time."

"So you'll be up to four cameras each," the director said, nodding. "I know you can handle it, Irene, and Dave has been showing promise, but you'd better slave the cameras for June and Harry so they only have to worry about the master. And I don't want to get in trouble with Flower, so half of you should be on break now."

"I'll sit down. June, why don't you join me, and we can do the girls against the boys."

Razood spotted his operators coming down the ramp, left his camera floating in place, and began to sprint toward the shuttle. Jorb laid out flat making a desperate grab for the Frunge's ankle with his tentacle, missed, and lost the race.

"Like a couple of overgrown kids," the Grenouthian director remarked as he started hopping toward the shuttle. Then he looked back over his shoulder and added, "Don't forget that you're doing double duty today. Shoot the crews shooting the appraisals, but if one of the specialists tells you they have a hot prospect and none of the show's crews are available, shoot that instead."

"Harry, zoom in on the meeting house," Irene said a few seconds later. "I think I see some Alts gathering."

Harry repositioned his cameras with tentative hand movements, tapped the control screen, and then tapped it several more times. "You're right. I must see a hundred

Alts, all carrying a box or a case. Flower must have gotten the word out to them somehow."

"Skywriting, the holographic kind," Dave told them. "I ran into Dewey last week and he mentioned that Flower had contracted with him to bring a giant holographic projector on his freighter and spend a night in orbit displaying messages about the *Antiques Tunnelshow* over the continent. He said it took so much power that he almost didn't have enough left in his fuel pack to make it back."

"I've been surprised by how seat-of-the-pants the director is running the show," Irene said. "He's usually a meticulous planner, but it seems that every week they're changing the format based on feedback from the Grenouthian network."

"Flower told me that they've decided on an early pivot to aliens," Harry said. "I asked her what the hurry was, and she said that based on the reactions to the commercials the Grenouthian network has been running, they're already confident in the concept. There's no point in tweaking the show for humans when the potential alien audience is thousands of times as large."

"Thousands of times?" June asked skeptically.

"Well, I know that the Vergallians outnumber humans by around a hundred to one, and the Grenouthians license their content to species beyond the tunnel network."

"I thought the tunnels were what made broadcasts possible."

"The Grenouthians sell a lot of content on memory chips for physical delivery and rebroadcast," Harry said. "I remember that from my time on *Everyday Superheroes*. And the Alts are all coming this way."

"Stay on the Alts until they reach where the show crew are setting up the tables and the cordons," Irene said.

"And here come the Old Way guests," Dave said, manipulating all four cameras he was now controlling so they pointed in the opposite direction of Harry's to where a line of ox carts and people were coming up the dirt road. "They must have been waiting for the shuttle to land so they wouldn't be in the way."

"Will all of the shows be held on planet surfaces or orbitals from now on?" June asked Irene.

"I don't think so, though everything is so fluid now that I wouldn't bet," Irene replied. "Flower told me that in addition to her stops at Earth Two being longer than everywhere else other than Earth and Union Station, the colonists here prefer to avoid modern transportation, so taking a shuttle up to orbit to attend a show wouldn't work for them."

"They almost look like two armies approaching."

"If everybody on Earth had fought with paintings and musical instruments, the Stryx never would have removed the Alts, and we'd be one species by now." Irene walked over to where her husband was controlling his quartet of cameras and said, "Two cameras are enough for the approaching Alts. Let's get these other two pointed back at the setup."

The *Antiques Tunnelshow* benefitted from a simple set, and after unfolding the tables and putting up the velvet rope lines to channel guests into the triage area, the staff and volunteers from the independent living deck raised printed signs above the specialist stations, as opposed to doing it with holograms. The Grenouthian director beckoned to the documentary crew to bring their cameras in as the guests began queuing up, and Harry's nose soon detected the distinctive smell of freshly baked bread.

"No wonder Flower told Bill and Jake to take the weekend off," he said to Irene. "The Alts and the Old Way bakers must be catering the show."

"Or they could be bringing things they made to give each other," Irene said. "You know how generous they are, especially the Alts."

"You see?" the Grenouthian director exclaimed, indicating the queue after hopping over to glance at the viewfinder screens on Dave and Harry's cameras. "You see? That's how you form a line. No crowding, and nobody trying to sneak forward. A chalk mark on the ground would have served as well as the ropes."

"We know that the Old Way colonists are more polite than most people, and that the Alts are nicer than anybody," Dave said. "But I've also heard aliens say that the Alts are the most boring species in the galaxy."

"Boring is a compliment when the alternative is making war. Why are Jorb and Razood concentrating their crews on the people who brought the printing press in the ox cart?" he asked in frustration. "Get over there and cover the musical instruments and household gadgets sections. The early appraisals are the ones with the most cultural surprises."

"The director seems to be a little wound up today," June observed as the Grenouthian hopped off toward the crowd around the double-treadle printing press.

"I don't think he likes the idea of using footage from the documentary crew on the show, but he doesn't have much choice," Irene said. "He tried recruiting more camera crews, but it's part-time weekend work, which is a hard sell on Flower." She held a hand up to shield her eyes from the sun and surveyed the tables that were slowly being surrounded by Alts and people. "You stick with Dave in case he needs you, and I'll supervise Harry. But keep it casual so nobody suspects you of working until we swap with the boys."

Harry guided his camera over to the musical instruments section and got them in position in time to catch Lena talking to an Alt who had presented the specialist with a woodwind and was waiting for an opinion.

"I've conferred with my colleagues," the specialist reported breathlessly, "and this is the finest Alt clarinet equivalent we've seen on the *Tunnelshow*."

"Really?" the Alt asked. "How many have been brought in?"

"Well, this is the first one on the show, but I meant it in the broad sense. The carving is gorgeous, the hardware is perfection itself, and even the paint is beyond reproach. Could I ask how you came to own such a wonderful instrument? Are you a concert musician?"

The Alt surprised everybody by blushing. "I play in the neighborhood pick-up orchestra if they need an extra, but I couldn't call myself a musician. I made it."

"You made this?" the specialist asked in amazement. "When?"

'I finished it last week, and I was worried the paint wouldn't dry in time to bring it in. I was a little concerned about the shape of the bell, but when I was star gazing a few nights ago, I was surprised to see a large hologram signed by Flower requesting that any Humanese-speaking Alts bring their handicrafts to the meeting house for a show. My trip here on Flower was such a good experience that I wanted to express my thanks by coming."

"Since you just finished making the instrument, you can't have had it appraised, but do you have any ideas about its value?"

"I believe it has a nice sound, but again, I'm no musician. I make them in my spare time. My grandmother taught me," he added as an afterthought. "Some of her woodwinds are played by highly accomplished musicians."

"Of course, but what I meant is, do you know what it would sell for in a retail setting?"

The Alt looked distraught and stumbled back a half step, almost as if he'd been struck. "Sell? For m-mo-mon-sell?" He croaked, unable to pronounce 'money' out loud. "There must be some misunderstanding. Would you like to have it?"

"I wish I could make you an offer, but we have a rule about buying items from our guests," the specialist said, mistaking the Alt's meaning. "In a music store, I would place an estimate of—"

"Stop," the Alt said, placing his hands firmly over his ears as he backed away. "It's yours. I have to be going." He rushed off in the direction of the border without a backward glance.

"What just happened?" the specialist asked, looking around to see if any of his colleagues had understood.

"You know," said an older specialist examining a violin brought in by a local member of an Old Way community. "I remember hearing somewhere that the Alts don't use money."

"Some of them get upset if you say the word," the violin's owner confirmed. "There aren't any lodging businesses on the Alt side of the border. You stop at somebody's home and they invite you in to stay. It takes a while to get a feel for how much work they'll let you do to defray the cost of your lodging without offending them."

"But he left without—excuse me," the specialist said to the graceful Alt teenager who was next in line. "Do you know the man who ran off?"

"Thanos," the girl said. "He doesn't mix much with Humans so he's overly sensitive."

"Could you return this instrument to him?"

"But he gifted it to you. It would be a terrible insult to return it now."

"Oh dear," the specialist said. "Maybe Flower keeps loaner instruments for travelers, and she'll take it. Is that a flute you've brought me?"

"Yes," the Alt said, but the trepidation in her voice was obvious. "I made it to give to Aashija, the Vergallian princess who takes care of our export business."

"I'm aware that your people contracted with the Vergallians to handle your business affairs on the tunnel network, but I don't understand how it works. You provide the instruments on consignment and get the proceeds, minus a commission, when it's sold?"

"Proceeds? Oh, you mean money. We don't use it ourselves, but if any Alts travel into the Human half of the continent or need to leave the world, Aashija will take care of their expansions."

"Expenses?"

"Yes, sorry," the teenager said. "I only know the word from lessons. I've never needed to say it out loud before."

"Would you be interested in hearing how much this flute you've made would bring in a retail setting?"

"Not particularly. I came for the same reason as Thanos, to thank Flower."

"I don't know if the director can use any of this in the show," Harry muttered to Irene. "The Alts have a way of taking the excitement out of everything."

"If not the show, I think it will find a place in the documentary," Irene said, and then her eyes caught an Alt couple carrying what looked like an antique Victrola mounted on a sewing machine table with the horn pointing up. "Over there, Harry. At the Gadgets and Technology table."

Lena was chatting with the Alt couple as Harry maneuvered the cameras into position with a little help from his wife. The specialist at the table must have gotten to the part about the price, because an older Alt who had brought in a sort of model helicopter powered by twisted rubber bands suddenly began to sing in a deep baritone that drowned out all the conversations in the immediate area. The appraiser finally got the point and desisted.

"Now that's the first one of whatever that is we've seen on the *Antiques Tunnelshow,*" the specialist said when the Alt couple set down their device. He crouched to study the mechanical linkages and was clearly puzzled by the narrow conveyor belt that folded out from the main mechanism. "So you put something in the horn up top and it gets shaped into—is it a brick-making machine? No," he contradicted himself immediately. "The mold and shaping plates aren't heavy enough for that. Does it form small loaves of bread or cakes?"

The female Alt covered her mouth with her hand to hide her giggles, but her husband managed to keep a straight face as the specialist felt around the inside of the large funnel on the top. "It's for making bricks of manure," he explained. "Dung is easier to transport when dry, and it saves on packaging that would have to be recycled."

The specialist, who had insinuated his entire head into the loading funnel for a better look at the screw mechanism in the throat jerked up straight. "How novel. I've seen machines that make manure briquets or pellets for burning in stoves, but not one that forms bricks. Did you build this yourself?"

"Yes, but it's a standard design that's been around for thousands of years. The conveyer arm follows a pattern card, much like a weaving machine, and it has a range of motion to allow for laying out a hundred and twenty bricks before the machine has to be moved."

"So the dung can dry properly."

"Exactly," the husband said. "Would you like to see it in operation?"

"That would be educational," the specialist said.

The Alt pantomimed shoveling some dung into the funnel, and then he began pumping the treadle with one foot. "You see how the loading horn is vibrating," he said. "That's to help keep the dung moving down to the forcing screw. Now I'll engage the conveyer—" the belt beneath the mechanism began moving, "—and you'll notice that it moves the belt to the next deposit position right before the paddle pushes out a new brick."

"Like a double action revolver."

"I'm not familiar with the term. Is it another word for a centrifuge, like the ones we use to separate liquid manure?"

"A type of antique fire—"

"—starting mechanism," Lena interrupted, stepping between the appraiser and the Alt. "We use circular flints for starting fires while camping. It's better than rubbing two sticks together."

The two Alts looked at each other, then burst into laughter. "It's wonderful that you've finally learned to laugh at yourselves," the wife said when she recovered her breath. "I never thought I would hear a Human quote from one of our oldest stories."

"I only remember the one line," Lena improvised. "How does it go again?"

"The story dates back over thirty thousand years, before the Stryx moved us to Alt, so it could be apocryphal. Weedon, the last of our people to trade with your ancestors, tried passing on our technology of starting fires with bow drills. But the Humans told him that they preferred to wait for lightning to strike a tree, and failing that, they could always rub two sticks together."

# Eleven

"It's a rush job," Dewey explained to Bill as they unloaded the cases of cookies and biscuits from his freighter. "When the holiday and gift baking companies on Earth saw a highly decorated biscuit tin from the nineteenth century get an auction appraisal of six hundred creds, they all decided to hitch their star to the *Antiques Tunnelshow*."

"Fine, but why pay a fortune to ship cookies to Union Station for you to bring here for expedited review?" Bill asked.

"It all comes down to marketing. The most effective way to reach alien influencers active in the Human food exports market is through the new *All Species Cookbook Magazine*. But they only review products from Earth that have received the cookbook's seal of approval."

"If they saw the tests M793qK makes me do, nobody would take the seal seriously."

"I'm sure the good doctor performs a full spectrographic and chemical analysis of all the candidate products," the artificial person said. "The physical kitchen testing you do is likely necessary to meet the tunnel network treaty requirement to maintain the franchise."

"I'm not sure I understand," Bill said, depositing another case of cookie tins on the floater pallet, this one addressed from somewhere in the Netherlands. "Do you mean that when the right to produce the new edition of the

*All Species Cookbook* was awarded to humanity, there was a requirement for humans to do all of the work?"

"A significant portion of the work," Dewey corrected him. "The new magazine employs Open University students from all the tunnel network members to help with species-specific artwork and sensibilities, like the seal-of-approval labeling work is done by M793qK since humans don't know enough about alien nutrients."

"Or human nutrition, to hear him talk." Bill started lifting the next case and had to adjust his grip and stance when he sensed the weight. "I wonder what's in this one?"

Dewey stared at the QR code for a moment and said, "Vacuum-packed dates. While they may be a dessert food, I don't see the connection with cookie tins, but I've never claimed to be a marketing expert."

"How much do you want to bet that M793qK makes me crush the cookies to determine their crumble factor? He's always coming up with new factors he claims that some species or another cares about. A few months ago, when we were evaluating pickles for Flower's new brand, he made me bite into thirty of them to determine the snap factor. I haven't eaten a pickle since."

"The B&L pickle brand was created by Botan and Lisa, a young couple from Bits who left Flower for the Miklat. You might have gone LARPing with them a few years ago."

Bill thought for a moment. "I don't remember," he admitted. "So many people come and go on Flower that their names and faces turn into a blur."

"That's the last one," Dewey said, placing another case on top of the others on the floater pallet. "There's a five-hundred cred bonus if the evaluations get done before the next show."

"For me?"

"For the business Flower set up that pays you and the Farling doctor. You'd have to talk to her about the split."

Bill shrugged. "Mondays are completely open for me these days. I was going to walk around the food court and the retail corridors scouting locations for my café, but if M793qK has time to do the evaluations now, I'm game."

"You guide the floater pallet up to the kitchen and I'll stop in and see the doctor," Dewey said. After Bill left, the artificial person walked back up the ramp into the freighter's hold, removed a black briefcase from a hidden compartment in the bulkhead, and handcuffed it to his wrist. Then he exited the freighter, instructed the ramp which doubled as the main hatch to rise back into the closed position, and headed for the lift tube.

When Bill reached the kitchen, he was surprised to find Jake in the process of flipping an omelet. "There's enough for two if you haven't had breakfast," Jake said. "It's an experiment. Flower sent me a case of B&L pickles and suggested they may go well with eggs."

"I just ate," Bill said thankfully. "But why did you come in here to make yourself breakfast?"

"We're doing a rush job for the *All Species Cookbook* today. You didn't know? M793qK texted me on my old phone from Bits. I started carrying it again because it's the preferred method of communication for all the aliens who eat here."

"I'm going to stack these cases on the counter so I can let the floating pallet return. Did the text include a start time?"

Jake consulted his phone. "Another twenty minutes, unless he shows up early. Do you want a coffee?"

Bill hesitated. "I better not. M793qK might want us to dunk cookies in coffee to test the sop factor or something crazy like that and I don't want to get over-caffeinated. I don't care what he and Dewey say. I know sometimes he's just playing with us."

The Farling doctor arrived a minute before the appointed time, which was cutting it close by alien standards. He had brought his black medical bag with him, which seemed odd, until he rubbed out an explanation. "I had to stop by the bazaar and treat a stab wound. You'd think Humans would have learned not to run with scissors by now."

"Is the patient okay?" Jake asked.

"Of course she's okay, she's better than okay," M793qK rubbed out on his speaking legs. "I removed a few gallstones for her while I was operating in the neighborhood. Now where are the biscuits?"

"I put all the boxes on the back counter, and it's not just biscuits," Bill said. "There are cookies—"

"Same thing," the Farling interrupted.

"—dates, and even teabags. I opened that case out of curiosity because it weighed next to nothing, and it's a couple dozen cans the size of oatmeal containers that have different scenes painted on them."

"Hand painted?"

"You know I'm no good at art stuff," Bill said, even as he closed one eye in thought. "I think it's, what did that specialist call it? Transfer printing?"

"Unlikely," M793qK said as he eased past Jake on his way to the back of the kitchen. "You probably saw a *Tunnelshow* discussion of transfer printing for decorating ceramics, a technology that was developed in England in the mid-eighteenth century and reached the height of popularity in the early decades of the 1800s. If we're talking about the same piece from the show two weeks ago, it was a Willow pattern from the Staffordshire potteries area. ReproMan dedicates half a floor to English pottery since it's in vogue with tourists from the tunnel network."

Jake and Bill both stared at the back of the alien's carapace with their mouths hanging open. "How can you keep all of that straight?" Jake demanded. "I need to write down recipes with over five ingredients."

"Then I suggest you undertake rigorous training of your memory. I'll bring you flashcards next time I come this way, no charge."

Bill trailed along as the Farling examined each of the cases, apparently reading the digital codes through his multi-faceted eyes without any technological aids. After examining all the cases, the alien returned to the first one and said, "Five of this, half-ten of the other. We may as well start at the beginning with the Dutch Butter Cookies." He sliced through the brown paper tape with one of his middle legs, flipped up the tabs of the box, and removed a large round tin.

"What's that on the cover?" Bill asked.

"A windmill. You've never seen one?"

"Not like that with a whole house attached. The one's I've seen look like propellors."

"You're thinking of more recent turbine technology," M793qK rubbed out on his speaking legs as he took a butter cookie from the crinkled paper that held a small stack and popped it in his maw. "The art depicts a traditional windmill with cloth sails, likely used for milling flour or pumping water for irrigation or drainage. The basic principle has been around on Earth for at least two millennia, starting with the Chinese, I believe."

"And what's wrong with the boy in that picture?" Jake asked, pointing at a different tin in the case.

"He's cold and weary after staying up all night with his finger in the dike, thereby saving his country. I think it would be fair to say that they don't make Humans the way they used to." The Farling took a second cookie and crushed it. "Good crumble factor, no need to test that. Have a taste, you two."

"A regular taste, you mean?" Bill asked. "I don't have to dunk it in hot liquid or throw it in the air and catch it in my mouth?"

"We're running a quality control service, not a circus, and I'm too pressed for time to go beyond the letter of our contract," M793qK responded.

"It's buttery," Jake said after taking a bite.

"Too sweet for my taste," Bill added.

"Excellent." The Farling moved on to the next case which was already open and produced one of the cans of tea Bill had mentioned. "Now we'll need that hot water. Three cups should do it."

"I'll get it," Jake said. He grabbed three cups from an overhead rack and headed for the instant hot water tap.

"We aren't going to test the tea bags for rip resistance?" Bill asked.

"You can rip one if it's important to you," M793qK replied magnanimously.

"Is something going on I need to know about? Did Dewey bring you good news from Farling Four?"

"Dewey always brings good news from my planet when he visits. Why would there ever be otherwise?"

Bill frowned. "If you're trying to convince me that you'll be the model employer from now on, it won't work. I'm still going to open my café as soon as the *Antiques Tunnelshow* commitment is up."

"I see you remain suspicious of me," the Farling doctor rubbed out on his speaking legs while simultaneously opening the next box. "Ah, tea biscuits. Can you identify the image on the tin?"

"The London Bridge?" Bill hazarded a guess, based on the word 'London' in the maker's name.

"Very good. And what made the London Bridge special?"

"Doesn't it have a song about it?"

"Yes, but I was referring to the fact that the original bridge was built with houses on it to help defray the cost of maintenance," M793qK explained. He took a cup of hot water from the tray Jake presented, added a tea bag, and set it aside for the moment. "The bridge became a destination market center, with two-story houses featuring shops on the first floor."

"I've never heard of putting houses on a bridge," Bill said. "Harry told me that there was a bridge with a roof on it near the town where he lived. He said that was to reduce maintenance costs too, and it seems more sensible than adding whole houses."

"The houses were added to the bridge for the money the inhabitants paid to live there, not to protect the roadbed from rain. What I'm trying to explain," he offered the open tin to each of the humans in turn to take a tea biscuit, "is that it's all about mercantilism."

"It?" Jake asked. "I must have missed something."

"Everything," M793qK said. "There would be no reason for any of us to be here on Flower if it wasn't for business. That's what makes the *Antiques Tunnelshow* so important."

"Flower could have found other shows to fill the con deck for twelve weekends," Bill said. "I know that she's expecting royalties from the Grenouthian Network and the Empire Convention Center chain if the show continues after we get to Union Station, but I didn't know you had a point in it."

"Multiple points, it was my idea. But as important as entertainment products are on the tunnel network, that's not where my interest lies. I'm in negotiations with the Grenouthians to make my planet a stop on the show's circuit in future seasons, and if it goes as well as I suspect it will, I'll exercise the option to launch a version in Farling space."

"Farlings collect antiques?" Jake asked. "I thought you were a super long-lived species."

"And your point is?" M793qK rubbed out.

"Well, I'd think you'd have to learn how to get rid of stuff or after a few thousand years you'd have nowhere to put it."

"Our lifespans are proportional to the ability of the individual to maintain his body. Members of the hierarchy can manage the task indefinitely, but most Farlings who reach maturity don't live any longer than Verlocks. That said, your supposition about possessions piling up is spot on, and throughout the Farling Empire, there's an active auction market for estate sales. It's the perfect match for the *Antiques Tunnelshow.*"

"Then why hasn't it been done already?" Bill asked.

"It has," M793qK said. "I remember three different versions that lasted for centuries, but entertainment properties all have a way of winding down when there are enough reruns to keep any sane sentient watching for more time than makes sense. There are minor differences in format," he continued, raising a limb to forestall Bill's objection, "but the basic concept of bringing antiques to be appraised is as old as the auction process itself, which predates the Stryx."

Jake wrapped the string of his teabag around the handle of his cup to keep it from coming out in his mouth and took a sip from the opposite side. "I'm not giving up coffee, but it has a nice flavor." He followed with a bite of the biscuit. "I guess those Londoners knew what they were doing."

Bill followed suit, but he dipped his biscuit in the tea first, just briefly before it could start dissolving. "I wouldn't cross a bridge for a cup, but it's not bad."

M793qK drank off his whole cup while resuming his lecture with his speaking legs. "The problem with family heirlooms is that they have no economic velocity. In some places and times, there may be taxes due when they pass from generation to generation, but on the whole, they may as well be carved potatoes. When somebody comes on the *Antiques Tunnelshow* with a pocket watch they found hanging from a nail in the corner of the basement when cleaning up the old coal bin nobody has been in for three hundred years, it represents ten Human generations of lost economic opportunity."

"It sounds like you're saying that everybody should convert their antiques to cash for the sake of business activity," Jake said. "But if they did that, the prices would collapse, and you'd be back where you started."

"And we're the shortest-lived species on the tunnel network," Bill added. "Any multi-generational hoarding we do has to have far less impact than it would with the advanced species. How old would a pocket watch passed down to you by your grandfather be?"

"I never met my parents so I wouldn't know," M793qK said. "Jake makes an excellent point. I'm not advocating for everybody to sell their family heirlooms for the sake of creating commissions for auction houses or so they can spend the cash on tourism. The same amount of cash, plus the commission, will be locked up by the buyer. I'm simply trying to point out that ignorance, while it may be blissful, is not economically efficient. Antiques, when they have a value, are an asset class, like the balance on your programmable cred or value of the inventory of a business."

"But almost everybody who gets an appraisal on the *Antiques Tunnelshow* says that they would never sell."

"Humans say a lot of things." The Farling neatly bisected the paper tape on the next box and extracted a large tin with a clipper ship in full sail depicted on the cover. Several other craft sailed around the sidewall on stormy seas. "Now we're getting somewhere." He pulled off the cover and the oily salty smell was almost overpowering. "Put out your hands."

Jake and Bill obeyed the instruction, and each was rewarded with a section of cashews, almonds, something covered in chocolate, and a glob of dried red berries.

"Don't we get any pistachios?" Jake asked as M793qK cleaned out that compartment of the tin.

"The shells are bad for your digestive tract," the doctor replied.

"That's why we take them off."

"Wasteful, especially when I'm here. You see, it's all a question of efficiency. My body is an advanced chemical factory, and I can digest nutshells along with any other organic matter. Given the caloric content before us, the best possible outcome would be for me to eat all of the pistachios and Brazil nuts."

"Weren't we supposed to be certifying these for the *All Species Cookbook* seal of approval and confirming the accuracy of the nutrition labels?" Bill asked.

"It's all good so far and I'll regurgitate a few samples for the mass spectrograph when I get back to my clinic," M793qK said. "How are the nuts?"

"Salty," Jake said. "I have a sudden craving for egg-nog."

"Then they're working as planned. And the art?" he rubbed out on his speaking legs while simultaneously masticating a mouthful of Brazil nuts still in their shells and holding up the tin's lid.

"It seems incredible that the ship doesn't get blown over on its side with all those sails. But what does it have to do with nuts?"

"Clipper ships were a common motif for the packaging of imported luxury items all around the world at one time. These tins are attempting to invoke a retro look to piggy-back on the *Antiques Tunnelshow* when it hits the Empire Convention Center circuit."

"It seems like a lot of planning just to sell some nuts," Bill said. "Don't people on Earth eat them?"

M793qK shoveled the remaining Brazil nuts into his maw and folded up the cardboard tabs of the case, a clear indication that he intended to take it with him. "Just to sell some nuts?" he repeated Bill's phrase. "Are you spending every evening agonizing over menus and sketching interior layouts for your café just to sell some coffee and cookies? There are three paths a sentient can take in life," he continued as he opened the next box and extracted a cellophane-wrapped wheel of dates which he passed to Jake. "Every lifeform in the universe must choose between advancing, standing still, or retreating. Why do you think Humans call the rest of us advanced species?"

"Because you've had advanced technology for hundreds of thousands or millions of years longer than we have," Bill said.

"But how do you think a species becomes advanced? By being satisfied with what they have, or by going backward, like the Kasilians did for many generations before the Stryx intervened by proxy? The way to advance as a species is to keep moving forward."

Jake finally worked a fingernail under the plastic and opened the package, and as he did so, he noticed a pull string that would have cut through the wrapper from the inside. He broke a few dates out of the circle and popped one in his mouth while passing the package to Bill.

"What about the Alts and the Old Way movement?" Bill countered as he took a date. "You usually say good things about them."

"Do you think that the Alts and other people who choose to live with limited technology in their day-to-day lives aren't advancing?" M793qK rubbed out on his speaking legs. His wings popped partially out of his carapace in amusement as he took the package of dates and placed it in his mouth, wrapping and all. "Unlike a certain species well represented in this kitchen, the Alts developed their own interstellar drive, and in general terms, I would assess their technological progress to be five hundred years beyond humanity's state-of-the-art. That they don't force that technology into every possible niche of their society is a choice, and one that demonstrates their social advancement is approaching that of the Drazens or Hortens."

"Maybe I'd use these dates for baking, but they're not great by themselves," Jake said.

"Same here," Bill said. "I probably shouldn't have brought up the Alts, but what about the Old Way movement?"

"They haven't become stagnant," the Farling said. "Their approach to preventive health care through diet and exercise is superior to any other Human population not coached by Flower and myself. Their focus is on relationships and personal growth, and they've found it useful to eschew modern communications technology while developing their society. I predict that in a few generations, they'll be sufficiently mature as a culture to be able to integrate more technology without losing their balance. In a thousand years, it may be difficult for an outside observer to differentiate between an Old Way community and a similar farming community on a Vergallian tech-ban world."

"But Vergallians are ruled by queens," Jake pointed out.

"That may be the direction the Old Way is headed as well," M793qK said. "A trillion Vergallians can't be wrong."

## Twelve

"The shuttle from Alfe is arriving in five minutes," Flower reminded Julie.

"I think Basil is working on a sentence," Julie subvoced in reply before continuing out loud, "Come on, Basil. Where is Mommy going?"

"Momma," Basil said dutifully, but his attention was on a twenty-month-old girl in a bouncy seat. "Basil bounce."

"I'll put him in the other one," one of the toddler activity coordinators told Julie. "The two of them would bounce and make faces at each other all morning if we let them. But M793qK caps bouncy time at twenty minutes for their age cohort."

Julie watched as the woman put Basil in the bouncy seat and secured the safety harness, and then she ventured, "Mommy goes to work now. Bye, bye, Basil."

"Basil bounce," the boy repeated as he enthusiastically pumped his chubby little legs.

"Four minutes," Flower said over Julie's implant. "I'm holding the lift tube capsule for you."

"Sorry," Julie subvoced, and hurried out of the crèche. The doors of the closest lift tube slid open at her approach, and three minutes later she emerged on the docking deck, just as one of the giant shuttles began nosing through the atmosphere retention field that kept the air in the open end of Flower's core. "How will I recognize her?"

"Yvella is the only Sharf on the shuttle. And she's traveling incognito, so don't make a fuss."

"Lena said that Yvella is the granddaughter of the Sharf emperor. I thought she'd be traveling with royal guards or something."

"Great-granddaughter," Flower corrected her. "Yvella spent the last year and a half on Earth studying your art and culture after the New Worlds Fair made such an impression on her. She picked up a half-dozen languages and probably knows as much about your art now as some of the specialists, but she'll be interning as Lena's assistant."

"Did Yaem talk her into coming?" Julie asked.

"She's here despite everything he could do to discourage her without raising suspicions," Flower said with a rare chortle. "He's worried that word will get back to Sharf Intelligence that he's no longer working for them in any meaningful way, but I doubt Yvella would care."

"It's hard to imagine that she won't notice Yaem is working for you around the clock if she attends the production meetings with Lena."

"Running Flower Studios is officially Yaem's cover job. Here she comes."

Julie started forward at Flower's words, and she immediately spotted the skeletal young Sharf glide-stepping down the ramp in fashionable boots with built-in magnetic cleats. Yvella was holding the handle of a rolling carry-on bag she must have purchased on Earth, since the advanced species all used floater technology in their luggage. The hard-sided case was covered with travel stickers from all over the world, reminding Julie of her days as an unwilling courier for the international drug syndicate.

"Yvella," Julie called softly as she approached the Sharf. "I'm Julie. Welcome to Flower."

"Thank you for coming to meet me," Yvella said, offering a hand with such prominent bones that Julie was afraid they would grind together if she applied the slightest pressure. "Flower told me so much about you on the shuttle."

"Flower exaggerates," Julie said. "Lena would have come to meet you herself, but guests are already queuing up for the show, and she tries to get a jump on things by chatting with them to see if there are any outstanding candidates for an in-depth interview. Did you enjoy your time on the orbital?"

"I was only on Alfe for two days, but I went to the salvage shop and I'm afraid I got carried away buying old jewelry. I'm looking forward to getting a second opinion from the specialists."

"Jewelry salvage?" Julie asked as she led the way to the lift tube.

"The main business on Alfe is breaking up old ships that come in from all over the tunnel network for recycling," Yvella explained. "Imagine how many lost earrings and bracelets build up over the service life of a small interstellar liner with ten thousand cabins. And sometimes they get freighters that suffered catastrophic failures, or even sealed containers that broke free of a container carrier. There's a fascinating museum if you get the chance."

"I'd heard it was on the Sharf deck and humans aren't allowed because we gawk."

"Ask Ada, that's what the orbital's artificial intelligence calls herself, to get you in. She broke ever so many rules for me."

"Yvella's cabin," Julie told the lift tube so the new arrival would get the idea of how it worked. "I see you've been all over Earth. Were you checking up on us for your great-grandfather, or was it a vacation?"

"Sort of independent study," Yvella said. "I kept a diary and saved images of all the interesting art I saw, and I'm hoping to write a dissertation over the next few years."

"Do you have a specific topic, or would you be writing about human art in general?"

"I have a hypothesis that all of your best work is aspirational."

Julie pondered for a moment. "In the sense that artists are trying to encourage the people who encounter their work to do better?"

"I mean that the artists who do the best work, from a Sharf point of view, are the ones who aspire to be better than they actually are, if you know what I mean."

"I'm not sure that I do."

"Anyone who masters a craft can create works that draw in an audience and manipulate its emotions. What Sharf want to see in art is themes that bring us together and encourage us to be our best selves for those around us." Yvella gestured for Julie to step out of the capsule first and then followed with her rollaway. "Humans aren't quite there yet, but sometimes your artists can step outside themselves to produce the works they would be capable of if they were better people."

"I think I know what you mean," Julie said, leading the way down the familiar corridor toward her cabin. "When I was writing my novel about the Old Way, I worked hard at seeing the world through their eyes, and it was an improvement over how I used to look at things. I have a Drazen friend, and when something makes me angry, I ask myself, 'How would Rinka respond?' and usually I end up laughing."

"Aspirational thinking," the Sharf confirmed with a nod. "Keep it up and one day it will be automatic, and you'll have become your best self."

Julie stopped in front of a cabin and swept her hand over the door pad.

"Hello?" a whistly voice inquired.

"It's Julie. I'm here with your new roommate."

The door slid open and the towering young Dollnick female stepped out and made a sweeping gesture back into the cabin with all four of her arms, like a model at a trade show presenting a new floater. "Come in," Shint said to Yvella. "I'm so happy to meet you. I've missed having a roommate since university."

"I'm right across the corridor if you need anything," Julie said. "First Administrator McAllister and his family are next door. I don't know when you slept last, and nobody expects you to start work immediately, but we added a day to the *Tunnelshow* this week because Flower is taking on a large load of recycled metal. The show will be starting in a few minutes."

"I was waiting for you to arrive before going to work there myself," Shint said. "You look fresh as a Sheezle bug larva, so why don't you come with us?"

"I will," Yvella said and gave her bag a little push, so it rolled into the cabin. "I had an excellent rest on Alfe so I'm good for the next three days. Is that how long the show lasts?"

"We only work eight hours a day," Julie told her.

"Don't worry, I'll stay up with you and we can get to know each other," Shint said. "The drawback to living with Humans is that they sleep all the time."

"That would be worshipful," Yvella said. "I love your matching purses. I could never pull that off with just two shoulders."

"Dollnicks have a saying that four arms are better than two, and today will be my first on-camera appearance. They're going to shoot Lena's Challenge and I'm the alien—" she made quote marks with the fingers of all four hands, "—expert."

"I often stayed up all night on Earth and watched reruns on demand of an old show that reminds me of the *Antiques Tunnelshow,*" Yvella said, falling in with the Dollnick as they followed Julie back to the lift tube. "Is Lena's Challenge a ritual humiliation of the host where she has to choose an original item from a group of fakes or put three antiques in order by value?"

"It's similar," Shint said. "Lena is presented with three antiques and asked to rank them by how desirable they would be to a particular species. Today it will be Dollnicks. Then the alien expert, me, says whether or not she got it right and explains why."

"Oh, that sounds fun!"

"I'm sure the director and Lena would be happy to have you participate in a future challenge," Julie told Yvella as they entered the lift tube. "We only have one other Sharf on board who I'm aware of, and he—"

"Is supposed to be keeping a low profile because he's a station chief for Sharf Intelligence except he's gone native," Yvella completed Julie's sentence. "My father sits on an Intelligence committee, and he told me all about it. They aren't quite sure what to make of the reports Yaem sends in because they're a strange mix of quality and obvious fabrications. For example, one will praise the Drazens, caution us about the Hortens, and give a levelheaded analysis of Human interactions with the rest of the species. In the next report, the Hortens and the Drazens will have swapped places."

"That sounds about right for those guys," Julie said. "My husband works with them, and they all have a good time."

Flower let the passengers out of the lift tube a spoke farther up the con deck from where the crowd was forming at the entrance. The Grenouthian director hopped out to intercept them before they reached the area where all the tables were set up for the specialties.

"Yvella," the Grenouthian greeted the young Sharf. "Yaem asked me to send his apologies he's not here to meet you but he's visiting the orbital on business." At this last word, the director rubbed the side of his nose with his paw, a universal sign for shady business of some sort, including all things related to intelligence.

"He doesn't have to hide from me," Yvella said. "I'm not here in any official capacity. I understand that Alfe is the only Sharf property on Flower's circuit, so I'll bet he wants to stock up on little things that he can't buy on board."

"I'm sure you're right," the director said and pivoted to the Dollnick. "Are you ready for your big day, Shint?"

"I'm looking forward to it," Shint said. "When do I find out the items that Lena will be asked to rank?"

"At the same time as Lena," the Grenouthian told her with a twinkle in his large black eyes. "She's unhooking the rope as we speak, so the guests will be spreading out among the specialist tables in a couple of minutes."

"What will Lena do next?" Yvella asked. "As her intern, I should report in, but I don't want to interrupt anything important."

"She doesn't have a fixed duty station and spends most of her time observing appraisals and chatting with people who display a good camera presence. If she finds a candidate for a feature interview, Lena will call over a camera crew and shoot it on the spot."

Julie escorted the new roommates to the appraisal area, handed them off to Lena, and then hopped in a lift tube and returned to Flower Enterprises. The grinning co-op student at the reception desk should have alerted her to the fact that something was up, but she put it down to Friday being the last day of the workweek and continued to her office. If it wasn't for the treadle sewing machine in the corner, she would have thought she'd taken a wrong turn.

"What happened to my desk?" Julie asked out loud.

"I got you a better one," Flower responded through an overhead speaker. "It's a Georgian Revival pedestal partner's desk, flame mahogany. Do you like it?"

"It's lovely, but what about all of my stuff?"

"I had a bot transfer it over. Don't worry, I kept the padded swivel chair you like so much, but I added a holographic projector to the base to disguise it as a period chair to match the desk."

Julie felt for the chair back to make sure she didn't end up sitting on air, then sat down and began exploring the drawers. "Does revival mean that it's a replica? Did you have it made for me?"

"Antiques aren't anything new," Flower said. "Even your ancient Greeks and Romans went through stylistic periods and revivals. The desk is over two hundred years old."

"You've been saving it for me since we stopped at Earth?"

"One of the colonists on Chianga brought it up for appraisal. When she said she wanted to sell because the family was moving to a Frunge open world as sales reps for Threads, the city they're from, I offered to save her the bother of bringing it back to the surface."

"How much did you pay?" Julie asked, and then winced when she realized how rude that sounded. "I'm just curious because of the show."

"Then ask the Grenouthian director to send you the appraisal footage," Flower said.

"How could this not have made the final cut? Was the owner—oh, wait. The specialists were all excited about that super tall thing they said was a secretary's desk from the 1700s and valued at four hundred thousand creds."

"The Human Museum on Chianga sent it up for the show, I think to show off to the other open worlds that they had it. Two antique desks in one show would have been a bit much."

Julie got out her tab, propped it in the holder, and leaned back a little in her chair. "It's perfect, thank you. I remember now that the director and Lena argued over where to put that secretary's desk in the final edit."

"The director insisted on opening the show with it and I believe he was correct," Flower said. "Even though it was much more valuable than the collection of original patents that he chose for the final appraisal, the director was concerned that the alien museums at our stops would get into a competition. If that happened, the show would lose the excitement that comes from a guest finding out that the painting they found in the trash is worth twelve thousand creds."

Julie nodded. "That makes sense. What's on the schedule for today?'

"Diplomacy. A Vergallian royal traveling incognito has arrived on board. I want you to recruit her for the *Tunnelshow*."

"Why is she hiding her identity?"

"Adlyn has had her share of troubles and made some enemies along the way, but she comes highly recommended by Baa," Flower said. "More importantly, she knows Vergallian tapestries."

"But how can she appear on the *Antiques Tunnelshow* if she's in hiding?"

"Adlyn is both a truthsayer and a face dancer, and nobody will try anything while she's here or on Stryx stations."

"She won't do anything to me, will she?" Julie asked nervously.

"There's a secret compartment in the desk that you open by—there's not enough time, I'll do it for you," Flower said. A panel flopped down from the front of one of the drawers revealing a narrow space holding a necklace on a silver chain. "Put it on but hide the pendant inside your dress so Adlyn isn't offended."

"What is it?" Julie asked as she put on the necklace and let the pendant slide below the high collar of the Victorian dress she'd taken to wearing on *Tunnelshow* days.

"A defensive charm that Baa sent along. Adlyn will be here in a minute. Be yourself, offer her the job as a specialist, and honestly answer any questions she may have. As a truthsayer, she refused to negotiate directly with me because she can't read my intentions."

"Where will she sit?"

"Grab a chair from the office across the way," Flower said. "I have the carpentry shop creating a pair of Georgian revival chairs to match the desk."

Julie jumped up and retrieved a chair from across the hall. As soon as she got it into place in front of her desk, a hologram snapped into place, disguising it as a period piece. Then she returned to the doorway just in time to see the receptionist escorting a shabby older woman who she wouldn't have been surprised to see living in a shelter back in Manhattan. The receptionist turned back after making eye contact.

"Adlyn," Julie greeted the Vergallian. "I'm Julie, Flower's special assistant. Please come in."

"Why are there holograms on the chairs?" Adlyn asked, half amused, half suspicious.

"To match the desk. It's new, I mean, to me. As of this morning."

"You seem disappointed by my appearance."

"Not at all," Julie said before remembering that the Vergallian would know she was lying. "Okay, I am surprised. If I had seen you living on the streets in the neighborhood where I grew up I would have taken you for another homeless person."

"How old do I look to you?" Adlyn followed up.

"It's hard to tell with people who live on the streets, but sixty?"

"Multiply that by ten and you'll be closer to the answer. Now tell me about the job."

Julie stared for a moment and then shook it off. "We're producing the *Antiques Tunnelshow* at each stop we make until we get to Union Station, at which point the production will be transferred to the Grenouthian network and start a circuit of Empire Convention Centers on Stryx stations. We're trying to fine-tune the show for aliens, I mean, non-human audiences, and it quickly became apparent that we needed specialists from other species. I understand you have an expertise in tapestries."

"If you call a hundred years hawking heirlooms from exiled royal families expertise, I have it in spades," Adlyn said. "I wouldn't be here if I wasn't interested in the job, but I wanted to hear it from a Human. I'll have to check to make sure that I'm still welcome on Stryx stations."

Julie's eyes widened at the thought of what one would have to do to get banned by the Stryx, but she nodded as if it all made sense. "If you don't mind my asking, can you, uh, disguise your identity without appearing to be human? The director is looking for a Vergallian tapestry expert more than he's looking for an expert in Vergallian tapestry."

"I understand." The skin on Adlyn's face began to twitch, and then ripple, and in a matter of seconds, Julie was staring at a Vergallian, who while clearly in her later years, still showed the unmistakable beauty of the upper caste and royals. There was a shiny streak along one of her sharp cheekbones as if she had been scarred by a weapon, and her hair was almost pure white. "Would this suffice?"

"Is it you?" Julie blurted and then reversed course. "You don't have to tell me. I couldn't help asking."

"I'm aware of that. It's really me, or as much of me as I can remember. Face dancing claims a price from those who practice it for centuries."

While Julie was answering the Vergallian's questions about living on board Flower, Lena was explaining the procedure of corralling guests for feature interviews to her new intern.

"And they're strangers to you?" Yvella asked. "Do you present a parchment of introduction?"

"They usually see me coming and turn away if they aren't comfortable with the idea of being interviewed," Lena explained. "Enough shows have been broadcast that the guests all recognize me."

"How do you choose the people to interview? If you're looking for beauty, I won't be able to help because Humans all look very strange to me."

"I can't describe how I choose, it's just a feeling, I guess. Maybe the way they relate to the object that they've brought. You see that guy in the blue shirt with the old sword?"

"He's not carrying it right," Yvella said. "There's no peace strap and it could—"

Somebody cried, "Watch it!" as the sword slid out of the scabbard the man had been holding with one hand in the middle with the hilt pointing down. It clattered onto the deck, and then the man almost stabbed himself while trying to get it back into the scabbard.

"I wouldn't have asked him for an interview because of the casual way he was carrying the sword and the expression on his face that looked like he's out for a loaf of bread," Lena said. "But that man with the manilla envelope. He looks interesting."

"Is he old?" Yvella asked. "I can't tell with the whiskers."

"I think he's in his eighties. Let's see what he has."

Shint intercepted them on their way to talk to the man and said, "The director wants you. Yaem is back and they're ready to shoot the challenge."

Lena sighed and redirected her steps to follow the Dollnick toward a circular table set up in the center of the appraisal area. Jorb was there with three cameras under his control, and Dave had set up a pair of floating cameras a few steps behind and to the side of the Drazen to document the making of Lena's Challenge.

Yaem set the third object on the table and caught sight of Yvella as he stepped back. The Sharf spy made a formal bow in the direction of his emperor's great-granddaughter, but he remained next to the table as if he expected to be part of the shoot.

The Grenouthian director popped out of the crowd, squinted up at the overhead lighting, and muttered something. The lights brightened noticeably. Then he went over to Lena and whispered in her ear for almost a minute before joining Jorb behind the center camera.

"You stay here," Lena said to Yvella. Then she accompanied Shint to the table. "Did the director give you any instructions?" she asked the Dollnick.

"He told me to wait until you made your guesses and then to rearrange the tokens in the right order," Shint replied. "Gold, Iron, and Aluminum. He said Yaem would do the lead-in."

"Right." Lena looked back at the central camera as she positioned herself close enough to Yaem to make dialogue natural without blocking the table. Another pair of cameras floated over the gathering people behind her, and she nodded and said, "Ready."

"Since we're stopping this week at Alfe, the only Sharf orbital on the Stryx tunnel network, we asked the local museum for three items," Yaem said, his eyestalks bending almost comically in the direction of the table. "The first is an ankle bracelet, gold with natural gemstones, made by the firm of Gzard and Gzard during the fourth Frunge Renaissance. The second is a permanent holographic schematic for the ductwork of a Dollnick Class Two colony ship, and the third is a platinum process print of a Drazen circus performer juggling knives. Lena," the Sharf paused dramatically, "your challenge is to place these tokens in front of the items in order of their desirability to a Dollnick collector. Gold for the most valuable, iron for second place, and aluminum for the least desirable."

Lena couldn't help making a face as she surveyed the items. "Is there a trick?" she asked. "Are any of them counterfeit?"

"They are all genuine articles, exactly as I described them."

"Does anybody have advice?" Lena asked the audience as she stole a look at the back of the framed print.

"Hologram first," somebody said immediately. "The Dollies love colony ships."

"Your Dollnick specialist is wearing an ankle bracelet," a woman observed. "Maybe it's a thing with them."

"Colony ship," somebody else asserted forcefully.

Lena nodded and put the gold token in front of the permanent hologram of the colony ship ductwork. Then she asked, "Anklet or clown?"

The crowd didn't have a clear opinion between the two choices, with one individual even suggesting that Shint's wearing an ankle bracelet was a trap. Lena picked up the iron token, vacillated, and then set it down in front of the anklet and slid the aluminum in front of the framed print.

"How did you make your choices?" Yaem asked.

"Well, Dollnicks do love colony ships, so the first one seemed pretty obvious. I don't know anything about platinum process printing, but I'd guess that it doesn't leave behind enough platinum to make the print intrinsically valuable, and I've learned enough Dollnick numerals to know that the print is 46 of 200, unless it's a date. The anklet must be pretty valuable for the gold and natural gems, even if it isn't to Dollnick taste."

"Shint?" Yaem said, motioning the Dollnick closer.

"You got one right," Shint said as she rearranged the tokens. "The ankle bracelet is both valuable and fashionable, and I can't imagine who left it behind in a ship to be salvaged. But you got the most and least desirable reversed." She moved the gold token in front of the print of the Drazen circus performer and the aluminum in front of the permanent hologram. The audience groaned.

"Is it because holograms can be easily replicated?" Lena asked.

"There is that, but the more important factor is that every self-respecting Dollnick already owns a full series of construction holograms from colony ships. They're often projected over the nest for infants, like Verlock Skies."

"I can't believe that the platinum printing process is that special," Lena said.

"It's not the process," Shint explained. "It's the subject. He's juggling."

"Dollnicks care about juggling art?"

"We love everything about juggling. Nobody does it better."

"Four arms are better than two," Flower said over Julie's implant.

# Thirteen

"Jorb?" Samuel inquired, reaching down to shake his Drazen friend who was sitting on the corridor floor with his back to the door of the Human Empire headquarters and snoozing. "Are you awake?"

"I'm always conscious of my surroundings," Jorb said, reaching for Samuel's shoulder with his tentacle to pull himself to his feet. "My well-honed friend-or-foe instinct must have identified you as a friend and allowed you to approach this closely."

"Why are you sleeping in the corridor?"

"Because you come into the office so late. I thought you got up at 0500."

"Only on the days we get together to spar," Samuel said. "Why did you wait instead of pinging me or coming back later?"

"I got an urgent message from the home office, and I thought it would be best to take care of it first thing," Jorb said. "Let's take a walk on the reservoir deck."

"You don't want to come in?"

"Too many bugs."

"Krey's hounds came in and swept the place on Saturday," Samuel said.

"What day is today?" Jorb asked.

"Oh. All right." A short ride in a lift tube capsule later, they exited on the reservoir deck and took a catwalk out over the water. "What's up?"

"We need to get a Drazen on the show."

"You run a camera crew every show so you'll be in the credits," Samuel pointed out.

"In front of the cameras, not behind them," Jorb said. "The home office is worried that when the Grenouthian Network takes over the *Antiques Tunnelshow* at Union Station, it will all turn into pay for play."

"But I'm not involved with the show in any way, other than officially hosting Shint and Yvella as guests of my family."

"The home office is sending a ceramics expert with three centuries of experience in the auction business. They want me to get her on the show now so that the Grenouthians are stuck with her."

"Does it really work that way?" Samuel asked.

"The Grenouthian network would need to show a good reason to let her go," Jorb said. "I want your backing."

"You have it, but with who? I can talk to the Grenouthian director or Yaem, but you know them better than I do."

"I'm not an emperor."

"Neither am—" Samuel stopped at his friend's skeptical expression and decided there was no point in revisiting the old argument. "Do you think my words will carry more weight with them than yours?" He leaned out over the reservoir to sneak a casual look behind them and wasn't surprised to see a large Cayl hound crouched low on the catwalk with an ear turned in their direction. "Is this all about owes?"

"I don't mind owing the director or Yaem one, that would bring us back to even," Jorb said. "But the home office doesn't want me owing more favors to M793qK."

"How is he involved?"

"The whole production was his idea. He's been setting it up for years through that ReproMan business of his. He pitched it to Flower and then they brought in the director and Yaem. M793qK either wants the *Tunnelshow* to tour Farling space in the offseason, or to set up a parallel operation there. And he owes the Human Empire big time for giving the Stryx an excuse to alter the tunnel connection rules even if he doesn't admit it."

"Didn't Julie tell me that Rinka has a point in the show?"

"She's a silent producer," Jorb said. "It turns out to mean no work in return for no control."

"I didn't realize that M793qK was involved in the show beyond sending his patients with valuable antiques when the real guests come up short," Samuel said. "I can go by the clinic and talk to him."

"He's there now," Jorb said and spun Samuel around to walk back to the lift tube. "Or maybe we should go the other way for a change?"

"Are you afraid of Krey's hounds? Wait, isn't that Razood waving?"

"It could be somebody impersonating him. We better get to M793qK right away."

"Samuel," Razood shouted, and for emphasis, he whacked the steel rail of a catwalk with a hammer from his belt, creating a resonant ringing. "We need to talk."

"Just remember that I asked first," Jorb said.

"Can you excuse us for a minute?" Razood asked the Drazen when the two parties met.

"I'll save you time instead. He wants you to get a Frunge on the show, Samuel."

"But you're already featured as a metalwork and mechanical devices specialist," Samuel pointed out to Razood.

"And Jorb's on call to do mining paraphernalia, but we're staying with Flower when the show transfers to the Stryx station circuit in another five weeks," the Frunge said. "We need a specialist for after the Grenouthians take possession. Fandaz has a childhood friend who's an expert in textile history."

"When can she get here?"

"Last night. She stayed with Fandaz."

"And you want me to introduce her to M793qK?"

"It's a little more complicated than that. She's sort of from an important family, and they would lose face if it came out that she asked to be on the show," Razood said. "But if you asked…"

"That's why I'm on my way to M793qK now," Samuel said.

"So you'll go see her afterward?"

Samuel stopped and looked at the Frunge, and then back at the Drazen for an explanation.

"He doesn't want you to ask M793qK," Jorb said. "He wants you to ask her."

"Ask who?"

"Mizet," Razood said. "You know, make it a personal favor."

"You'll owe me one?"

"I'll owe you two, but you'll owe Mizet one. That makes it okay for her to leave her academic career and her family home to travel with the *Antiques Tunnelshow*."

Samuel noticed that both of Krey's hounds were now listening in, and from the expressions on their faces, they were as puzzled as he was.

"I ask Mizet as a personal favor if she'll become the Frunge textiles expert on the *Antiques Tunnelshow,* and then I go to M793qK—"

"I've already got her past the Big Three and Flower," Razood said. "They need a Frunge who knows fabrics. It's all about somebody with enough standing asking her to accept the job."

"I didn't think anybody in the Frunge Empire knew who I was," Samuel said.

"Of course they know who you are," Jorb said. "Razood sends them reports detailing the progress of the Human Empire every week even if he has to make something up."

"It's been easier coming up with content since the first class graduated from your government school and started setting up pilot ministries," Razood said. "Can I ping Fandaz and tell her you'll meet them at the Blue Tea Café in a half hour?"

"I guess I can't imagine M793qK keeping me that long," Samuel said. "Any special instructions?"

"Make sure you use the phrase 'personal favor.'"

"Come on," Jorb said, pushing Samuel into the lift tube capsule. "Let's get to the clinic before Forgath shows up asking you to promote the Horten games expert who got here at the same time as the other two."

"Should I be expecting visits from anybody else?" Samuel asked.

"The Vergallians and Dollnicks are already covered, though I get the impression that Avisia and Adlyn have some bad history. And the Sharf already scored Lena's intern, even though they aren't tunnel network members. I wouldn't be surprised if Yvella takes over from Lena in four or five decades."

"Yvella is that young?"

"Lena is Human," Razood said patiently. "She can only work into her seventies before the labor laws push her into part-time."

"How about the Verlocks?" Samuel asked as they exited the lift tube up the corridor from the clinic.

"The Grenouthians and the Verlocks have an understanding about opportunities like this that dates back millions of years. It pays to be an older species. I'll wait out here."

The clinic door slid open as Samuel approached, and an alarm went off when he passed through the medical scanners at the entrance.

"You need more exercise," the synthesized voice produced by the Farling doctor's pendant greeted him.

"We're teaching four classes of ballroom dancing a week, plus I go to the dojo every Friday before work and spar with one of the guys."

"It's not enough," M793qK rubbed out on his speaking legs. "You should be exercising every day at your age. If you can't figure it out yourself, I'll draw up a program and give it to Flower."

"I get it," Samuel said. "You don't have to threaten me. We were thinking of putting on two more ballroom classes a week to separate the graduates from the students, and I've been talking with Avisia about getting together for a weekly duel."

"Make it twice a week and start jogging in the morning before work." The Farling doctor pulled a large envelope out of a cupboard and handed it to Samuel. "Here. I want you to bring this on the show."

"Is it the first x-ray ever taken?"

"Good guess, but no. It's a historical document. Let the specialist open the envelope, it's fragile."

Samuel re-flattened the ears of the metal clip holding the flap that he'd just stood up. "Is it a practical joke to make us look bad? A judgment from a witch trial, something like that?"

"If you don't want it broadcast, the director will cut it for you," M793qK said. "My suggestion is that you bring your Minister of Antiquities along. Now, who does Jorb want to parachute into the show?"

"A ceramics expert, three centuries of auction experience," Samuel said. "I didn't get the name."

"Fine. You owe me one."

"Jorb said you owe us for the tunnel getting connected to your world."

"Are you planning to hold that over my carapace forever?" the doctor rubbed out, and his pendant synthesized his voice with a tone of injured complaint. "Besides, you're not doing me a favor by bringing that on the show," he added, indicating the envelope Samuel was holding. "I'm doing you a favor by passing it along."

"I just found out that the show was your idea," Samuel said. "How many points do you have?"

"A Farling never tells."

"Is it all about money? I thought you had more than you could spend."

M793qK finished mixing some bubbling chemicals in a beaker and quaffed the result in a single gulp. "That hit the spot. On Earth, I have more money than I can spend, but I have ships under construction that will cost more than—less said the better. But it's not why we're all pushing so hard on the *Antiques Tunnelshow*."

"You mean you, Flower, and everybody from Harry's cafeteria," Samuel said. "I thought it was a business."

"It is a business, but it's also much more than that. By the time the show has been around a few centuries, I predict it will have visited every imperial palace on the tunnel network, and not a few estates and habitats belonging to important families and business consortiums as well. The last time something like this came along was around ten thousand years ago when the Hortens ran their fiftieth galactic gaming tour. Can you imagine the size of the brackets? The tournament took seventeen years, but the *Antiques Tunnelshow* has even more potential because the only talent required to participate is hoarding."

"You're saying that it's a diplomatic mission?"

A tinkling bell sounded, and M793qK said, "My next patient is here. Tell Jorb that he owes me one off the books."

Samuel recognized a dismissal when he heard one, and as he turned to leave, multiple alarms went off as a woman whose face was squinched up in a grimace limped through the medical scanners. He stepped aside to let her pass and found Razood waiting in the corridor.

"Jorb had a student coming so he couldn't wait," the Frunge blacksmith said. "What took you so long?"

"M793qK was explaining why the *Antiques Tunnelshow* isn't just another entertainment franchise."

"Do you think we'd all be scrambling to have a permanent presence on the show if it was?"

"Are these specialists you guys are pushing to get on camera actually intelligence agents?" Samuel asked. "M793qK said he expects the show to start doing location shoots like they did on Earth Two. I thought it was going to visit all of the Empire Convention Centers."

"If it's a success on the Stryx station circuit, it will get invitations from everybody who has a venue that they want to show off," Razood said as he hurried Samuel toward the lift tube. "It's not that big a deal for the tunnel network because we already have extensive tourism and know how to get along with each other, but it's a chance to show the flag wherever sentients collect stuff. The Frunge have official diplomatic relations with less than one percent of the spacefaring species in the galaxy because we don't have any trade with them and nobody goes there. If the *Antiques Tunnelshow* hits the sweet spot we all think it can, it could prove a catalyst for interspecies relations for hundreds of centuries."

"But you're all rich already, compared with humans, anyway," Samuel said. "Why should it matter to somebody whose family has been living in the same place for longer than modern humans have existed that some old vase they were using as a flowerpot is worth a couple of thousand creds?"

"It's not about the money, it's about winning. Everybody loves to win, except for maybe the Alts, and they're the exception that proves the rule. The members of the advanced species don't need anything from each other, though we save a lot of resources by being members of the tunnel network and part of an unbeatable defensive alliance. As your mother-in-law could tell you, even our stories don't make a lot of sense to each other without extensive editing. Abs Press only works with literature from tunnel network species, who have a lot more in common with each other than random civilizations that the Stryx haven't touched."

Samuel led the way out of the capsule toward the Blue Tea Café while he considered the Frunge's words. "I thought that humans were the only ones who got excited about finding stuff in the trash that turns out to be valuable."

Razood let out a creaky laugh. "Humans are the only species I'm aware of that *puts* valuable items in the garbage. I suppose it's not surprising since you must generate around ten times as much trash as the Hortens, who with their cleanliness phobias, are the second most wasteful aliens on the tunnel network. But even the most advanced species misplace things from time to time. And this is where I stop."

"At the Vergallian boutique?" Samuel asked in surprise. "Are you buying a gift for Fandaz?"

"I'm turning around and going back to Colonial Jeevesburg," the Frunge blacksmith said. "I have a big order of replica dragoon's pistols to make for some gamers. It wouldn't be proper for me to be present while you're asking Mizet your favor. She might think that you're under duress."

"All right," Samuel said. "I'll see you Friday morning at the dojo." He continued down the corridor and scanned the tables in the Blue Tea Café before entering. To his surprise, he saw his wife and the Cayl emperor's granddaughter sitting with Fandaz, the owner of the café, and a second Frunge whose hair vines were woven so tightly that her elaborate updo didn't require a trellis. Vivian waved and said something to the others as soon as she spotted him.

"Good morning," Samuel greeted them all, taking the open stool that his wife indicated and turning to face the new Frunge arrival. "You must be Mizet. Welcome to Flower."

"It's my pleasure, Imperial Highness," Mizet said in the scratchy English of a Frunge who had learned the language recently but wasn't used to speaking it. "Your wife was just showing me pictures of Princess Rose. She's as cute as a Hzax."

"Thank you," Samuel said, bobbing his head. He glanced over at Krey to see if the Cayl who served as the Human Empire's mentor would give him any cues or have Flower relay a message to his implant, but she was sipping an orange tea through a long straw and was clearly attending as a passive observer. "How was your trip?"

"Interesting," Mizet said. "Purchasing a commercial liner ticket to rendezvous with Flower would have delayed my arrival until your next stop, but I was able to travel as supercargo from Union Station on a freighter. My companions were a Drazen ceramics specialist and a Horten who had brought along such a variety of travel games that we ended up staging a micro-tournament with the ship's owner as a fourth. I was surprised that an artificial person would be so comfortable bluffing."

"Dewey," Vivian said, though Samuel had already guessed by that point that the transportation had been arranged by Flower. "I explained that he was created on a gaming world and had experimented with personality upgrades, including a professional gambler."

"Mizet could have paid for all the extras at school on her winnings if we had played for money rather than pins and needles," Fandaz said. "It's not surprising that she ended up specializing in the history of textiles."

Everyone at the table looked at Samuel expectantly, and Vivian tapped his foot with hers under the table.

"What a coincidence," Samuel said. "The *Antiques Tunnelshow* has been a showcase for antiques from Earth, but I know that our specialists are out of their depth when people who have completed Frunge labor contracts or live on your open worlds bring in semi-metallic textiles and other advanced fabrics. I know we've just met, but could I ask, as a personal favor, that you consider taking a position with the show?"

The petals of Mizat's hair vines turned dark green, adding new accents to the complex weave. "I would be delighted," Mizet said in her scratchy English.

"Witnessed," Krey growled around her straw.

"Don't hurry off," Vivian said, grabbing Samuel's wrist as he shifted on the stool in preparation for getting up. "There's another coincidence coming."

"Dotat," Mizet called out, waving toward the entrance. "Over here." She turned back to Samuel and said, "I asked Flower to ping him when you arrived."

Samuel nodded as if it all made sense to him, leaned close to Vivian, and whispered, "Do I ask him as a personal favor?"

She shook her head and whispered back, "He's here by way of Ortha via Mornich and Marilla."

The Horten, whose skin was shading toward an intermediate yellow with nerves, took the remaining seat next to Krey, making six at the table that was intended for two.

"Can I get you anything?" the owner of the Blue Tea Café asked the newly arrived Horten. "We have a steam sterilization unit for mugs."

"Do you have distilled hot water?" Dotat asked.

"I could make some," Fandaz offered.

"Just kidding, I'm not one of *those* Hortens. A cup of anything boiled would be fine."

"Samuel?"

"Do you have Instant Inca?" Samuel asked. He knew that the Blue Tea Café didn't serve fresh brewed coffee, but the instant blend from Drazen Foods was better in any case.

"Two Instant Incas coming up," the owner said and excused herself.

"Your family all asked me to say that you better be planning on spending the week at Mac's Bones when Flower arrives at Union Station," Dotat said to Samuel without further preamble. "A very large Cayl hound indicated that if you take too long about it, he'll come over to Flower and drag you, or so young Marilla interpreted the elaborate pantomime for me."

"Are you related to Marilla?" Samuel asked. He guessed that the age difference between the gaming specialist and the Horten girl who owned a minority share of Tunnel Trips might have been a few hundred years.

"No, though we'll be in-laws several times removed when she marries Mornich, as I'm a cousin of sorts to Ambassador Ortha," Dotat explained. "I got to know Marilla a little while I was consulting for Tunnel Trips on the restored Horten liner they've put back into service. They wanted the gaming room to be authentic. Paul turned out to be more knowledgeable about our Nova game than any alien I've ever met, so it was a pleasure working with them both. Your father too."

"I'm glad to hear it," Samuel said. "One of the milestone requirements for the Human Empire to progress was starting an interstellar passenger liner service with majority human ownership. It's a lucky thing that a liner turned out to be one of the last ships in the auction lot that Aisha bought from the Stryx for Paul."

"The universe works," Mizat said, and then started coughing from pronouncing the 'k' sound, leaving it unclear whether she'd ever intended to conclude with, "in mysterious ways."

Dotat nodded. "Your mother has become a huge fan of the *Antiques Tunnelshow,*" he told Samuel. "I watched it twice with your family while I was there. Your sister only cared about the dresses and a pair of ruby slippers that came on, but the ambassador was very interested in furniture and books. She gave me to understand that she has quite a collection of rare books, though I had the strange impression that the rest of your family wasn't so sure. But maybe I'm not good at reading Human faces."

"Remind me not to play poker with you," Vivian said, and Krey nodded her agreement.

"You're making me homesick," Samuel said with a laugh. "I can imagine sitting around with my family and the hounds watching the show. The funny thing is I haven't made it through a full episode yet because something always comes up."

"Did you see the collection of gaming hardware that a Human from Bits who's living on Flower brought in?" Dotat asked. "The show doesn't have a good games specialist, so the owner had to explain how the technology worked. That's when the ambassador suggested that I offer my services."

"She did? I mean, that sounds like something my mother would say. Have you talked with the producers yet?"

"Everything was arranged through a Horten middleman. Forgath is his name. And I understand that Tunnel Trips is adding Farling Four to the schedule for liner service."

Samuel glanced at Krey, who was showing her fangs in an amused grin. "Why doesn't that surprise me," he said.

# Fourteen

"You've had what in the freezer since we stopped at Earth Two?" Bill asked Harry.

"Gooseberries. Flower doesn't grow them."

"And we're going to wrap them in foil?"

Harry glanced at the recipe Bill was displaying on his tab.

"That's one of those funny old English spellings, either that or the name changed," Harry said. "My mom called it Gooseberry Fool, even though she made it with whatever tart berries were at hand."

"And you're sure they ate this in Shakespearean times?" Bill asked.

"That's what Flower tells me, and I don't argue with the management. It's a sort of custard, at least the way we're making it. Jake is babysitting this morning, but he'll be here for the next two days in my place."

Bill scanned the recipe and made a face. "I don't like this bit about adding sugar to taste."

"I already did a sample run with some gooseberries I thawed out at home and they're pretty tart. Do you mind the metric units? Jake told me he prefers them."

"A kilo of gooseberries, two liters of cream, eight eggs, and a teaspoon of nutmeg," Bill read out loud. "If we added vanilla, it would be eggnog."

"The cream makes it heavier, and there's fruit instead of booze," Harry said. "I got the red gooseberries, which are sweeter than the green, and the first five bags are all thawed out. I'm calling the bags a kilo each, even if the Old Way farmer who sold them said they were two pounds and change. They've been washed, and they were grown without pesticides."

"What about the crusts, or are we going to serve the custard in cups?"

"We'll use the small glass dipping bowls that we have so many of. It's Horten glass, so they're light, but they won't break."

"What would they have used in Shakespeare's time?"

"I don't know," Harry said. "Wood bowls? I'd have planned on a pastry crust, but people would be tempted to eat them with one hand and make a mess. With a bowl and a spoon, they'll have to put down what they're holding, and it will reduce the chance of accidents."

"I guess nobody wants gooseberries and pudding all over their antiques," Bill concurred and looked back at the recipe. "Does scalding the berries mean we're supposed to get the skin off?"

"It probably meant blanching back when the recipe was written down, but I don't bother. It's enough to cut off both ends and make a purée. Use a knife with sharp serrations, so you don't put so much pressure on the berries that the contents ooze out. Here, you do half."

The men set to work on the contents of the bag and soon covered the bottoms of two large pots with trimmed gooseberries. "Are we going to have to refrigerate these after we cook them?" Bill asked. "If we add them to the cream and egg mixture hot, things could get dicey."

"They'll have cooled down quite a bit by the time we thicken the custard, and then it will have to cool as well," Harry said. "Don't add too much water because it will dilute the berry juice. A couple of splashes will do."

Bill stirred his mixture with a wooden spoon on medium heat, copying Harry's technique. After ten minutes, the older baker turned off the heat and grabbed a pair of stainless-steel sieves from the overhead rack.

"We're draining them now?" Bill asked.

"No, we'd lose too much of the juice. Fill up the sieve over another pot and mash the berries through to create a purée. The back of one of those large metal spoons should do a good job." Harry spent several long seconds contemplating the two pots of purée once they were prepared. "You know, I think we should split this into four batches before folding it into the custard. I want swirls, like ripple ice cream, and if we try to make too big a batch, we may end up with cups that are all cream unless we mix it until it's uniform."

"Got it," Bill said. He spooned half of the gooseberry purée back into the pot he'd cooked it in and set both aside on the counter to cool. "A liter of cream and four eggs each. Seems like a lot of liquid to thicken."

"Flower had a bot deliver the cream twenty minutes ago, so it's fresh and it's never been refrigerated, which will help. And I'd swear these Dollnick heating elements reach through the pot into the food somehow, like a microwave."

"It's superior technology," Flower told them. "And I'd recommend bringing up just one tray of the Gooseberry Foyl at a time. I have years of data from hosting cons, and people are much less likely to accept a pudding or custard than they are cookies or slices of cake."

"How about ice cream?" Harry asked, sneaking a wink at Bill.

"Ice cream is its own category."

Ten minutes later, Bill asked, "Is yours thickening?"

"It was pretty thick to start with," Harry said. "We don't want to end up cooking it, but a few more minutes can't hurt. What do you think of the sweetness?"

"I added one tablespoon of sugar, but the cream is already sweet, and so are the gooseberries, though they also have a bite."

"Have you eaten breakfast yet?"

"Why?" Bill asked, perking up considerably. "Did you make something?"

"Leftover cheese Danish from Flower's Paradise yesterday. I grabbed four pieces and put them in the fridge."

"I love leftover Danish."

"You know what?" Harry said after they finished their snack. "If that custard still pours easily, let's fill the glass bowls now and fold a little purée into each separately. I'm not confident that it will work if we do large batches and try to spoon it into the cups."

"Works for me," Bill said.

It took them another half hour to prepare eighty small Gooseberry Foyls, but they got the swirling effect that Harry wanted. They loaded them all on one tray, slid it into the large fridge, and since the show wasn't opening for another hour, Bill decided to let them cool that long after Harry left to help Irene. He spent the time looking at Flower's corridor maps overlayed with lease expiration dates for retail spaces. A few minutes before the hour, he got the tray out of the fridge, sent a silent prayer to the Horten glassmakers who had discovered a way to make it so light, and then realized that he hadn't accounted for eighty metal spoons. Then a four-armed bot entered the kitchen and Flower spoke through its speaker as it held out a tray-sized device.

"It's a weight reduction sub-tray," Flower told him. "You don't have to dial in the weight, it's set on automatic to assume fifty percent of the load."

"Why not all of it?" Bill asked as he set his heavy tray on top of the sub-tray.

"Because the tray would float up to the ceiling."

"Good point." The sub-tray was an exact fit, and the bulky floater unit below the center wouldn't be noticeable to anybody taller than Bill's waist. He took the tray from the bot and hefted it experimentally. "I like it. Why don't waiters use these all the time?"

"Haven't you ever heard of the benefits of exercise? Dollnicks have always been careful to deploy weight reduction technology only where it's required to prevent injury. The rule in industry is that if something is too heavy, you should pick it up with a partner."

"How about people who work alone, like delivery guys, or independent traders?"

"There's an exception to every rule. The bot will trail after you to collect the bowls and used spoons."

Guests were already passing through the triage area when Bill arrived on the con deck, and he soon discovered that Flower had been right about people preferring finger food. Only one man in the queue tried a Gooseberry Foyl, and he had brought an intricately carved chair for appraisal which gave him a convenient place to sit. The specialists were too busy to stop and eat, and other than Jorb, he failed to find any other takers.

"It's the two-hands requirement," the Drazen explained after he finished his third bowl. "I can control my floating camera with tentacle gestures, but you won't get any other crew members unless they go on break."

"Harry is going to be disappointed."

The bot trailing with the dishpan came up to take the third empty from Jorb, and Flower spoke again from its speaker. "Give me the tray, Bill. We'll mark this one up to experience. I'll take these to the middle school cafeteria."

"Does that mean I have the rest of the day off?"

"Just the Human I was looking for," a synthesized voice said behind him, and Bill turned to see M793qK holding out a familiar black leather bag. "Do you want to pick something, or should I choose it for you?"

"Don't you think you're being a little obvious?" Bill asked. "Everybody who isn't talking to a specialist is going to see you giving me something."

"How many people do you see looking in our direction right now?"

Bill snuck a look around them and saw nothing but the backs of heads. "Have you deployed some sort of stealth technology?"

"I asked Flower to project a hologram of you with a tray of Gooseberry Foyl," the Farling rubbed out on his speaking legs. "Quick, take something before everybody notices that you aren't moving."

There were only two items in the medical bag, and the last thing Bill wanted was to appear on a broadcast of the *Antiques Tunnelshow* with a velvet pouch full of jewels, so he took the plate showing the profile of a manly-looking woman with a crown.

"What should I say when the appraiser asks where I got it?"

"That you were shopping for decorations for your café and you bought it from an alien for five creds."

"I can't lie like that," Bill said.

"I already deducted five creds from the next bonus I'm going to give you so technically it's true," M793qK said. "Don't look so nervous. It's a fake."

"Oh, that's okay then. When I watched the last show with Julie, I realized that I like the appraisals where people find out they bought a fake because I feel like I'm learning something useful. When it turns out that the picture they bought at a rummage sale for the frame is worth more than they make in a year, it's more like fantasy."

Eight hours later, a few dozen members of Flower's paradise who had been volunteering at the *Antiques Tunnelshow* gathered in the common room after dinner to screen raw documentary footage from the show. Irene, Harry, Dave, and June sat at the table that was usually set up for guest lecturers, and Nancy waited at the podium until the seats were full and the doors were closed.

"Welcome to Friendly Friday," Nancy said in her schoolteacher's voice which had lost little power with aging. "In keeping with tradition, on the third Friday evening of every month we have cooperative members talk about a project they're working on. Tonight it's Irene, who I think everybody knows by now, and her documentary camera team. I don't pretend to know anything about the immersive industry, so I'll yield the floor to her expertise."

Nancy stepped down to a polite round of applause and went to sit with her husband, Jack, who had saved her a seat in the first row. Irene squeezed Harry's hand and then got up and moved to the podium.

"Just to make sure there's no confusion, the documentary we're shooting, tentatively titled, 'The Making of the *Antiques Tunnelshow,*' is a Flower Entertainment production. We're all working for the Grenouthian director, who is also directing the *Antiques Tunnelshow,* so he's always on location to provide us with guidance. He'll also do the final edit, which is the most important part of the production."

"Does working as camera crew count against your volunteer time, or do you get paid?" somebody asked from the back of the room.

"You'll hate us, but both," Irene said. "I'm not quite sure how Flower squares that particular circle, but my husband may know. Harry?"

Without moving from his seat, Harry said, "We aren't earning scale for camera operators, or a unit director in Irene's case. When people of a certain age work more hours than strictly allowed by Dollnick labor law based on the actuarial tables for our species, Flower can get around it by letting us volunteer, providing the pay rate is reduced by fifty percent, or that our earnings are donated to a charity of our choice."

"You can see why I try not to think about it too much," Irene said, drawing a laugh from the retirees. "I'm still learning how the Grenouthian director makes his editorial decisions when cutting hundreds of hours of recordings down to under an hour, and the choices he makes are often based on very subtle cues. Without further ado, Flower?"

A large holographic projection appeared at the front of the room showing the Grenouthian director peering at the viewfinder display on a floating camera. Then the hologram panned away to a table where a man was taking a ceramic bowl out of a box and brushing away strands of packing material.

"How did you come to own this lovely bowl?" the specialist asked as he turned it over to check for marks on the bottom.

"Bartered for it a few weeks ago," the man said. "A trader I know at the fair on Roshent had a pair of them that he got from another trader for six cases of baked beans and the actuator from a Frunge wingset, though I got the impression that the mechanism was only good for parts. I think he said that she got the bowls from a Horten trader, but I might be confusing it with a different trade."

"I take it that you're an independent trader yourself."

"Born and bred. I primarily deal with tools and specialty foods, but I've been collecting and trading bowls for the last decade. I traded a complete set of hand-forged chisels for the two bowls, and I'm a little worried that they're replicas because of the lack of marks."

"Do you have the second bowl?" the specialist asked.

"Yes, but it looked identical to me. Do you want me to dig it out? The woman at the entrance told me not to bother."

"That's because she was just directing traffic. I can tell you that this is what the Drazens call a thread bowl, which was used to collect the bits of thread clipped off after tying a knot while sewing."

"Why would they do that?" the trader asked as he brushed the packing from the second bowl.

"Snip the extra thread or save it in a bowl?" the specialist asked.

"The second one."

"Drazen thread is all spun from natural fibers so it can be recycled into stuffing or used for rag in paper production." He studied the two bowls for a moment and then shook his head. "They aren't a pair, which leads me to suspect these were mass manufactured."

"But they're identical," the trader said. "I even took an image with my implant and ran a comparison."

"Here's a little hint about Drazen ceramics where a figure is depicted," the specialist said, touching each one with the eraser end of a retro yellow pencil he was using as a pointer. "When you put paired bowls side by side, the figures should be facing each other. If we do that with your bowls," he continued turning them to face the other, "one of the figures is upside-down."

"Sounds like I got taken for a ride. Are they worth anything?"

"I don't see enough of these to categorize them definitively, so I could only give you an estimate for the decorative value, which would be a few creds each. But let me consult with my Drazen colleague who recently joined the *Tunnelshow*. I believe she's finishing up with that bronze dragon. Minka?"

The Drazen specialist at the next table, whose tentacle was drooping after she was forced to explain to the third human that day that the Imperial Dragon they had purchased from a shady dealer was a copy, turned in their direction and seemed to brighten up when she saw the bowls. She spun around the potter's wheel on her table so the ceramic plaque reading "Back in a minute," was facing out, and went to join the human ceramics specialist behind his table.

"Lovely," she said in Drazen as she studied the bowl. The trader, whose implant gave him the translation, suddenly looked a lot happier. "How did you come by these?"

The trader recited his tale a second time, throughout which the Drazen continued studying the bowls. When he finished, she said, "What you have here is a mother-daughter set of thread bowls, which is why they are identical rather than paired. They aren't particularly old, the style of that ribbon they have wrapped around their tentacles dates them to the late Choot period, approximately four thousand years ago on your calendar. These were made in large quantities," she continued, turning both bowls over, "and they're unmarked, other than mother-daughter dots, here and here."

"Those little pinholes?" the human specialist asked. "I thought they were natural flaws."

"No, and you'll notice that they occur at the same point in the radius of the lower rim, so they were purchased at the same time. If one of these were sold in a sewing shop today, I'd estimate it at fifty or sixty creds, as they are hand-decorated, and the work is first-rate. But since you have the matched mother-daughter bowls, I think you're looking at a hundred and fifty creds."

"Thank you, Flower," Irene said, and the hologram disappeared. "How about a show of hands? How many people believe this segment will appear on the show in edited form?"

"That was my camerawork," Dave said proudly.

"And how many think it will be included in the documentary?"

Again, most of the hands went up.

"Well, I hope that you're right because I'm rooting for it as well. Flower?"

A new holographic projection appeared, this one showing a whole family group holding up a tapestry depicting a calvary charge that would have looked right at home in the great room of a drafty castle.

"What we have here is a classic tapestry from a Vergallian tech-ban world," the specialist said. "Can you tell me how it came into your possession?"

"Dad was in the mercenary cavalry on Ashban," the teenage daughter who was holding up the center said. "We saw it on the last market day before we left the planet, and my mom decided to buy it for him as a surprise."

"Was it displayed openly like this, or was it rolled up?"

"Rolled up and sticking out of a barrel with several other tapestries. The old Vergallian running the stall started yelling at us when we unrolled it enough to see what it was."

"Do you think that's because people came into his shop all day making a mess?" the specialist asked.

The girl looked at her mother, who said, "I'd be surprised if he got a customer once a week. The tent was old and worn, and the lantern was turned way down as if he was trying to conserve fuel. He was talking at us the whole time we were there, and while I only know a few thousand words of Vergallian, it was enough to tell that he was a very grumpy character."

"Do you remember how much you paid?"

"Of course, it was only two weeks ago. He wanted two hundred creds, which was my entire budget for souvenirs after twenty years on Ashban, and I couldn't talk him down one thin cred. I don't think he really wanted to sell it or anything else in his tent either."

"I know the type," the specialist said. "More of a collector than a tradesman. We're starting to see quite a few tapestries on the *Antiques Tunnelshow,* and the best examples come from Vergallian tech-ban worlds. This one has some wear issues that impact the price, around the edges there, and you can see a wine stain on the flank of the white stallion—"

"I thought it was blood," the father interrupted.

"Wine," the specialist said. "But a good conservator could fix that and the other minor issues. The quality isn't quite what you would expect if it had been sewn in a royal household to commemorate a particular event, and I've seen very similar pieces, with small differences, that were produced by women's sewing circles in villages as a group activity for the winter that also earned them holiday money when the tapestry was sold. Do you have any idea what this would be worth today on the auction market?"

"We're hoping more than two hundred creds."

"I think you're safe there. I consulted with my colleagues, and while the Vergallian specialist who recently joined us was called away for a few minutes, I think I can safely put an auction estimate of six hundred to eight hundred creds on this tapestry in the current condition."

"Idiot," a voice proclaimed, and the focus shifted to an older Vergallian woman holding a takeout bag from the vegan café in the food court. "In the future, I recommend that you stick to quilts, preferably the newer ones from the Old Way movement." She set her meal on the nearest table and strode over to the tapestry. "Did you think that Princess Alwiss was a man with long hair? This is the *Charge of the Dispossessed,* one of the classic scenes from the Fall of the House of Ashban. Where did you get it?"

"Ashban, Lady," the man said, recognizing at once that he was speaking to an upper-caste Vergallian, if not a member of a royal family fallen on hard times.

"Let me look at the back," Adlyn said, brushing past the specialist. "If it were the original, my advice would be to leave it with us and start running. Maybe the detectives from the Imperial Museum would leave you in peace. Maybe. But I haven't heard of the capital being sacked, so my working hypothesis is that it's a student copy."

"A student created this whole tapestry as an exercise?" the human specialist asked in astonishment. "It would take years."

"Years of visiting the Imperial Museum every evening when they allow students in for copying. Yes," Adlyn continued, taking the end of the tapestry from the former cavalryman and turning it toward the camera so the back would be visible. "The student worked his name into the dirt road by tying knots in a pattern. If you connect them, it reads in Vergallian, 'Dipyor, Graduation Project,' and gives the date. That was less than four hundred years ago so there's a good chance he's still working in the field."

"We bought it for my father to remember his time on Ashban," the teenager said. "We aren't going to sell it."

Adlyn shrugged. "It's a good example of student work, and for somebody with the wall space who knows how to get out blood stains, I'd place on this tapestry an auction estimate of two thousand Stryx creds."

"I still think it's wine," the chagrined human specialist muttered.

"Thank you, Flower," Irene said as the audience in the hologram and the room burst into applause. "I believe this segment would work well in the documentary, but I don't think it will make the *Antiques Tunnelshow*. Any thoughts?"

"That Vergallian was pretty snippy," a woman commented. "All of the other specialists manage to sound upbeat even when they're proclaiming a forgery."

"I served a contract as mercenary cavalry on a Vergallian tech-ban world, and another term as a tithe collector so my kids could grow up there," a man said. "I could see right off that it was a historical tapestry because the flags were troop-specific and out of date."

"Maybe the human tapestry specialist should have waited until the Vergallian returned," Jack ventured. "It seems counterproductive to risk making a mistake because of the order of people in line."

"That's what I told them," Harry said. "Most of the specialists will wait if they know somebody more qualified will be available, but the tapestry guy was cocky."

## Fifteen

"I have the new numbers from the Grenouthian Network," the director said, waving a tab in his paw, even though the screen was dark. "The alien specialists are a hit, and viewers prefer when we shoot on location rather than on the con deck."

Yaem swore under his breath at a text on his smartphone and turned the device over so he couldn't see the screen. "What was the drop rate?" he asked.

"Negative double digits. Viewership increased through the hour."

"Why are viewers starting late?" Lena asked. "Is it a time zone thing?"

"No," the Grenouthian director said. "It can be streamed in full any time after the start of the broadcast, but when viewers ping their friends to watch, they want to stay in sync so they can discuss what they're seeing. And your challenge is a big hit."

"I guess people like seeing me mess up. I haven't gotten the order right yet."

"When is the Verlock expert due to join us?" Julie asked.

"At Timble, when we pick up the Grenouthian appraiser," the director said. "They know each other from imperial swap meets."

"What are those?"

"Didn't you have them on Earth? How does one tribe of Humans who sold their cultural treasures under a bad government or economic duress recover them from another?"

"I don't think they generally do," Lena said. "Sometimes artifacts that were stolen by conquering armies or colonial governments are eventually restored, but I can't imagine anybody giving back items that were legitimately purchased."

The director scratched the side of his belly and looked at Yaem, who was toying with his upside-down phone, his mind elsewhere. "YAEM," the director bellowed.

"Sorry," the Sharf said when he saw the others staring at him. "All of the artwork for—there's no reason for me to burden you with my problems. What was the question?"

"The Humans have never heard of imperial swap meets."

"Really? Then how do they get back historical artifacts that fell off the floater?"

"Let me get this straight," Lena said. "Every year all of the advanced species get together and trade relics that they've acquired from each other's empires?"

"We currently do it once every century or so, depending on demand," the Grenouthian explained. "Imperial swap meets aren't for any old valuables, they're specifically reserved for items of historical significance, including some which belong in imperial museums and university collections. It takes hundreds of years of training to become a swap fest specialist."

"Has your species sold off that many of its treasures over the years?"

"We've had interstellar travel for seven million years, mistakes happen. But what makes the job challenging isn't learning about our historical artifacts, it's mastering everybody else's."

"Why is that important?" Lena asked. "Does the swap fest specialist pick out the alien pieces to bring?"

The director shook his furry head. "The tricky part isn't picking out which artifacts our species wants back or guessing at what you may want from our collection. It's the bartering."

"I get it," Julie said. "If you have Britain's original Magna Carta, you're not going to give it back for a comb some emperor's mistress dropped at an embassy ball."

"A crude comparison, but apt. If we aren't judicious with our foreign relic reserves, we could run out and not have anything to barter in the future if something important shows up at a swap fest. Then another species might get it."

"Why would another species want—oh."

"There are a limited number of priceless historical artifacts in existence, and most of them remain in the possession of the species that created them," Yaem said. "The swap fest is a major entertainment event, and there are always a couple of important pieces, but a lot of the action is in articles that are only valuable for historical reasons, like personal diaries of visiting diplomats that get left behind, items found in abandoned colonies, family heirlooms of expatriates and explorers who never return home. It adds up at a steady rate."

"There's a game if you're curious," the Grenouthian director said. "It was originally created by the Verlocks to spot negotiating talent in youngsters. Nobody starts out with a major artifact that's held in the imperial collection. You have to work your way up to it by bartering large numbers of less significant items."

"How many tunnel network traditions like that I've never heard of are there?" Lena asked.

"Don't look at me," Yaem said. "The Sharf aren't tunnel network members."

"And I'm not a mind reader so you'd have to make me a list of the periodic interspecies events you're aware of before I could answer," the director said. "The ambassadors take care of all the usual business that comes up, but every profession, craft, and academic organization, holds some sort of event on a regular basis, to get their intellectual property straightened out if nothing else. How many interspecies associations are listed in the current catalog, Flower?"

"Seven thousand and fourteen officially registered with the tunnel network," the ship's artificial intelligence came back immediately. "There are many times that number with one or more tunnel network members that are based in non-aligned empires and regions of space."

"But there can't be that many different professions and trades unless you're breaking them all down to the specialist level," Julie protested. "Or is that what they're doing?"

"It can turn into a hassle if you're not careful," Yaem said. "I must have joined a dozen organizations since I started working for Flower, but most of them only hold an event once a decade or so, and attendance isn't mandatory."

"Same here," the Grenouthian said. "The only membership I take seriously is the Empire's Choice Awards Academy, but it pays to join the groups relevant to your profession for the publications and the discounts."

"He's not kidding," Yaem jumped in. "When I book travel and the agent asks if I have any memberships, it takes five minutes to go through the list."

"Is there a group for show hosts?" Lena asked. "If I'm going to continue doing this, I should look into it."

"Why if?" the director asked bluntly. "The *Antiques Tunnelshow* is a lock for an award in the newcomer category next year. I already nominated you for Best New Human."

"I miss researching stories and doing in-depth interviews. I've talked to some nice people who come to the show and heard some interesting family histories, but it's not the same as investigative journalism."

"Look, you have a chance to make this show your own. Do you think that the network tells Aisha what she can and can't do on *Let's Make Friends?* At some point, the face of a show becomes bigger than the show itself, and when that happens, if you want to make the *Antiques Tunnelshow* about the Apologist music scene—well, that wouldn't work, but I'm sure you get my meaning."

Lena weighed the alien's words before replying. "How long do you think it will take for me to gain some editorial control?"

"Five seasons," the Grenouthian replied bluntly. "Three to determine that the show isn't a flash in the pan, and two more for the initial power struggle between the director and the producers to settle out. And don't forget that it will take a hundred episodes or more before most viewers will be able to pick you out of a lineup of Human females with the same color skin and hair. The less you look like them, the more they'll think Humans all look alike."

"Yes, I've heard that," Lena said. "All right, I'll try thinking about what I want in the longer term. Will you and Yaem maintain any association with the show after it transfers to the network?"

"I doubt they would take my texts," Yaem said. "If they had smartphones, that is. There was a time—"

"The delegation from the ISPOA is here," Flower informed Julie by way of her implant. "I have to enter the tunnel in two hours if we're going to arrive at Timble on time, and I don't think they'll be happy if they have to come along for the ride."

Julie waited for Yaem to finish his rant about the good old days before he acquired a smartphone, and then she announced, "John is back with a delegation from ISPOA. They may want to talk about all the counterfeits we've been seeing that were manufactured by Horten pirates."

"As long as Myort isn't along," the director said and rose to face the door. "Myort. Long time no see."

The Huktra dragon variant with his wings tucked tightly acknowledged the Grenouthian with a head bob. "Director. You've come a long way since playing the female parts in regional theatre."

Julie would have sworn that the director's fur bristled, though it was already cut so short that it was hard to tell. "John," she greeted the EarthCent Intelligence agent. "Are the two of you it?"

"Nobody else wanted to make the trip, and their species all have assets on Flower keeping an eye on things," John said. "We knew the timing would be tight so it didn't make sense to bring so many representatives that half the time would go on introductions. For anybody who doesn't know Myort, he's the Huktra ambassador and cultural attaché on Earth. He gets away with doing both jobs because he only sleeps a few hours a week and he's a master of disguise."

"I know my way around a personal holographic projector," Myort said modestly. "I'm sure that the director doesn't want me coming along to Timble, so if there's no objection, I'll run down the list of complaints and injunctions that have been sent to ISPOA for action, mark them all as settled, and we'll be on our way."

"The Inter-Species Police Operations Agency is investigating our show?" Lena asked, addressing the question to John rather than the imposing alien.

"Investigating is too strong a word," John said. "We're here on more of a fact-finding and informational mission."

"Facts for us, information for you," Myort added as he crouched on his haunches at the end of the table which had no chairs suitable for his bulk or wings. "Which do you want first?"

"Information," the director and Yaem said simultaneously.

"I don't have to tell you that jealousy is a green-eyed monster, but every major producer of reality immersives on the tunnel network is rushing to get their own version of the *Antiques Tunnelshow* into production. Thanks to advertising and your tie-in with the Grenouthian network, your lead is probably insurmountable. But you know what that means."

"Legal challenges," the director said, showing his blunt teeth in a snarl.

"Most of the complaints and injunctions are pure delaying tactics that might as well have been filed by legal interns for all the effect they'll have, but a few of the issues raised have the potential to impact distribution in the empires of the production companies filing the complaints," Myort said. "There's nothing at the governmental level—bringing on specialists from all of the species helped you there—but if the Horten Entertainment Association or the Drazen Immersive Consortium can tie you up in court for a few cycles, that would be enough time for them to start producing their own versions of the show. If they bring on a Human host, it's possible that most viewers won't even be aware of the switch."

"It's always the young species who screw everything up," Yaem said, and then hastened to add, "No offense, Julie, Lena."

"None taken," Lena said dryly. "What are the specific allegations they're making to ISPOA, and why didn't they go directly to court?"

"As you might imagine, situations like this come up whenever somebody starts producing a new entertainment franchise that looks like it has mass-market cross-species potential," Myort said. "To prevent empires from weaponizing their courts, the tunnel network treaty makes ISPOA the first stop for all inter-species criminal complaints."

"But aren't these civil complaints?"

"I can answer that," John said. "ISPOA doesn't deal with civil complaints. Unfortunately, the entertainment industry is so powerful in most empires that they've been able to criminalize aspects of piracy and intellectual property infringement for precisely this reason."

"Let's get down to specifics," the Grenouthian director growled.

Myort produced a hand-held holographic projector from his belt and directed it at the ceiling over the conference table. A scene from the show at Break Rock appeared where the appraiser put a value of forty creds on a Horten gamemaster guide in poor condition that had been brought in by one of the hackers from Bits.

"The Horten Entertainment Association has filed an intellectual property infringement claim on behalf of the publisher of the gamemaster guide which cannot be reproduced in any form under Horten law," the Huktra said. "It's an archaic law that dates back to before they joined the tunnel network that nobody bothered decriminalizing because it never comes up."

"But the specialist didn't reproduce the guide," Lena argued. "He appraised it as a whole and as individual character sheets, since they're often unbound and sold that way to gamers who only care about one character."

"In doing so, the specialist flipped through all twenty pages on camera. The resolution of the immersive cameras is high enough that if we zoom in," he did something to the hand-held projector and the hologram expanded, "you can read all of the text."

"I can't read any of it and my implant isn't giving a translation."

"It's in a Horten role-playing language, you'd need to download the vocabulary," Yaem told her.

"The Hortens create new languages just for games?" Julie asked.

"All the advanced species do," Myort told her.

The Grenouthian director slumped in his chair. "I knew I should have edited that out, but Break Rock was a bust for antiques, and we were depending on M793qK's patients to present his treasures. But wait. How old is that gamemaster guide?"

"Not even six hundred years," Myort said. "Horten gaming guides are in copyright for the life of the creator plus one hundred and seventy-three years and Plork died less than a century ago."

"Are you here to serve us with an injunction?" Julie asked. "Will it only apply to Horten gaming guides, or to all of their intellectual property?"

"It doesn't work like that," John said. "If the complaint sticks, the Horten Entertainment Association can ask that the *Antiques Tunnelshow* be banned from their empire until the matter is resolved in court. ISPOA doesn't like being dragged into these commercial disputes, which is the main reason they assigned me the task of leading the delegation. They've basically put the ball in your court."

"Can we head them off at the entrance to the warren?" the Grenouthian director asked. "Buy the rights from the heirs of the game's author?"

"ISPOA can't take an official position," Myort said and performed an exaggerated wink that caused the upper lip on the left side of his snout to pull up to reveal his fearsome fangs. "Otherwise, I'd suggest working through your new specialist, Dotat, who is extremely well-connected and has an obvious bias toward making the *Antiques Tunnelshow* a success."

"What's the intellectual property issue with the Drazens?" Julie asked.

"They made several specious complaints that I won't bore you with, but there's a criminal charge related to profiting from the exploitation of looted historical artifacts that John can explain."

The EarthCent Intelligence agent took a short iron rod with a flat point and a peened top out of his satchel and passed it to Julie, who adjusted to the weight just in time to keep it from scratching the table. She handed it on to Lena, who passed it to the Sharf. Yaem licked the side of the spike and said, "This has been in contact with wood treated with chemicals to prevent rotting," before offering it to the Grenouthian, who looked like he was squeezing his head between his paws.

"I knew there was something off about that Human," the director moaned. "Jorb told me that it didn't seem likely a contract worker could have afforded Drazen mining artifacts, but I was desperate to get something topical on the show while we were at Break Rock."

"Is it a chisel?" Julie asked. "I don't remember seeing the appraisal."

"A spike. I added it at the last second after I showed everybody what I thought was the final cut. You'd have seen it if you'd watched the broadcast."

"Do you mean like a railroad spike?" Lena asked. "I thought the advanced species all got rid of their railroads before they discovered interstellar travel."

"Not at all," the Grenouthian said. "Steel rails and wheels are beloved technology to engineers throughout the galaxy. They're primarily used in industrial applications to reduce friction and wear for very large and heavy machines with a limited range of movement, like container cranes at a spaceport. But the spikes the Human brought in were from a rail system in a mine, the kind the Drazens still use to transport ore underground for traditional reasons."

"If they're just iron railroad spikes, what's the big deal?"

"Based on the style and precise metallurgical composition of the spike the man brought in, Jorb said it dated to the original settlement of Two Mountains."

"Was it stolen from a museum?" Julie asked.

"Even worse, an operational historical site," John said grimly. "My Drazen contact in ISPOA told me that they hushed it up because it was an isolated case, but a group of humans who had completed a labor contract toured the First Shaft on Two Mountains before leaving the planet. The next safety inspection, which took place a week later, revealed that several spikes had been removed from the track, apparently as souvenirs."

"Who steals a spike from a track in a Drazen Historical Heritage site, especially a track that's in use by tourists?" the Grenouthian bellowed. "It's beyond comprehension."

"What can we do to fix the problem?" Lena asked.

"Displaying one of the looted spikes on the *Antiques Tunnelshow* was adding insult to injury," John said. "The Drazens want the spikes returned, and they want the men who took them to apologize. ISPOA has a seize-and-hold order in place, and EarthCent Intelligence is cooperating. But it appears that one individual, the Dale Howard who appeared on the show, went from Flower to Union Station, and then took passage to Farling Four."

"M793qK has as much to lose as any of us, so his retainers will run the man to ground," Yaem said. "Give me all of the details and I'll pass them along."

"We're in trouble if the thief has moved on to another Farling world where one of M793qK's enemies is in control," the director said darkly. "Is that everything, or do you have more bad news?"

"There's a royal warrant out for your Vergallian specialist's detention, dead or alive, but it's only enforceable on a dozen or so planets in the Empire of a Hundred Worlds, and I'm sure Adlyn has the sense to steer clear of those," Myort said. "She finished on the wrong side of a succession war, the usual Vergallian tragicomedy. The rest of the complaints are less critical in that there are no smoking guns, so you can drag your heels until the Grenouthian network takes over the show and it becomes their problem."

"More illegal profiteering?" the director speculated.

"Exactly. Human travelers have a willingness to pay cash to strange aliens in dark alleys without questioning whether said aliens own the items they're selling at a tiny fraction of the value. When those artifacts appear on the show, you become complicit."

# Sixteen

"You have the wrong Vergallian," Adlyn told Vivian. "I haven't been a girl since your world ran on whale oil."

"Girls night out is a chance to get together for an evening and do something as a group. That's where the name comes from."

"A group of girls and one old royal in exile."

"I told Yvella and Shint you were coming," Vivian tried again. "They're both excited about how much they can learn from you."

"Sitting in a faux-Frunge café drinking colored tea that tastes even less interesting than it sounds?" Adlyn retorted. "I don't think so. If you wouldn't mind removing your foot from the threshold, you're keeping the door from closing."

Vivian steeled herself and said, "You'd be doing me a personal favor."

The Vergallian, who'd started retreating into her cabin, turned back. "On the other hand, who am I to turn down the Human empress, a Dollnick prince's daughter, and the Sharf emperor's great-granddaughter? Did you invite Julie and her Drazen friend who's raking in the creds with her lullabies?"

"Julie and her husband are chaperoning a date for Razood and Fandaz, and Rinka is babysitting for both of us."

"Your husbands don't participate in childcare," Adlyn stated.

"They do, but our School of Government is holding a debate tonight and Samuel has to be there."

"All right. Tell Yvella and Shint to meet us at the LARPing studio. Shint is welcome to bring her protector. He can tank for us."

"You want to go LARPing?" Vivian asked in confusion.

"I already have the time reserved and I'm not rescheduling," Adlyn said. "Do you have any idea how hard it is to find an open slot rather than joining a party?"

"I'm more of a dancer than a LARPer. Which reminds me that you're welcome as a guest instructor for the Vergallian ballroom class we're holding for students four evenings a week. I know that it will look less like a dance than a mob to you, but…"

"Let's just leave it at the pregnant pause, shall we? Krey and Avisia are meeting us at the studio in ten minutes."

"Ten—deal," Vivian cut herself off when she caught the look of impatience on the Vergallian's worn face. "We'll meet you there."

Shint and Yvella were thrilled with the change of venue for their outing, and the Dollnick specialist pinged Lume to inform him he was invited. Vivian pointed at her ear to let the aliens know she was talking over her implant and informed Samuel and Rinka of the change in plans and her uncertainty about when she would be back. Then she pinged Flower and subvoced, "What kind of adventure did Adlyn choose?"

"She asked for an environment, not an adventure. It appears you're going for a dungeon crawl in a real Vergallian dungeon."

"I guess with two Vergallians for guides we'll be okay."

"Bad guess," Flower said. "Adlyn asked Krey to attend as a witness, but I can't say any more on the subject without violating a confidence."

When Vivian and the two young aliens she was officially hosting arrived in the locker room for the LARPing studio, both Vergallians were already there, changing into the lightweight protective gear worn by duelists. Somebody started whistling a tune from the other side of the central row of lockers, and Shint whistled something back that Vivian's transplant translated as, "This looks serious."

"It's between the royals," Lume replied in Dollnick. "I brought a first aid kit."

"There are standard dungeon crawl outfits in the lockers, all Frunge multi-fit," Flower informed Vivian over her implant. "The red lockers hold barbarian kits, the green lockers are rangers, the blue lockers are for mages, and the black lockers are for assassins. Stop me if you hear anything that interests you."

"I'm sorry, I'm still processing this," Vivian said out loud. "Flower told me that there are Frunge multi-fit outfits in the lockers and they're color-coded. If you girls want to change, just tell her what kind of character you want to play and there's probably a color for it."

"I'm fine with anything," Shint said and opened a locker at random. "Ooh, it looks like I'm a scribe."

"Ranger," Yvella said after opening a locker of her own. "Believe it or not, I've never worn a multi-fit costume. Is it nanofabric, like the SBJ Fashions boutiques?"

"It's not programmable like that and I don't think it's made of nanobots," Vivian said. "Somebody explained to me that the fibers are activated by your body heat so they shrink to size. When they're cold, they're so baggy that a Verlock could get into them."

"What about my arms?" Shint asked.

"Do you think I would stock multi-fit costumes that weren't suited for Dollnicks?" Flower asked through an overhead speaker grille. "Put your upper arms in the sleeves and feel for inside pockets below them with your lower arms. If you push through, the pocket will unfold into a sleeve."

Krey padded into the locker room followed by both of her Cayl hounds. "They can't get enough of LARPing," she said apologetically. "If I came without them, I'd never hear the end of it."

"Is everybody decent?" Lume whistled from the other side.

"No!" Shint practically shrieked, and then she giggled in a breathy fashion. "Just a minute, Protector. I've never worn one of these before."

"I'll go ahead and prepare the dungeon," Adlyn said, fixing the younger Vergallian with a hard glare. "You know, exactly like last time."

Vivian waited until the older Vergallian had entered the LARPing studio before asking Avisia, "Can you tell me what's going on? I'm supposed to be responsible for these two, and it won't reflect well on the Human Empire if something bad happens."

"It's a LARPing studio," Avisia said, and drawing her rapier, covered the tip with the palm of her other hand and thrust. The blade drooped like a strand of wet spaghetti. "Noodle weapons. I would have preferred to do this without an audience beyond the mandatory witness, but nobody asked me."

"You don't have to fight her," Krey observed as she removed an enormous battleaxe from a locker and showed it to the hounds, who growled in approval. "I was given to understand that the outcome will have no impact on either of your social standings."

"Adlyn is the one who can't admit she's wrong," Avisia said, shaking her rapier until it suddenly stiffened up so she could slide it back into the scabbard. "I don't blame her, but I didn't have a choice in the matter myself. It's not like I accepted the assignment on Flower with better prospects waiting for me back home. Nobody likes to be reminded of this sort of affair, and I'm practically in exile as well."

Shint finally got her lower arms through the sleeves and Lume came around from the other side of the lockers wearing a black assassin's outfit with enough throwing knives in two crossed bandoliers to keep four arms busy. The party entered the Live Action Role-Playing studio and immediately found themselves in a stone-paved tunnel lit only by guttering candles in damp nooks.

"This is creepy," Yvella said happily. "It reminds me of a castle tour I took on Earth."

"I wanted to visit for the New World's Fair but my family was against it," Shint said. "I sort of used that as leverage to get this opportunity because even a father can't say no every time."

A clattering sound that might have been a falling stone sounded from up the tunnel.

"Everybody remains behind me," Avisia said in a low voice, unsheathing her rapier again. "Remember, you're only here as witnesses. Don't get involved."

Krey growled at her hounds who were inching forward along the walls of the passage, trying to slip by the Vergallian, and they settled down on their haunches. Vivian attempted to raise Flower on her implant without pointing at her ear, but the Dollnick artificial intelligence failed to respond. They followed several steps behind Avisia as the tunnel sloped downward. The air became so damp that the walls showed seepage and rivulets of water running into shallow gutters before disappearing through regularly spaced gratings.

"I don't want to do this again," Avisia muttered under her breath as the soft click of a stone being placed on the floor came from somewhere ahead of them. She raised her voice and called, "Guard. Is that you? The watch reported that you never signed out. If you're drunk again, I'll have no mercy."

Silence greeted her, but both hounds tilted their ears forward as if they could hear something that escaped the bipeds. Vivian glanced at Krey, and the Human Empire's mentor's furry ears were also twisted forward.

The only candle illuminating the way forward was suddenly extinguished, leaving the tunnel sunk in gloom. Avisia removed an object from her belt and tossed it into the darkness, at the same time hissing to her companions, "Close your eyes."

Vivian caught the beginnings of a flash as her lids closed, and when she opened them again, there was a uniformed body on the floor a few steps ahead of Avisia. The Vergallian moved forward in the light of the flare that was now producing a steady glow, crouched, and felt the guard's neck. "Dead," she pronounced.

"That Tursjil offered me personal offense," Adlyn's voice came out of the darkness. "Go back to raise the alarm and I'll let you live."

"You know I can't do that," Avisia said, her knuckles whitening on the hilt of her rapier. "I pledge on my honor that your appeal was submitted to the Council of Queens. I don't approve of everything my family has done, but my loyalty is unquestioned."

Adlyn stepped into the light, and the fencing pads Vivian had watched her put on had somehow morphed into a tattered dress that wouldn't have interested a ragman. Her face appeared several hundred years younger than it had been in the locker room a few minutes before. Adlyn's off-hand was covered in blood and holding a short dagger that looked like it had been improvised from a scrap of metal sharpened by running it against a stone, while her dominant hand held the rapier that was missing from the guard's belt.

"I am leaving," Adlyn said. "The last time we did this, I spared your life, but you complained that I treated you dishonorably. With these witnesses and ample time to review your words, what say you now?"

Avisia drew a dagger with her right hand and began moving forward with the rapier in her left en garde, and then she stopped. "You magicked me," she complained in a voice that somehow came out sounding like that of a teenager. "I was ready to face you and then I woke up on the tunnel floor with my oldest sister pouring water on my face."

"I spared your life," Adlyn repeated. "After you were down, I struck the back of your scalp hard enough to draw blood and left it to you to say what you would."

"But to do *that* in a duel. It's an execution offense."

"We've had this discussion before. In a fair fight, I would have left you dead on the floor and made good my escape. You weren't even finished with your schooling, and you had no chance against me."

Avisia started forward again and then she seemed to wilt. "I don't want to do this again. I withdraw my words."

"Witnessed," Krey growled before the Vergallian could change her mind. The dungeon faded away and was replaced by a pleasant meadow that Vivian recognized as the neutral starting point for players who had entered the LARPing studio before choosing a quest. Krey's hounds immediately lit out after a holographic rabbit and Vivian pitied the bot that gave the hologram substance.

"Can we go on a quest now?" Shint asked. "I've never been."

"Me either," Yvella said. "But no skeleton warriors. They remind me of my great-great-grandfather in the last century of his life. What do you think, Empress?"

"I only watch the Professional LARPing League because of my twin brother," Vivian said, without explaining why Jonah wanted an extra pair of trusted eyes on the human players. "I'd prefer something above ground after that dungeon."

"Agreed," Adlyn said. "I spent enough years in dungeons not to go adventuring in them for fun."

"How about a woodland chase?" Lume suggested. "We have an edge with the hounds."

"Any objections?" Krey asked. "Flower, a woodland chase quest, if you please."

"Are you tanking for us, Lume?" Avisia asked.

"I'm more of a finesse assassin," the Dollnick said. He tossed one of his throwing knives in the air, then all four of his hands blurred into motion and rapidly emptied both bandoliers so he was juggling two dozen blades in a glittering arc. Then, just as rapidly, he began pulling them back and sheathing them.

"That was worshipful," Yvella said.

"He's no schoolboy juggler," Shint concurred.

"I'll tank," Krey offered, unslinging her battleaxe. "Try not to hit me with any knives, Lume."

An angry-looking unicorn trotted out of the woods, a string of jewels wrapped around its horn. It stared at the party for a moment and snorted, as if it was considering impaling them all one by one. But then the hounds returned from their rabbit hunt, and the unicorn bounded off, leaping higher in the air than Lume was tall.

"Hold!" Vivian cried before the others all took off running after the unicorn. "Maybe we should just go to the tavern."

"What's wrong?" Avisia asked. "With all that ballroom dancing you do you should be able to run for miles."

"I've seen that unicorn in the Professional LARPing League broadcasts. Flower must have borrowed it from Libby the last time we stopped at Union Station. Nobody has ever caught it."

"A challenge," Krey growled, though Vivian noticed that the Cayl emperor's granddaughter, who was faster than a hound in a sprint, didn't show any signs of gathering herself for a run.

"She's right," Adlyn said. "In here, I seem to be a full mage, and that unicorn has an aura like Baa's cat. A string of holographic jewels isn't worth the damage it would do to us."

"You know Baa?" Vivian asked.

"We've had business dealings."

"I've never been in a tavern," Yvella said, accepting the change of plans with her usual puppy-dog enthusiasm. "Will there be a brawl?"

"I could start one," Lume offered.

The hounds looked at each other and then took off running in the direction where they'd last seen the holographic rabbit. Krey slung her battleaxe and said. "Tavern it is. Maybe they'll have music."

As it turned out, the tavern not only had music, but line dancing, which Shint and Yvella took to like they had been waiting for it their whole lives. Lume bought two pitchers of small beer, as none of them were serious drinkers, and Vivian found herself sitting between the two Vergallians, with Krey and Lume across the table.

"So what are you going to do next?" Adlyn asked Vivian.

"Next, this evening, or next with the empire?"

"The Human Empire. Exiled royals hear things, and it sounds like the Council of Queens intends for the princesses they sent to Earth to push your empire forward."

"I suppose they want us to take over from EarthCent and start representing Earth so the princesses can go home," Vivian said.

"Perhaps," Adlyn said after taking a sip from her beer. "Or they may have concluded that you'd make a fine daughter-in-law."

"But I'm already married. Unless you mean the Human Empire would make a fine daughter-in-law to the Empire of a Hundred Worlds. Obedient, without affecting the line of succession."

"You and Samuel are making progress the last few months," Lume said. "Hosting young Shint and Yvella is a good example of that, but you need to engage more with imperial families of the other empires."

"But we have nothing to offer them," Vivian said. "Thanks to Flower, M793qK, and the Grenouthian director, we've made a bit of a splash in the entertainment industry the last two years, but our role has been limited. First we sponsored the documentary festival, and now the *Antiques Tunnelshow*."

"I'm not supposed to get directly involved," Krey said. "Can you explain it to her, Adlyn?"

The older Vergallian woman took a sip of her small beer and made a face. "Buy me a decent glass of wine."

Krey nodded to Lume, who got up and headed for the bar again. Avisia took another sip of her beer and then got up and followed him, carrying the glass with her as if she intended to dispose of the contents.

"You and your husband need to play the part," Adlyn said bluntly. "You're supposed to become the figureheads for an entire species, but you act like a young couple with an embarrassing day job. How many times have your pictures appeared in the Galactic Free Press?"

"I don't know," Vivian said. "Too many."

"As a couple, twice. Once for your wedding, and once when the Human Empire established its headquarters on Flower. I did a search and there are no published pictures of you with your daughter. Yvella is only an emperor's great-granddaughter, and she's in the Sharf Gazette almost every day, even if she has to send them selfies."

"Look," Krey said, extending a claw to point at a Sharf with what looked like a nonfunctional crossbow over his back. "That's the third time I've seen him hanging around near Yvella."

"Do you think he's stalking her?" Vivian asked.

"Only in the paparazzi sense. He's probably capturing images with an implant."

"And Yvella understands that it's part of the price of being in the emperor's family," Adlyn said. "You may think that the job of starting an empire is about meeting Stryx milestones and building a governmental infrastructure, but that's all work for technocrats. The job of the imperial family is to put themselves out there so the empire has a focal point. You don't see Vergallian queens living in cottages and shopping in the market because that's not what the population expects of its leaders. Does Earth have a history of populism?"

"You can say that again," Krey told her.

"Then that may explain it. Take it from somebody who was raised to be a—" Adlyn glanced toward the bar. "I'll put it this way," she began over again. "Do you think the Stryx pushed you and your husband forward because you're uniquely qualified to administer a startup empire, or because the two of you are the best-connected Vergallian ballroom dancers humanity had available?"

Vivian froze for a moment, and she felt the blood draining from her face. "I don't know if I can do that," she said in a whisper. "I've never been one of those people who likes being stared at."

"I'm a truthsayer, not a psychologist, so I can tell that you're sincere. But I've also been around long enough to know that you wouldn't be in the position you are today if you didn't have the potential within you to handle the job without melting down. Thanks to dancing, there's nothing wrong with your posture, and if you need help dressing to impress, I'll remind you that your sister-in-law is a partner in SBJ Fashions. Now, get up there with Yvella and Shint so the nice paparazzi can take your picture."

"She's right," Krey said, giving Vivian a pat on the shoulder. "Now go, or I'll have to give you a nip on the ear."

Vivian went to join the young aliens in the line dance, and Lume returned with the drinks. "Avisia said she had to leave early," he told them. "I think that encounter in the dungeon shook her more than she let on."

"Her three older sisters were the problem," Adlyn said. "Avisia was a girl when it all happened, but she had more sense than the rest of those—what's the point of talking about it now? If I could wave my magic wand and never have been a royal, I would."

Lume tapped a ring on the little finger of his lower left hand and the line-dance music faded as an acoustic isolation field snapped into place. "You're the top Vergallian on our watch list, not that anybody would ever see you coming with your mastery of face dancing," the Dollnick told Adlyn. "I suspect you've had more impact on the future with your freelancing around the tunnel network than if you had chosen to reclaim your rightful throne."

"I'm tired," the Vergallian said. "I'm thinking of this specialist job as a way of easing into retirement, though I suppose they'll expect me to spot all of the cursed objects that come on the show as well."

"The Grenouthians?" Lume asked.

"The Stryx. I'm tempted to ask Samuel to introduce me to his mother so the two of us old ladies can compare notes about our careers as tools."

"Better to be a chisel in the hands of a master carpenter than a forest fire," Krey quoted an old Cayl saying. "I sometimes wonder what I did wrong to be appointed the Human Empire's mentor, but then my grandfather's words come back to me, and I console myself chasing my hounds around the reservoir deck."

"What did Emperor Brynt say to you?" Lume asked.

Krey sighed. "Grandpa said that the path to true knowledge starts with being able to recognize those who have it so you'll know who to ask when you hit a dead end, and there are always dead ends. The Cayl Empire operates independently of the Stryx, but they warned us off accidentally destroying ourselves on more than one occasion. After the Human Empire is up and running, I'll return to my life, and if my descendants should ever need extraordinary help, maybe my service will be remembered."

## Seventeen

"Are these alien potatoes?" Jake asked Harry.

"Purple potatoes were around on Earth long before the aliens showed up," the baker replied. "Fashion is as much a thing with food as it is with clothing. I have a book about it if you're curious."

"Sure, zap it to me."

"It's paper," Harry said. "It doesn't zap."

"Oh, from the library. I don't know. Is it baby-safe?"

"Julie brings books home from the library all the time," Bill joined the conversation. "We don't let Basil chew on them, but I'm sure Flower would have said something if they were hazardous."

"If you haven't gone to the library lately, you should," Harry told them both. "They still pick up abandoned collections every time we visit Earth, and they have enough books about cooking in general and baking in particular to fill a regular library. You might even consider grabbing a few hundred for decorations in your café, Bill."

"You mean, pile them up in the corners or something?"

"I was thinking of shelves on walls at different heights with discarded industrial parts like gears for bookends. Didn't you ever have bookshelves at—sorry, I forgot how you were brought up."

"That's all right," Bill said. "I guess I thought bookshelves were a library thing. Julie only brings a couple of books home at a time. She returns them after she reads them."

"There were some bookshelves on Bits for old computer language bibles," Jake said doubtfully. "I've never heard of anybody having hundreds of books in their home."

"Ask Samuel or Vivian," Flower interjected. "Samuel's mother is famous for buying old books and then pressing them on guests, and Vivian's mother runs a publishing house that makes all of their translated alien romances available on paper, even if it's only print-on-demand."

"I was waiting for you to say something so I could ask about catering the show today," Bill said. "I was thinking of making those cookies that the Grenouthian director—"

"No," the twenty-thousand-year-old artificial intelligence cut him off. "The director has been living around Humans for years, so he's developed a taste for some of your baked goods. The Grenouthians on Timble would spit out anything with sugar or white flour. Recreating desserts from Human history was an experiment, and it created several minutes of interesting background shots for the show over the course of the season, but we're sticking with crowd-pleasers today. That means colorful fruits and vegetables tastefully arranged."

"What are these black ones?" Jake asked.

"One of the Grenouthian varieties of carrot-like root vegetables, but don't taste it," Harry warned. "It won't poison you, exactly, but it will be a couple of days before you're interested in eating again."

"This looks childish to me," Bill said, stepping back from the arrangement he'd just completed using a mix of fruits and vegetables grown on Flower along with Grenouthian varieties that Dewey had brought in soon after they came out of the tunnel at Timble. "Are you sure about this, Flower?"

"The rainbow is a universal sign of hope among tunnel network species, and it's one of the classic patterns the Grenouthians expect to see for platter service."

"A hundred platters a day seems like an awful lot," Harry said. "Isn't it enough to feed thousands of Grenouthians?"

"If they're hungry, a hundred adults would go through it all in one sitting," Flower said. "Bill and Jake will be setting the trays out on stands, which is the Grenouthian way of letting everybody know that the contents are intended for snacking, not meals. Dewey will shuttle over new loads of freshly sliced fruits and vegetables as soon as the Old Way and Alt volunteers finish preparing them."

Bill set his finished rainbow tray in front of the giant roll of cling film and pulled out enough to cover the whole thing. The protective film pulled taut around the edge of the tray with such force that if he'd held it upside down, none of the slices would have moved.

"That's four finished, and two duplex trays are all that Jake and I can carry unless we use that floater," Bill said.

"Leave now and you can go over to the orbital with Harry and the camera crews," Flower said. "And remember, the director will be on edge working in front of so many Grenouthians from the industry that rejected him before he joined the ship. Don't argue with him or question any directions he gives you because it would be a severe blow to his status if any of the local Grenouthians are within earshot."

Bill remembered Timble from a previous trip when he'd made deliveries of repaired gaming hardware from Bits to human actors living on the immersive production orbital, but he wasn't prepared for the giant mall area to be so packed with furry aliens that it was easy not to notice the humans at all. As soon as he and Jake set their trays on the telescoping stands and removed the protective film, Grenouthians descended on them like a swarm of locusts, and Bill began to wonder if Flower had underestimated the demand.

"Why don't I handle the replacement trays as Dewey brings them and you take a look around," Jake suggested. "We can swap places in the afternoon."

"Thanks," Bill said. "I have to admit I'm curious to see some appraisals. I don't even recognize most of the stuff the bunnies are carrying."

"Sort of makes sense that different species would have different ideas of what's worth saving through the generations. I saw a Grenouthian with a giant jar of what looked like colored grains of rice that I would have thought was a holographic seascape if he hadn't passed so close."

Bill found a raised area further up the deck where he could see over the crowd of taller aliens. He spotted the floating immersive cameras operated by Harry and the rest of Irene's documentary crew set up around a group of specialist tables with bilingual holograms reading, 'Entertainment Memorabilia' and likely the equivalent in Grenouthian. Bill headed in that direction, primarily because the camera operators all had ample space to move, as if they were surrounded by invisible force fields. Everywhere else he looked, the deck seemed to be packed solid with a sea of white fur.

"Bill," a voice shouted in his ear as he pushed through the crowd, and a tentacle pulled on his shoulder. "It's a madhouse in here. We need your help with the cameras."

"I'm not a camera operator," Bill told Jorb as the Drazen half-led, half-dragged him in a different direction. "I never learned."

"You don't have to do anything other than stand there and look at the viewfinder screen. Your camera is slaved to mine for the reverse angles, but the Grenouthians keep bumping into it on purpose."

"I thought they had more respect for immersive productions than any other species on the tunnel network."

"They do," Jorb said grimly. "Little Grenouthians dream about working on crews, which is why they have unions that prohibit unattended camera operation. They're completely freaked out by Irene and her documentary crew. They've never seen Humans behind cameras before."

"So you want to make them even angrier by putting me behind a camera?"

"They aren't angry, they're shocked, and the reason they keep bumping my reverse angle camera off the shoot is because there's nobody behind it. I only need you long enough for Lena's interview and then I'll find another body."

Bill let Jorb position him behind a floating camera that was pointed at a table where Lena was waiting with a man in his thirties who was dressed in a lab coat and carrying an antique microscope. As soon as Jorb got back behind his camera and another alien who Bill didn't recognize manned a third, the volume of sound suddenly dropped to a background murmur as an acoustic shield of some sort snapped into place.

"Tell me about this costume you're wearing," Lena said to the man.

"It's from the role I played in a Grenouthian documentary about the advance of medical science on Earth in the

Nineteenth Century," the man said. "It's part of a series the production company is doing titled, *'Humans. They're Trying Their Best.'*"

"That sounds a bit more charitable than some of the Grenouthian hit documentaries I've seen that make fun of us from start to finish."

"Yes, my mother was very proud of me for landing the part, and she said that if my grandfather was still alive, he wouldn't believe how far we've come."

"Far from Earth?" Lena asked.

"I mean professionally," the man said. "My family has been on Timble for three generations, and my grandfather and my mother both played in dozens of immersives, dramatic documentaries, and straight dramas."

"Is the microscope a family heirloom?"

"My grandfather used it as a prop when he played a mad scientist developing a plague that was targeted to wipe out the people from a country that kept on winning the team sport where they kick the ball around the field. Most of his roles were like that, but he always did his best to bring humanity to the part, even though the Grenouthians kept casting him as a stereotypical mad human."

"Did he ever tell you why he put up with it?" Lena asked.

"It's acting work, and all of the roles for humans in alien productions at that time were stereotypes," the man explained. "Grandpa believed that it was important for human actors to show that they could perform on the galactic stage and to try to be bigger than the parts they were given. I remember watching old immersives with him when I was a boy, and he would point out scenes where he and other human actors were able to subvert the intention of the writers and give viewers the impression that our lives are just as valuable as theirs, even though we don't look the same or live as long."

"You said that your mother was also an actor."

"She still is, though she complains about type casting. Her Grenouthian agent keeps sending her up for supporting roles as a mother or a grandmother. Mom used this microscope as a prop when she played a chemist working in the fast-food industry to develop addictive substances that led to obesity and sickness."

"I'm not sure whether that constitutes an advancement over a mad scientist trying to create a plague to wipe out the supporters of another nation's football team."

"Strangely enough, it was, and she said that her father cried when he saw the finished documentary. The director let her bring real complexity to the character. Mom played it like she wasn't aware that she was doing anything wrong and had been educated to believe that scientists could create foods that were better than anything nature had to offer, including breast milk."

"It's still an issue on Earth, but that's starting to change," Lena said. "Drazen Foods and its competitors have made healthy eating fashionable among youth. I understand that the Vergallian princesses who are coming to Earth to assist the current governments are pressing for new food standards that will eliminate artificial flavors and coloring."

"My grandfather used to say that the Grenouthians weren't being hard on Earth to be mean, but because by their standards, we really were savages. He had a theory that all the aliens would start coming around once we lived on their worlds and space structures for a few generations, abiding by their rules, and raising our children away from all the historical and cultural baggage back home."

Bill felt a warm belly press against his back, and a voice whispered in his ear, "Implant?"

"I can understand if that's what you mean," Bill said without turning. Thanks to similar encounters on alien worlds and orbitals in recent years he was getting used to it. Bill felt something slipped into the back pocket of his jeans, and the voice said, "Keep this in your pouch until you see the doctor. He's expecting it." Then the warm pressure of the belly went away, and Bill casually checked to make sure whatever had been put in his pocket wasn't sticking out.

Lena thanked the actor for his cooperation, added a few observations of what she'd seen on Timble so far, and then Jorb called, "Cut." The camera Bill had been pretending to babysit followed after the master unit that the Drazen guided toward to the next shoot.

"Are you catering today?" Lena asked Bill.

"We brought over some fruit and vegetable platters and Flower will keep them coming, but it's more of a whimper than a bang," he said with a wry smile. "As of Monday, I'm done working for other people."

"I'd heard that your baking is a cover job and you're an undercover agent of some sort. I was going to cultivate you as a source."

"Cultivating sources is supposedly my job," Bill said. "Julie told me you're trying to figure out a way to combine investigative journalism with hosting the *Antiques Tunnelshow.*"

"Without any success to date," Lena said with a sigh. "But I've been presenting news one way or another since I was a child, and maybe a few years of trying to make everybody around me better would be good for my karma. I didn't do any prep for that interview, and I never saw the actor before in my life, but I think I learned more about how the Grenouthians view humans than I did when I spent weeks on a story about a reenactment preserve that they set up near my hometown on Earth." She pointed at her ear and looked around as she listened, but she couldn't see anything other than white fur. "Can you give me a homing beacon?" she asked out loud. "He's right here. I'll bring him."

"Me?" Bill asked, even as it occurred to him that she would know he was listening in.

"Julie wants us. She was approached by a Grenouthian who she knows from Flower's business dealings, and she thinks he would make a good interview subject."

"Can you use two interviews in one show?"

"I never know with the director, but it's for the documentary," Lena said. "They're setting up in a room, and she's broadcasting a location beacon so I can find them. That way."

The Grenouthian was carrying a black attaché case, a sure sign he was involved in the legal profession. Harry and Irene had already arranged their cameras, and Julie was standing behind one of them looking flustered. As soon as Bill entered the room, she said, "Swap with me. I have to be out on the floor."

Bill took his wife's place behind the camera, being careful not to touch anything, and Julie introduced Lena to the alien before taking her leave. Irene said, "Any time you're ready."

"Can you tell us what you're doing on Timble?" Lena began.

"What?" the alien asked. "Have we started? Don't Humans say 'Action' when they start shooting?"

"Sorry," Irene said. "Action."

"Can you tell us what you're doing here on Timble?" Lena repeated.

"Important network business," the lawyer replied. "I'm here to see you about your contract."

"Flower assured me she sent word to your network that I'm being represented by an agent on Union Station."

"Terrible error," he told her. "Just because Aisha and Jonah use the same Chert agent doesn't mean that—is this a name thing?" he cut himself off.

"What do you mean?" Lena asked.

"Aisha. Jonah. Lena. Your names all end in the same annoying sound that hurts my throat to pronounce. There's no such thing as coincidence, and three times makes it a rule."

"The agent was recommended to me by the First Administrator of the Human Empire. He's related to both Aisha and Jonah."

"You don't have to tell me who's who in Humanity," the lawyer said roughly. "Fine. You want to give five percent of your earnings to an agent in perpetuity instead of trusting the paw that feeds you, suit yourself."

"Five percent?" Lena asked. "Samuel told me he thought it was fifteen."

The Grenouthian's black eyes bulged as he stared at her in surprise. "You thought the agent was going to take fifteen percent and you still agreed? I would have left my job to represent you for fifteen percent."

"Are you sure you want to say that on camera?"

The alien blinked, having forgotten about the documentary in the heat of the moment, and then he shrugged. "I'm a lawyer, not a director or a producer. I go where I'm compensated."

"Flower's next stop is Union Station," Lena said. "Was it that important to try to talk me out of representation that you couldn't have waited a few days? My understanding of my pilot season contract is that I can elect to extend it for fifty years when the show transfers to the network's control."

"Work to rule, you don't want to do that," the Grenouthian told her bluntly. "It means an adversarial relationship, and your Chert agent will be the first to confirm that. But the contract wasn't the only reason I was sent to see you," he continued, and pulled a familiar-looking book from his attaché case. "Read it, study it, know it."

"*Alien Antiques for Humans*? When did this come out?"

"It hasn't been released yet. Think of yourself as a Beta reader."

"The author is staff," Lena said. "Does that mean it's by the editors of the Galactic Free Press?"

"Maybe. The reason the network is paying me travel time to get this book in your hands a few days early is so you don't damage your brand by making a fool of yourself at the first show on Union Station. The director has done a clever editing job so far to cover the mistakes you've been making, which is fine for a Flower Entertainment production, but it's not how the Grenouthian Network operates."

Lena opened the book, glanced through the chapter summaries, and felt herself blushing. "You don't care about individual artists or brands?"

"Care? That's an odd word to choose, but I suppose Humanese lacks the proper vocabulary for what you're trying to express. We, and the other advanced species, honor and value artists and creators in our cultures. But we've been getting feedback from audiences who are baffled by human appraisers saying something to the effect of, 'This is the best example of early-mid-late pottery I've seen. If it had the famous brand, it would be worth a million creds, but without a mark, you may as well use it for a dog bowl.'"

"We aren't that bad," Lena protested as she flipped through the pages looking at the helpful hints and pull quotes. "It's that we value original works appreciably more than copies."

"Do your dead artists get royalties in their afterlife?" The Grenouthian paused to think about what he'd just said, and Bill suspected he'd witnessed the birth of a new religion. "That would make an interesting theology."

"No, but you can't be arguing that a mere copy is worth as much as the original."

"Why can't I?" The lawyer pulled a large gold pocket watch out of his pouch, and for a moment, Lena thought he was intentionally channeling the White Rabbit from Alice in Wonderland. "Here," the Grenouthian said, passing it to her after opening the case. "What do you make of that?"

"It's beautiful," Lena said. "I've seen some fancy watches on the *Antiques Tunnelshow,* but this is in a class by itself."

"Seventy-three natural jewels, over a hundred complications, and it includes three stopwatches that can run simultaneously for billing multiple clients on a busy day. There are millions of these in use, and after a black attaché case, it's the first thing every lawyer buys. They cost more than ten cycles rent for a furnished office, but can you guess why?"

"Even though there are millions of them? Are the jewels that valuable?"

"The materials cost nothing next to the labor," the Grenouthian explained. "These legal pocket watches are handmade by masters of the craft, and they represent hundreds of hours of machining and assembling. Do you see that screw head there on the—yes, that one. I'll wager it took the maker ten minutes to cut a thread on that screw. In a retail setting, the standard model sells for over ten thousand creds, because that pays for a master craftsman, his overhead, the store's overhead—need I go on?"

"But if somebody brought the original on the *Antiques Tunnelshow*..." Lena couldn't stop herself from saying.

"Original? There's no one original. A pocket watch like this is the culmination of millions of years of perfecting a craft and a product. You may as well wait for a Human to bring the original stone axe or arrowhead on the show."

"I never thought of it that way, but how about pieces that are more about the aesthetic than the technical expertise? A painting—"

"Read the chapter," the Grenouthian cut her off. "A master craftsman doesn't spend his career making the same watch over and over again, but producing the occasional classic design to the highest standard is a way of acknowledging that we all stand on the shoulders of giants. Your artists have an unhealthy obsession with trying to be the first at something so they can become the great new hope of your critics who are desperate for something to discover. The network wants to make sure that you understand the difference between Human antiques and the historical artifacts and family heirlooms of the advanced species that you'll be seeing beginning next week."

"I'll start reading it tonight," Lena promised. "You won't get an argument from me on the brand names. I've seen people bring in everything from jewelry to stained glass lampshades where the appraiser tells them if only it was by XYZ it would bring a hundred times as much at auction. But you mentioned historical artifacts. Does that mean you value a chair from—" she multiplied the number she originally intended to use by a thousand, "a million years ago more than a modern replica?"

"If you're talking about a lawn chair for the beach, I'd pay more for the replica if it was in better condition. If you mean the chair the emperor was sitting in when he signed the tunnel network treaty, it's in a museum, and it's priceless. If somebody had the bad sense to try to pass off a replica as the original, I'd be the first to bring legal action. But if they want to sell replicas of the emperor's chair for dining room sets, where's the harm? They're worth what a chair is worth."

"And that's a cut," Irene said when the Grenouthian picked up his attaché case and began hopping toward the door without another word. "I'm sure the lawyer was exaggerating about the director having to edit out your mistakes, Lena. He would have mentioned something in a meeting."

"You've lived in space for more than five years and you meet a lot of aliens while shooting documentaries," Lena said. "Did you know that they have a different way of looking at art than we do?"

Irene laughed. "Aliens have a different way of looking at everything than we do, but I can tell you this. The Grenouthian director brought me along to operate a camera when he did a commercial for Flower Textiles. There were hundreds of stitchers operating treadle sewing machines to fill bespoke orders for SBJ Fashions, and I know enough about stitching to have been wowed by the quality of the dresses they were turning out. They cost more than the throwaway fashions we used to buy on Earth, but they're also much higher quality, dresses you can wear all your life and hand down to your daughters."

"Is that a catalog of recent releases on the back cover of your book?" Bill asked Lena. "Check and see if they have *Opening a Café for Humans*."

# Eighteen

"Drube," the manager of the Empire Convention Center introduced himself to Julie in the lobby. "Where are the major point holders?"

"They're taking a look at the setup in the Meteor room," Julie said. "I think our Grenouthian director wanted to see if we needed to bring along the tables we've been using."

"The day that any convention center I'm managing runs out of folding tables is the day the Stryx declare that the tunnel network was all an elaborate prank on the Flopsies," Drube said indignantly. "I'm sure we can match or beat anything Flower had to offer on her con deck."

"Including her unsolicited advice?"

"No," Drube said with what passed as a wry grin among Dollnicks. "I've heard enough about Flower to know I can't compete with her on that account. Did you bring the camera crew to document the Antiques Flea Market?"

"Our Grenouthian director brought them, but, yes," Julie said. "I didn't hear about the flea market idea until we were in the tunnel on the way here. I appreciate your providing us with passes for Preview Day."

"Two hands wash the other two hands, and the idea came from your side, not ours."

"Really? I wonder why Yaem and the director never mentioned it to me."

"The artificial person who brought us the concept and all of the relevant data from Earth was acting on behalf of M793qK," Drube said. "The Farling doctor used to be at the top of the our emergency call list when he had a clinic on Union Station. Aren't you going to introduce me to the documentary crew?"

"They don't have implants," Julie explained. "But the woman closest to us is Irene, the unit director, and that's her husband trying to keep his camera from wandering off. The other couple are Dave and June."

The Dollnick strolled forward, and if his arms had been long enough, he would have shaken hands with all four of the camera operators at the same time. "Harry as in Harry's Fruitcake?" he asked in whistly English. "We can't keep it in stock at the bar."

"Guilty," Harry confessed. "At this point, I'm just the name behind the brand, Flower does all the work. How did you guess it was me?"

"Do Human names repeat?" Drube nodded to himself. "No wonder your species always seems so confused."

"Are you saying that other species have names that don't repeat? It doesn't seem possible, especially when you only use one name and it's short. I know a Lume, and many of the alien names I hear are only one syllable, but there are a lot more of you than there are of us."

"Which Lume?"

"Tall Dollnick, travels with us on Flower," Harry said, not sure whether everybody with four arms knew that Lume was Flower's station chief for Dollnick Intelligence.

"You aren't pronouncing the name right, or maybe it would be more accurate to say that you're leaving out all of the tones and accents that make it unique," Drube said. "When I learned Humanese, I was puzzled by the lack of acoustic range, but on the positive side, it allowed somebody like me with no talent for languages to easily pick it up. Alien diplomats complain about the difficulty of learning to whistle Dollnick," he added, almost as if he was proud of the obstacle his language presented to the other advanced species. "Ah, Lena. And you must be Scott," he greeted the approaching couple. "It's a pleasure to meet a Human who isn't height-challenged."

Julie left the *Antiques Tunnelshow* host chatting with the gregarious Dollnick with whom she'd be working in the near future and entered the Meteor Room, where she was greeted by a pure soprano note sung by Rinka in a far corner. Yaem was standing with the Grenouthian director, both of them looking at a handheld meter and nodding at the waveform displayed. "Cut," the director called.

"You could have just asked me instead of lugging that meter along," M793qK rubbed out on his speaking legs. "My hearing is perfect throughout Rinka's vocal range, and I can sense interference patterns with my speaking legs."

"I like meters because they lack a playful sense of humor," the Grenouthian director said. "Is everybody here yet, Julie?"

"Lena and Scott just arrived, and Irene's documentary crew is waiting. You didn't invite Jorb and Razood?"

"They're sick of looking at antiques so I gave them the day off. They'll have enough work tomorrow shooting our final show before the handover, especially with the observers from the Grenouthian network breathing down their necks and making snarky comments."

"How can you talk that way about your own species?" Julie asked.

"It's true," the director said. "We're superior to Humans at everything, and unfortunately, that includes being obnoxious when we put our minds to it."

"Well, I'm ready. How do we get into the flea market?"

"You walked right by the holographic sign when we arrived," M793qK told her. "You would have noticed it if it had been moving. That's the problem with peripheral vision in Humans. It's geared to spotting threats, but you'll walk right by a lion if it stands perfectly still."

"What were you measuring?" Julie asked Yaem to change the subject.

"The passive background noise coefficient of the room," the Sharf said. "The Empire Convention Center publishes a table of numbers, of course, but we wanted to make sure it was accurate with the divider in."

"The *Antiques Tunnelshow* doesn't need the full Meteor Room so they split it in half and put the Antiques Flea Market on the other side," the director said, pointing at what Julie had thought was just another wall. "You have to hand it to the Dollnicks when it comes to flexible interiors."

"The two of them are having trouble letting go," M793qK explained to Julie while they waited for the Drazen choirmistress to walk back across the large space. "When you've been involved in as many startups as I have, you reach the point where every successful exit looks like a new beginning."

"The room is flat," Rinka announced when she was within speaking distance. "If I'm ever asked to sing here, I'll have to remember to refuse."

"They're Dollnicks," the Grenouthian director reminded the choirmistress. "They don't care about the passive performance of rooms because they reshape everything with those audio manipulation fields they're so fond of."

"Let's go find out what we missed by not attaching a flea market to the *Tunnelshow*," Yaem said, waving open the exit doors to the lobby. "To be honest, I don't care if it's a money maker. If we'd taken on producing it, I would have gone three months without sleep."

M793qK put a limb on Julie's shoulder to hold her back so they brought up the rear of the group from Flower. "How does Lena feel about the format change?" he rubbed out on his speaking legs. "I would have told her back when I entered negotiations with the Empire Convention Center, but they wanted complete confidentiality in case it didn't happen, and they know she freelances for the Galactic Free Press."

"Lena thought it would be fun," Julie replied. "She told me she has a lot more experience shopping for bargains in outdoor markets than going to antique auctions, and she's looking forward to being able to talk about a subject where she isn't the least knowledgeable person in the room."

"I gave the Dollnicks the idea because I used to enjoy visiting flea markets on Earth in disguise. It's also a way to complete the dramatic arc for guests on the *Antiques Tunnelshow* who say, 'But we'd never sell it,' after receiving an appraisal. Now they can run next door and trade it in for what they really wish their relatives had left them rather than lugging it home and being miserable."

Irene waited with her camera crew at the lobby entrance to the other half of the Meteor Room to shoot Julie and the Farling doctor as they approached. "Do you want me to keep a pair of cameras on you?" she asked Julie.

"No, please," Julie said. "I'm browsing to see if I can find anything Bill might want for his café. He's planning an eclectic all-species look."

"Then we'll park the cameras and take a look around ourselves," Irene said. "It may sound funny, but after three months of shooting antiques, I have the crazy urge to buy one."

"Do you think it will be packed inside for Preview Day?" June asked as she handed over control of her camera for Irene to park it up and out of the way where the next deck met the bulkhead, the generally accepted location for parking cameras.

"Not a chance," Dave told her. "I've worked sales at enough trade shows to know that you never want to try to set up the morning of a show. Preview Day is an excuse to sell tickets to let a few early bird shoppers in while the vendors are setting up."

Irene presented her plastic entry chit to the young Dollnick at the door who was reading something from his tab. He barely looked up before tapping the door pad with his upper left hand. The sound of hundreds of voices arguing in a dozen languages hit the retirees in a wave. Dave grinned happily and led the way into what looked like move-in day on a university campus where all the students had been assigned to a single large room.

"This is a madhouse," June said. "I've never seen so many aliens who looked like they were ready to kill each other."

"It will settle down once they get the tables sorted out," Dave said. "Nobody wants to set up next to a vendor who's selling superior versions of essentially the same products."

"But isn't it all antiques?" Irene asked. "How could two vendors have the same ones?"

Harry laughed. "After three months of documenting the *Tunnelshow* you still ask that? It seemed like every fourth person had the same movie memorabilia or vase. I don't know when the Ming Dynasty ran China, but I suspect the empire fell because they were so busy making pottery that they didn't have time to defend their borders."

"We aren't going to learn anything standing here all morning," June said. "Why don't we take a look around? Maybe I'll see something my daughter or granddaughter would like."

"Nothing for yourself?" Dave asked.

"I already downsized once when we left Bits, I don't want to go through it again."

A Verlock who was slowly setting out rows of small stone carvings on a table tapped a translation pendant when he saw that June was interested in the little animals. "Ten – percent – discount – for – Preview – Day," he grated out.

"What does this one cost?" June asked, holding up a little animal carved from a dark red stone and polished to a mirror finish."

"One – eighty."

"Creds?!"

"Four – million – years – old," the Verlock intoned at his glacial pace. "Something – cheaper?" He rummaged through a box and brought out a piece that looked nearly identical to the one June was holding. "Twenty – seven – creds."

"That's still more than I can afford for a little figurine," June said, replacing the one she was holding on the table, and then asked out of curiosity. "How old is that one?"

"Sixty – thousand." The Verlock rummaged through his box one more time and brought out a small stone animal that he set between the other two. "Four – creds."

"I can't tell the difference between them. Can any of you?" June asked her friends. Irene and Harry examined the three pieces and shook their heads, but Dave said, "The most expensive one seems more lifelike to me. I can't put my finger on it, but the cheapest one looks dead."

"Good – eye," the Verlock said. "Human – knockoff."

"You're selling human copies of Verlock stone art?" June asked.

"Something – for – every – purse. Wrap – it – for – you?"

"No, I'll just take it." June handed four creds to the bulky alien and accepted the copy. "Thank you."

"Why did you buy it?" Dave asked as they walked away.

"After he spent all the time with us, I didn't want to leave empty-handed. Besides, how often will I get the chance to say that I bought a cheap human knock-off from a Verlock?"

Two aisles over, Julie asked M793qK, "Why do these vendors seem so different from the independent traders, both aliens and humans, who set up in Flower's bazaar?"

"They don't have ships," the Farling explained. "All of the merchants you see here have stalls on one of Union Station's market decks. Bartering or selling goods in their particular specialty is what they do every day. Independent traders spend more time traveling than working markets, and very few of them carry the same cargo twice."

"Their lives are more dramatic," the Grenouthian director added, examining an old lamp stand that looked a little like a bunch of carrots and then rapidly putting it back in place when the vendor looked in his direction. "I've told everybody working the cameras during our last show to keep their eyes open for a big dramatic moment to finish on."

"Like the appraisal where somebody brought in that music festival poster from the 1960s and the specialist discovered an Old Master behind it because the frame had been reused without removing the canvas stretcher?" Julie asked.

"I mean real drama, not some random Human finding out that they're rich through no effort of their own. If it weren't for the antiques and the specialists, most of our appraisals would be about as exciting as watching somebody check whether they've won the lottery."

"Don't worry," M793qK rubbed out on his speaking legs. "I have a good feeling about this show."

"Ringer?" the director asked, his whiskers twitching. "I checked the numbers and we're right on the edge. It would be risky to bring in another one."

"Let's just say I have access to confidential information and I seized the opportunity to crush two plague viruses with one grain of sand."

"Over here," Yaem called to Julie, who was glad to have an excuse to leave the Farling and the director to their scheming. "You should buy this for Bill."

"What is it?" she asked, examining the three metal plates connected by a complex hinge. "Some sort of waffle iron?"

"I've had what Humans pass off as waffles. This is a Sharf double-decker waffle maker. Once the waffles are cooked, the through holes line up, and the syrup is channeled from the top waffle to the bottom waffle in a controlled manner. And you can stack them as high as you want, though if you go beyond eight or ten layers, by the time the syrup gets to the bottom the waffles are cold."

"Five creds," said the Drazen who had started setting out his inventory which consisted mainly of kitchen wares. "I have another one somewhere, and if you buy the pair, you can have them both for nine creds."

"I'm not sure my husband will be making waffles in his café," Julie said.

"I'll order them," Yaem told her. "Tell you what. I'll buy the irons, keep one for myself, and you can tell Bill that his is a business-warming present."

"Your husband is opening a café?" the Drazen asked, and Julie noticed his tentacle starting to twitch. "Look no further, everything I have is perfect for you. In fact, why don't you buy my whole inventory and save me the trouble of putting it out? Say, two thousand creds?"

"I don't have that kind of money, and I don't think my husband would appreciate my making the decision for him," Julie said. "The waffle iron is interesting, but what he asked me to look for was mismatched mugs and teacups, to give his café a homey feeling."

"Mismatched cups and saucers? I have boxes of the stuff, though you don't have enough thumbs for classic stoneware."

"My friend Rinka has a two-thumb set, and I know my husband was looking for one. It's going to be an all-species café."

"Don't go anywhere!" the Drazen commanded. "Where's my brother with those other—Lork, I've got a hot one!"

"Please tell me they're looking for cups and saucers," Lork said, heaving a box onto the table. "If I have to carry these back to the Shuk after this show and set them up again I'm returning to hard rock mining. You didn't warn me that retail was so brutal."

"Look," the first Drazen said to Julie. "You can see how this is all wearing on my brother, and I don't want to make him unpack it all and then pack it up again two seconds later when you decide to buy, which you will. How about twenty creds for the box, and we'll call it a mystery lot."

"Twenty creds is over a hundred eBucks," Julie protested. "I could buy two boxes of mismatched cups and saucers at any flea market on Earth for that, and probably the same in Flower's bazaar."

"These aren't Human cups and saucers," Lork said, pointing at an alien scrawl on the box. "It says right there, 'Assorted crockery, Drazen, Frunge, and Horten."

"I wrote that myself when I was packing it," the first Drazen asserted. "There's a Verlock Obsidianware mug in there with just a small chip out of the handle that's worth at least ten creds on its own."

Julie felt the hard front of M793qK's carapace against her shoulder as he leaned over her. "Take it," he rubbed out on his speaking legs. "Bill can't wash dishes and serve people at the same time. He's going to need enough settings for three times as many sentients as the café will hold, and more, if you include species-specific crockery. What's he going to do if a flight of Huktras come in? They can barely get the tip of a claw through the handles on Human-scale mugs."

"Huktra?" Lork asked, his eyes lighting up. "Where's that heavy box, Torg? I unloaded it first to get it out of the way."

"I was using it as a seat. The odds of a Huktra coming to an Antiques Flea Market are low since they run the risk of knocking things over with their wings and tails and then having to buy them."

"Ten creds for the Huktra crockery," Lork told Julie. "I don't want to have to carry it back."

"We'll take it," M793qK said. "What else do you have?"

When Julie finally got the aliens away from the Drazen stall, they were weighed down with two boxes each, and the director had several ceramic pieces shaped like rowboats stuffed in his pouch that he said Bill could put on the shelf to make Grenouthians feel welcome, even if he never learned to make flaming ices.

"Should we bring all of this to his new location, or save it for a surprise at the opening," Yaem asked the others.

"Bill hasn't settled on the spot yet," Julie said. "He's got it narrowed down to three possibilities."

"It's not hard to predict which one he'll choose," M793qK said as he deposited both of his boxes on one of the rental mulebots waiting in a line at the exit. "He'll go with the one Flower pretends is the worst choice. She's a master of reverse psychology."

"Then let's get back to Flower and ask her where to unload this stuff," the Grenouthian director said. "I have a grand finale to prepare for. I'll tell Irene to shoot a few hours of the flea market at random and I'll edit it down to a thirty-second montage."

# Nineteen

"The *Antiques Tunnelshow* is coming to you today from the iconic Meteor Room in Union Station's Empire Convention Center," Lena addressed the imposing battery of immersive cameras, which in addition to the Grenouthian network's on-location crew, included representatives from all the major news services. "Starting next week, production of the *Tunnelshow* is being transferred from Flower Entertainment to a partnership between the Grenouthian Network and the Empire Convention Center chain, which will take us on a circuit of Stryx stations and beyond. I also want to thank the Human Empire for their support, and the imperial family is with us today to cut the ribbon for the first Empire Convention Center show. Without further ado, I give you Princess Rose."

Vivian, wearing a designer gown she'd first seen a half-hour earlier at SBJ Fashions when her sister-in-law had ambushed her with it, tried to keep her smile from turning into a death's head grimace as she led her daughter forward to cut the ribbon. Vivian retained her grip on the handles of the oversized golden scissors which were too heavy for a three-year-old to support and guided them into position. "Now, Rose."

The little girl, her face screwed up in concentration, pushed the handles together with her mother's help, and the ribbon separated, drawing cheers from the crowd in the lobby of the Empire Convention Center. Then Samuel came forward and picked up Rose so she wouldn't get trampled in the rush to the triage area, and a Grenouthian with an open attaché case appeared at Vivian's side and gave a discreet cough. Vivian slid the golden scissors into the case, glad to be free of the weight.

"Over here," Blythe called to her daughter from the other side of the hip-high glass barrier. "Samuel can step over, but you better go around in that dress. Let's get a coffee before we go in."

"I'll meet you there," Vivian called back, pointing in the general direction of the food court. She felt like a salmon swimming upstream as she worked her way out of the crowd flowing into the Meteor Room, and she was glad that Samuel had taken Rose. A few people stared at her openly, and one older woman even did a little curtsey. Vivian bobbed her head in return, uncertain how to respond.

"She seems to be holding up well so far," Blythe said to Samuel as they waited in the Coffee Bar.

"Rose is a trooper," Samuel said, balancing his daughter on his lap. "She's dealing with the title change better than any of us."

"I was talking about Vivian. She looks like an empress in that dress. Dorothy did a fantastic job."

"If I know Jeeves, SBJ Fashions will get a commercial out of it. They're probably going to work 'Imperial Family' into their advertising, like all the Vergallian designers who serve a royal family."

"Somebody curtseyed to me," Vivian reported as she carefully arranged her gown before sitting next to her mother. "I didn't know what to do or say."

"Just smile and nod," Blythe said. "Do you remember the advice I gave you before your wedding?"

"Close your eyes and think of the Human Empire," Vivian said, and they both laughed as Samuel's ears turned pink.

"We didn't have a Human Empire back then," he protested. "It wasn't even on the menu."

"I was teasing, but now that you've brought it up, I better go order."

"I got you a coffee and croissant," her mother said. "The waitress suggested deciding for you because everybody went to see the ribbon cutting. They're opening up again now, so there's going to be a delay."

"Ice cream," Rose contributed.

"Yes, we ordered you a small banana split, but you have to promise to be very careful with the dress Aunty Dorothy made for you."

"I think you've forgotten how kids eat at that age, Mom," Vivian said. "We'll ask the waitress for a bib."

"I'll keep a napkin ready and work mop-up duty," Samuel said. "Now, for real, what was the advice?"

Vivian sighed. "Mom told me to trust the process."

"Trust the process? What does that mean?"

"It's something Clive says when he knows that the aliens are all two steps ahead and the decisions he's making at EarthCent Intelligence are already preordained," Blythe explained. "Everybody in your family and ours has been touched by the Stryx, Samuel. I've never felt them pushing me to do anything I didn't want to do, but I've definitely felt them nudge."

"It's like that Station Scouts exercise where you lean back until you lose your balance and let another scout catch you," Vivian said. "Trust the process."

"I'm not afraid of the work," Samuel said. "Being called 'Emperor' just rubs me the wrong way. I'm afraid people will think I'm putting on airs."

"It's part of the job," Blythe said seriously. "Somebody has to do it, and I may be biased, but I don't know anybody more qualified than the two of you." She took a padded envelope out of her purse and passed it to Vivian. "A gift from your Aunt Chastity. She said to take it on the show and get some free publicity."

Vivian peeked in the envelope and groaned. "Oh, no. Is that a natural ruby pendant? Are those natural diamonds? It must have cost a fortune."

"She coordinated with Dorothy and the necklace goes with your new wardrobe. And don't forget that everything you wear becomes part of history for the Human Empire. Thousands of years from now, that dress you have on will be in a museum."

"Not the necklace?" Samuel asked.

"The current empress will be wearing it."

"Crown jewels?"

"Don't look so shocked," Blythe said, enjoying a laugh at the obvious discomfort of her daughter and son-in-law. "You've both met enough royals in your lives to know that they're no different from—well, maybe the Vergallians are—but you get my point."

Between the bib, strategically spread cloth napkins, and Samuel's watchfulness, Rose's dress was preserved intact for an appraiser in the distant future. Blythe offered to take her granddaughter to the EarthCent Embassy to visit Samuel's mother. Due to the crowds and haphazardly wielded antiques, Vivian agreed.

"You can pick her up at Mac's Bones later," Blythe said, once she was on her feet. "Your brother is helping Joe prepare a picnic, and my mom told me that you're expected to stay for a minimum of three days."

"Yes, ma'am," Samuel said.

After her mother left, Vivian cast a critical eye over her husband's outfit. "You should be wearing a jacket," she said.

"Dorothy told me that the dress-shirt-only look is big right now, and it would have looked strange with the backpack full of framed documents from the governor-general's library."

"If you had a suit, I'd feel less overdressed."

"Wait until you're wearing those jewels," Samuel said with a laugh.

"Just for that, I'm asking my mother to buy you a wristwatch," Vivian said as they got up and headed for the Meteor Room. "One of those ridiculously expensive ones that the specialists drool over on the *Tunnelshow*."

"As long as it's not a museum piece. When that actor from Timble found out that the watch that had been passed down in his family was worth two hundred thousand creds, I thought he was going to cry. I heard that the manufacturer from Switzerland sent a tunneling network telegram to Lena asking her to use her influence to get him to sell it back to the maker for their museum."

"Lena mentioned it when Julie invited her for our girls night out. The guy agreed to sell it to them for over a million eBucks and a condominium in Zurich, but she said he was pretty upset about the whole experience."

"Because he didn't really want to sell his family heirloom?" Samuel asked.

Vivian shook her head. "Because he wished he'd never found out what it was worth. He only took it on the *Antiques Tunnelshow* because he was hoping that if he got some camera time it would help him land better parts. Instead he ended up with enough to retire, and while it's the last thing he wants to do, he told Lena that he doesn't think he can go back to hustling all day every day to land bit parts and try to move up the ladder."

"I guess there are right times and wrong times to find out you don't need to work for a living."

The Grenouthian at the door waved the imperial couple through without asking to see their guest tickets. To their acute embarrassment, some of the guests waiting in line had witnessed the ribbon-cutting ceremony, and the whisper, "Make way for the Emperor and Emperess," went up in a dozen alien languages. Even the humans ended up getting out of the way when they saw the designer dress, and blushing like schoolchildren, Samuel and Vivian found themselves propelled past everyone into the triage area and directed to the first open table.

"Emperor, Empress," an unfamiliar Frunge specialist behind the table asked them. "What have you brought in?"

Vivian was too embarrassed to show the costume jewelry Samuel had brought back from the New York city-state's advising princess, so she produced the necklace her mother had given her. "It's a gift from my aunt," she said. "I haven't even had a chance to wear it yet."

"Very nice. They look natural to me, but there's a full scanner at the appraisal table for testing. Fine Jewelry and Gems." He looked expectantly at Samuel, who placed the backpack with all the documents he'd received from Governor-General Mayhew on the table. The Frunge pulled out a framed certificate at random and said, "Historical Documents and Treaties or Celebrity Autographs."

"You first," Vivian said when they exited into the area with all the specialist tables. "I'm too nervous."

"You're nervous?" Samuel asked. "I'm afraid the specialist is going to expect me to know all about the history of New York and I'll look like an idiot. The governor-general must have looted a museum to decorate the mansion's library."

The same "Make way" treatment played out when they approached the Historical Documents table, and Samuel was doubly embarrassed to see Jorb and Razood maneuvering six cameras into position under the direction of the Grenouthian director, with Irene's documentary crew just behind them. The Verlock specialist took one look at the framed documents unloaded from the backpack and deferred to his human colleague. The specialist spent five minutes examining the collection, asking Samuel questions the whole time, and then he straightened up and faced the cameras.

"This is the most impressive collection of New York historical documents I've seen since I visited the governor-general's mansion for a fund-raising event," the specialist began. "In fact, it appears to be the same collection."

"That's right," Samuel said. "Governor-General Mayhew loaned the Human Empire these documents and asked me to bring them on the *Antiques Tunnelshow*."

"All of these are priceless, so in keeping with our policy on pieces that will never go on the market, I won't talk about values, but I'd like to point out how foundational these documents are to New York history."

Twenty minutes later, Samuel thanked the specialist and repacked the framed documents, even as he wondered how much screen time the Grenouthian editor would give it, if any. The cameras under Razood's control had moved away less than a minute into the specialist's lecture, with the documentary unit consisting of Dave and June in hot pursuit. They all ended up at the Craft Art table, where the Cayl emperor's granddaughter was presenting a framed sampler.

"This is so exciting," the specialist said. "I'll date it the early 1800s, Vermont. I won't ask if it came down in your family because you're, uh…"

"Cayl," Krey supplied her species name.

"Where did you acquire this piece?"

"When Flower visits Earth, I try to visit as many craft fairs and antique shows as possible. I found this sampler in an old wooden chest filled with other pieces the dealer was selling for the frames."

The specialist looked like she was going to faint. "You mean he didn't know what it was?"

"He had no interest at all in art," Krey said. "He thought that the glass and the frames had value, but he didn't think it was enough to justify his putting in the time to throw out all of the old art and clean them up."

"How much did he want for the frame?" the specialist choked out.

"Two eBucks. I offered him twenty eBucks for the whole lot, and he agreed, providing I pay another fifty for the wooden chest, which he believed was quite the find."

"Did you bring any of the other framed pieces?"

"I only collect samplers," Krey said. "I left the chest and the rest of the artworks on consignment with a gallery in Manhattan that specializes in folk art."

"I see," the specialist said weakly. "Well, I'm sure you know that this is a school-girl sampler, created as a sort of graduation project to demonstrate her mastery of home crafts, along with the literacy that comes of knowing the alphabet. We believe it's a uniquely human form of—you're shaking your head."

"I'm not aware of any species that doesn't make samplers. Young females on Vergallian worlds must produce hundreds of millions a year. My sampler was quite a bit larger, as the Cayl alphabet includes over two hundred letters, and it's traditional to prove a theorem in the lower part."

"Prove a theorem?"

"Yes," Krey said. "I chose one that corresponds with Fermat's Last Theorem in your mathematical vocabulary, though my great-grandmother pointed out that I could have eliminated a step."

"I see," the specialist said, though her eyes gave lie to her words. "The sampler you brought in today is the finest to come on the *Antiques Tunnelshow* and the best example I've seen outside of a museum. Do you have any idea of the value?"

"Appreciably more than two eBucks."

"In the right auction today, I would appraise this schoolgirl sampler at between a hundred and fifty thousand and a hundred and seventy thousand creds," the specialist said in a rush. "How does that sound to you?"

"It seems reasonable," Krey said.

"For insurance, I'd value it at two hundred thousand creds."

"I'll tell my hounds, but they'll probably expect more treats."

At the jewelry table, Vivian handed over her new necklace and asked Samuel to turn around so she could extract from his backpack the package of costume jewelry that Governor-General Mayhew's Vergallian princess had purchased in Manhattan thrift shops as shopping therapy. The Dollnick specialist placed the new necklace in the scanner and whistled in approval.

"All natural stones," he confirmed, holding the necklace suspended in the hands of his upper two arms while using his lower hands to point out the features. "The atomic coding matches our records, and I see somebody purchased this lovely piece here on Union Station last cycle, so I won't ask if it's been in your family long."

"It was a gift from my Aunt Chastity," Vivian said.

"Chastity Papamarkakis? The publisher of the Galactic Free Press and one of the co-founders of InstaSitter? That explains how a Human could afford it. Do you happen to know how much she paid?"

"Of course not. It was a gift."

"Thirteen thousand and fifty creds, with the fifty going to the Stryx station librarian to permanently register the atomic code," the Dollnick said. "The price is embedded."

Vivian was speechless that her aunt would spend that much on a piece of jewelry, but Samuel said, "I've heard of molecular coding, but not atomic coding. Is something engraved on the back of the necklace that we didn't notice?"

"Atomic coding is used by licensed miners to mark natural stones as soon as they're extracted. The code is tied to the video captured by the miner's helmet cam for further confirmation if you want to view the moment of discovery. The stone cutters and jewelers add their own codes for video authentication to the atomic matrix. Given that even primitive species can synthesize diamonds and other gemstones that can't be reliably differentiated from natural stones, atomic coding is the only solution."

"What's to prevent somebody from faking the codes?"

"The same thing that restrains counterfeiting of all types," the Dollnick replied. "Enforcement. Do you have more jewelry in the package?" he asked Vivian.

"Costume jewelry," she said, pouring it out on the table. "None of the pieces cost more than ten creds, but the friend who asked my husband to bring them on the show was hoping to learn something about the styles they're imitating, all of which were new to her."

The specialist had gone rigid as the costume jewelry poured out of the bag, and Samuel wondered if they'd offended him. Instead, the Dollnick began whistling like an alarm going off, and Samuel's implant translated it to mean, "Vergallian jewelry specialist needed immediately."

Three aliens responded to the call, only one of them Vergallian, and they went into a huddle, examining the pieces Aazil had given Samuel, who intuited that the princess had played some sort of trick on him. The specialists seemed to be arguing about something, but eventually, three aligned against one, and they ran the jewelry through the scanner. Then they went back into a huddle, occasionally casting looks in Vivian's direction.

"Do you think they're all stolen?" Vivian whispered, her fingers digging into her husband's arm. "Is it a trap to make the Human Empire look bad?"

"I don't think so," Samuel said. "It's the last show Flower Entertainment is producing, but that means the Grenouthian director still has editorial control, and I'm sure it's not his goal to embarrass us."

"You're saying we should trust the process," Vivian surmised.

"I don't think we have a choice."

"Well," the Dollnick said after the aliens agreed on an arrangement to display the jewelry. "That was a clever trick you played on me, but I suppose it will create more interest for the viewers than if you had walked up and told me you'd brought all of the Human Empire's crown jewels."

"I honestly thought they were purchased in thrift stores on Earth," Vivian said. "There were receipts in the bag."

"With handwritten Vergallian script on the back of each. Did you read them?"

"I speak Vergallian, but I couldn't make out the script," Samuel said. "I assumed it was some sort of shorthand."

"Royal shorthand," the Dollnick confirmed. "What you've brought are gifts for the Imperial Family of the Human Empire from the Council of Queens and Fleet Command, which make reference to services rendered in healing their long-standing schism. All these pieces were previously included in crown jewels registered with the Stryx, but the atomic coding shows that they have been transferred to the Human Empire. Since none of these pieces have been on the market for hundreds of thousands of years, we had a bit of a disagreement over the valuation, but we think a conservative estimate would be four to five million creds for the collection."

"I let my three-year-old daughter play dress up with them," Vivian squeaked.

The Grenouthian director signaled Jorb to bring his cameras to heel and follow him to the collectibles area, where almost all of the guests were human. "The man with the helmet and the cardboard box," the director told the Drazen. "Stay on him. I'll get Irene and Harry on the other side so they can catch both of you in the frame for the documentary."

"That good?" Jorb asked. "What does he have in the box? The original Tarzan?"

"What's that?"

Jorb stretched upward with his tentacle and swayed his body to pantomime swinging from something. "The only Human who figured out how to move around in a jungle. There's an old cartoon from Earth that's popular with Drazen children."

The director gave a noncommittal grunt and pushed through the crowd to where Irene and Harry were shooting a couple of specialists trying to put the furniture back into the dollhouse that one of them had tipped too far over while looking for a label on the bottom.

"Irene," he said. "I want you to get the Collectibles table, and make sure that Jorb is in the background."

"Where Geoffrey Harstang is helping with the science fiction memorabilia?"

"That's the one. I tried getting Razood to come over, but he's ignoring my pings and texts. I think he saw the collection of swords the marshal of the Horten dueling club brought in. Make sure you catch the reverse angle in case I have to use it for the show rather than the documentary."

"Right," Irene said and called to her husband. "We're moving to Collectibles. You're on the reverse angle, so I'll slave your camera after mine are set."

The next appraisal was the tenth in a row for one of two SciFi franchises that were active from the late twentieth century up to the date of the Stryx opening Earth. Irene wondered what was supposed to be so interesting, and then she spotted M793qK leaning against the next table over which was dedicated to antique medical instruments. His multi-faceted eyes were fixed on the middle-aged man who was next in line for memorabilia. Irene wondered if the doctor was concerned about the helmet the man was wearing, which had some dangling tubes going directly to the area of the mouth that looked like they should be connected to life support.

"Nice helmet," Geoffrey complimented the man. "It looks like the ones I describe in my first series."

The man put the box on the table, removed the mouthpiece from the faceplate, and said, "My mom made it for me when I was a teenager because I was too embarrassed to go cosplaying with her at cons with my face showing. She passed away last year, and I inherited the collection from her. When I found out you'd be working at the Union Station *Antiques Tunnelshow,* I took it as a sign that she wanted me to bring it all to show you."

"An advertisement for the *Antiques Tunnelshow* listed my name? It was just last week that I agreed to appear as a SciFi and Fantasy memorabilia specialist."

"I got a message through GenePost that I'd won the *Antiques Tunnelshow* lottery, with a free roundtrip ticket to Union Station and a room in the Empire Convention Center hotel. But I doubt I would have come if it hadn't included your name at the top. Mom was a huge fan of the *Galactic War College* series."

"It certainly turned out to be my most popular work," Geoffrey said. "I didn't know that GenePost had any connection to the *Antiques Tunnelshow*."

"I don't know if it does," the man said. "I only signed up and had my blood sample taken a few weeks ago, but since then I've found that it's a great way to get messages to my kids who left Earth. Mom would laugh at me because she was into that whole Aquarius and Free Love movement where all of humanity is brothers and sisters, and it was considered selfish to insist on a special relationship with your children."

"I remember them. A sort of late twenty-first-century hippie revival. I lived for a summer in one of their communes on the coast before I joined the mercenaries. Nice people, most of them, but almost too laid-back for me." Geoffrey sorted through the memorabilia in the man's box as he spoke, checking the paperback novels and memory chip envelopes for inscriptions, and shaking his head at the various ticket stubs to talks he had given more than forty years earlier, and an old handheld gaming unit of the same type he'd had as a teen. Then he frowned at the tape holding the game's battery compartment closed, felt for the edge of the chair, and suddenly sat down.

Irene kept Harstang, the helmeted man, and Jorb all in the frame, and she noticed that M793qK had repositioned himself closer, and that his black medical bag was open.

"Do you know where she got this?" Geoffrey asked the man quietly.

"I'm not even sure it's part of the collection, but everything was in the same box."

"Would you mind taking off your helmet?"

"What?" the man asked. "Oh, I forgot I had it on." He pulled the helmet off, and Irene gasped as the old SciFi author turned white as a ghost.

"Your mother's name was Tranquility," Geoffrey said in a hollow voice, and tears began running down his wrinkled cheeks. "We were together for one summer, and then she stopped answering my texts and calls."

"Mom had a smartphone?" the man asked, squinting against the light now that he didn't have the frosted visor over his face. "Hey, you look kind of familiar."

"You look like me seventeen years ago. And I was eighteen when I met your mother."

# Twenty

"JB's Empire Café," Captain Pyun read from the large copper letters embedded in the plate glass. "That's got to be the fanciest sign I've seen on Flower."

"Razood insisted on doing the copper work after Forgath came up with the glass and Flower agreed to cut windows into the corridor," Bill said. "I was going to go with a hologram, but when I leased this space and had to do everything from scratch, the aliens from Harry's cafeteria started competing on who could contribute the most."

"You're the only café on the library corridor, and having the print-on-demand machine in the alcove spitting out books will bring people in. Lynx told me the publisher rented back the space the machine occupies so you'll have a little extra income every month."

"They used to run a whole publishing operation out of this space, but they were acquired by the Galactic Free Press and moved their editorial operations to Union Station the same week that Flower Entertainment handed the *Antiques Tunnelshow* over to the Grenouthian network. I committed to adding paper and toner to the machine when the alarm sounds, but the rest of the maintenance for the printer is outsourced, plus I get ten percent of every sale."

"From an empty space to a café in just thirty days," the captain said. "You've come a long way since we first met at *The Spoon* seven years ago."

"We didn't meet at *The Spoon,*" Bill said. "You bought me a meal there after you found me going through the food court's recycling bins looking for food."

"Captain, Bill," Brynlan greeted them as he shuffled up to where they were standing outside the café. "I hope the reason there's nobody else here is because I'm early."

"The grand opening isn't for another ten minutes," Bill said. "Julie is waiting for the last minute to bring Basil so he doesn't get cranky too soon."

"Lynx and Em are in the library," Woojin told the Verlock. "I think most of your colleagues are in there as well looking for old books about Earth's military that they can use as filler for intelligence reports about humans when things are slow."

"I won an honorable mention at our last Espionage Awards Dinner for my analysis of the Great Wall of China and why it ultimately failed," Brynlan told them as a pair of aliens emerged from the library. "I'm currently working on a mathematical model for the rise and fall of the Roman Empire in my spare time for my own enjoyment."

"Look what we found in the discard pile," Jorb said, displaying a leather-bound book in a language Bill didn't recognize. "Rinka is going to take it on the *Antiques Tunnelshow* if we ever end up somewhere it's shooting. I bet it's worth a fortune."

"We're going to preserve it, not sell it," Rinka said sternly. "I can't imagine how Humans could be so careless of an original book of Gregorian chants that must be twelve hundred years old. It's written in neumes, which are the foundation of your modern staff system for musical notation."

"I've been waiting to see the two of you together to ask if the name of the café is okay with you guys," Bill said to the Drazens. "Razood designed the sign so I can take out the 'Empire' when the time comes and you open the Singing Dojo across from us."

"That's so sweet of you to remember our second-level compatibility test. But you know, even a Stryx librarian can't predict the future at that level of granularity, with the names of grandchildren and businesses that don't exist yet. You shouldn't let the experience conscribe your actions."

"Except for us being happily married," Jorb said, trying to entwine her tentacle with his own. "I'm sure the station librarian got that part right. And you did agree that Borl was a good name for a son."

"Stop that!" Rinka said, jerking her tentacle away as the Drazen version of a blush turned her skin two shades darker. "Julie and Basil just exited the lift tube. Try to behave yourself."

The Grenouthian director came out of the library as Julie approached, herding three floating immersive cameras which he positioned around the entrance to the café with a casual wave of his paw. Harry and his wife followed, Irene carrying an antique device with one hand while trying to read an old booklet at the same time. She was intercepted by M793qK who emerged from his clinic two doors down and offered her a flat cartridge.

"Will it work?" Irene asked. "It all seems so complicated."

"Less complicated than unrolling film from a camera and mailing it across the globe to be developed and printed," the Farling doctor told her. "It's amazing that Humans went to the trouble of inventing photography when they could have waited a century or so and gone to charge-coupled devices to do everything digitally without the mess."

"The book says the prints will take around sixty seconds to develop after I expose them to air, and then I have to treat them with a chemical to fix the image."

"I used my own recipe, so that won't be necessary," M793qK said. "The emulsion also self-regulates the light exposure, so you don't have to worry about the missing flash attachment."

"Your instant film cartridge won't focus for me?" Irene asked playfully. She handed the booklet to Harry, unfolded the camera, and inserted the cartridge. Then she sighted the café entrance through the viewfinder and said, "I miss having a screen to see what I'm shooting."

The rest of the aliens from Harry's cafeteria came out of the library with Lynx and Em, the latter carrying a stack of books and bringing up the rear. Julie arrived, handed Basil to Bill, and then strung caution tape across the doorway.

"Just Married?" Lynx asked. "Was the store out of ribbon?"

"This is left over from Vivian's honeymoon suite," Julie explained. "Rinka and I were her escorts, and I couldn't just throw it out."

"Here comes the imperial family," Avisia said. "If you invited any other Humans, they're going to be late."

"Jake is already inside watching the stove for me, and Fandaz came early to make a big samovar of Frunge tea," Bill said. "I didn't want to start inviting everybody I know from Flower's Paradise, or I wouldn't have known where to stop."

"I can't believe Vivian wore the dress," Julie whispered to Bill in delight. "I thought she'd chicken out."

"What's that sparkly thing in Rose's hair?"

"A tiara. All the cool three-year-old princesses have one."

"Congratulations," Samuel said to Bill and Julie. "If you ever have leftovers you're trying to get rid of, bring them by Human Empire headquarters. Our co-op students are like a swarm of hungry locusts."

"Do you have the scissors?" Vivian asked Julie.

"I thought you had a special pair for openings," Julie said.

"The Grenouthians loaned those to me. Oh, here they come."

A four-armed bot floated above the little knot of aliens and humans, rather than going around, and handed Julie a modest-sized pair of silver scissors.

"They're white gold," Flower explained through the bot's speaker grille. "Dollnicks prefer it to the yellow."

"Twenty-thousand years ago, maybe," Lume said from where he was standing in the back. "You're showing your age."

Vivian checked that Rose was able to support the scissors by herself, and then guided the three-year-old through cutting the "Just Married" caution tape. Everybody cheered, Irene snapped a picture, and then Flower's hovering bot reclaimed the scissors before Rose could run with them.

"Everything is on the house today, and I don't want to hear any arguments about it," Bill announced. "I have a bean soup going on the stove for non-grain eaters, and I'll be bringing out a half-hot, half-salty pizza in about fifteen minutes. Dipping bowls for re-washing vegetables at the table are available on request."

"Can an old captain get a donut and a cup of coffee?" Woojin asked as he entered the café.

"Coming right up. And what will our future captain be ordering?"

"Coffee and a donut sounds good," Em said at the exact same time as her mother.

"The distant future captain will have decaf," Lynx added.

The aliens rushed for the all-species seating section before placing their orders, and Lume claimed the antique barber's chair that he had purchased for Bill. He used the chrome foot pedal to pump it up to a reasonable height and then sat down with his knees parallel to the floor rather than humped up like they would be with a normal human chair. "This is living," he declared. "A Dollnick could polish off a whole brandy-soaked fruitcake in a chair like this, though only on a special occasion."

The Grenouthian director motioned his cameras into a parking position out of the way and claimed the oversized beanbag chair for his own, while Yaem and Avisia each took a standard-looking straight-backed chair from a lot of eight Bill had purchased at the flea market for a discount because the matching table was missing. The Horten gave the stainless-steel and glass fiber chair he chose a quick dusting with a handkerchief before sitting and then turned a shade of light purple when he noticed the other aliens looking at him in askance. "Old habits die hard," Forgath said.

Nobody competed with Brynlan for the boulder he picked as his seat, and then Jorb and Razood whisked the cloth off the table next to the barber's chair and demonstrated how the steel tabletop could be tilted to create a Farling leaner.

"You shouldn't have," M793qK rubbed out on his speaking legs as he tested the weight-bearing capacity. "I could almost believe it was engineered for me."

"It was a one-horsepower table saw from the early twentieth century," Razood explained. "I removed the electric motor, which still works, and hit the table with some Sharf Protect to keep it from rusting."

"I shall try to imagine a circular saw bisecting the underside of my carapace whenever I lean against it."

Julie approached with a large tray and began handing out cups of tea. "Fandaz sent these over," she said, consulting the little pictograms drawn on the mugs to correspond with each recipient. "She said she knows how you all like your tea."

"With bourbon," Lume said, and sniffed the mug she gave him. "Yup."

When Julie got to the Farling, she hesitated, and then said, "I don't want to spoil the mood, but there's something that's been bothering me, and Bill said I should ask."

"Are you late?" M793qK asked and shifted his gaze to her abdomen. "I'm not sensing any pregnancy hormones in the air."

"It's too soon. I'm just starting to wean Basil."

"What Humans don't know about their biology I could write a library on."

"It's about Geoffrey Harstang," Julie pushed ahead, knowing that if she let the Farling physician distract her with non sequiturs she'd never get to the question. "I know that the Grenouthian director wanted a big finish for the last episode of the *Antiques Tunnelshow* we produced, but ambushing an old man with his grown son who already has grandchildren? You could have given him a heart attack."

"I was right there to take care of any medical emergencies, and there's no right way to introduce a man to the retired son he never knew he had," M793qK responded mildly. "I only learned of Jeff's existence a few weeks ago while I was calibrating the GenePost DNA sequencers and ran a few recent samples against the database to make sure everything was working properly."

"I'll bet you never forgot a DNA sequence you saw in your life," Avisia said as she raised her cup for another sip.

"You'd lose that bet. My life has been very long and full of genetic detective work."

"But there had to be a better way of doing it than on camera," Julie protested.

"I don't agree," M793qK said. "The knowledge that they had an audience might have prevented them from reacting badly if they had reasons for not wanting to see each other. Remember, I had no way of knowing that Harstang was unaware of his son's existence. He might have buried the knowledge in his subconscious."

"But you manipulated the son—"

"I sent him free tickets and an invitation to attend the *Antiques Tunnelshow* with Geoffrey Harstang's name prominently displayed. How could I know that the mother collected memorabilia from the lover of her youth? I included Harstang's name to warn off the son in case there was bad blood."

Julie had the feeling that the Farling was leaving something out, but she needed to check on the other guests, so she let it go. As soon as she was out of hearing, Avisia began rubbing her index fingers together in an imitation of speaking legs, and in a fair imitation of M793qK's speech pendant, said, "How could I know that the mother collected memorabilia from her old lover?"

"I'm curious about that myself," the Grenouthian director said. "Had she made recent purchases?"

"I treated a data vendor from the Free Republic back when I was on Union Station, and in lieu of a fee, he bartered me a pack of data chips that he claimed included all the personal information and transactions ever saved to Earth's cloud as of that year. You know how bad the Humans are at data security. I identified the son's mother, ran her against the data, and she began buying Harstang memorabilia through online auctions soon after the boy was born. I suspect she intended to tell him but kept procrastinating until it was too late."

On the other side of the café, Vivian asked Julie, "What were you arguing about with M793qK?"

"The ethics of using Geoffrey Harstang's reunion with the son he didn't know he had for a big finish to the show," Julie said. "What are the two of you playing?"

"I cutting Basil's hair," Rose said, patting the boy's head with both hands because she didn't quite have the coordination to make snipping motions with her fingers.

"Smile," Irene said, and her camera's motor whined to life and spit out a picture. She handed it to Em, who had already watched the picture of the ribbon-cutting develop before her eyes, and thought it was the most miraculous technology she'd ever seen.

"It's doing it again," Em exclaimed, showing the print to her mother. "It's like fading in reverse."

"Fading in," Lynx told her. "Are you going to make instant photography your new hobby?"

"Maybe, unless you let me get an implant so I can take images of what I see and send them to Flower to save for me."

Irene moved on to where the aliens were all sitting and drinking their spiked tea and she took a picture of the grouping. She handed the developing print to M793qK and said, "I thought you might want to see how your coating worked."

"Perfectly, I'm sure," the Farling said, but he accepted the print and began waving it with one of his limbs.

"Sixty-second-picture us," Jorb said, getting up and going to stand between Razood and Avisia. "Bill can frame it and put it on the wall so that customers know important aliens come here."

"If that's the goal, you've got the camera pointed in the wrong direction," the Grenouthian director said as the motor came to life and spit out another picture. He got up and went to stand between Brynlan and Lume. "Action."

"How come I'm the only one in the picture with M793qK," Forgath complained. "The Humans who see these will all think that Hortens are weird."

"Is everybody having a good time?" Bill asked as he set a brandy-soaked fruitcake, still in the box, on the low table the aliens were loosely grouped around. "Rinka said she's going to sing Drazen café songs, but she had to go home to get her…" he trailed off in choking sounds.

"Don't try to pronounce it," Jorb told him. "Call it a mandolin, since that's the closest Human instrument."

"You look a little shell-shocked," Lume observed. "I'll bet you didn't think that Flower would ever let you go out on your own."

"She did come up with last-minute job offers the last two times I told her I wanted to open my own café," Bill said. "But I'm glad I waited because this way I opened without having to borrow any money. Jake agreed to work part-time if I need him, and Fandaz will loan me her employees who want extra hours if I get a surge of business just for being new. I'm the only full-time employee for now."

"You're not an employee," Avisia told him. "You're the owner."

A pair of Cayl hounds barreled into the café and skidded to a halt between the antique padded barstools with the brass bases that were currently unoccupied. Krey and Dewey followed, with the artificial person apologizing for being late.

"Everything was backed up at Farling Four," he explained. "We had a tunnel slot that would have gotten us here two hours ago, but a visiting delegation from Tyrel was there and G32FX ended up declaring a planet-wide vacation day for challenge races."

"That five-letter fool let himself get sucked into racing against gryphons?" M793qK rubbed out on his speaking legs. "Everybody knows they have hollow bones to cut down on their mass."

"He didn't race himself," Dewey said. "G32FX wouldn't let any Farlings with more than three letters in their names compete, claiming that the Tyrellians had been through a long tunnel trip and wouldn't be at their best."

"Clever beetle," Captain Pyun whispered to his wife. "M793qK chose well."

"The Cayl elements garrisoning the mixed-species areas of Farling Four send their regards," Krey told Samuel and Vivian. "And I was asked to bring you an invitation to attend the coronation of the new Tyrellian emperor."

"When is it?" Vivian asked.

"The exact time hasn't been set yet as the current empress is taking her time about leaving the eyrie, but the next gryphon in line, who headed the delegation visiting Farling Four, thought his mother would be ready to retire within a decade. She's been hinting at it for over a century."

"Does the dauphin emperor realize that the Human Empire only exists on paper?" Samuel asked.

"You have to stop thinking that way," Krey told him. "The proximal reason for your invitation is that the Tyrellians have started watching the *Antiques Tunnelshow,* and they saw Princess Rose cutting the ribbon on Union Station. The dauphin emperor was favorably impressed."

Dewey set a box on the counter, scratched both of the Cayl hounds behind the ears, and asked Jake if he could make a couple of pots of instant oatmeal.

"Sure, there's a whole sack that Bill must have bought for cookies," Jake said. "Should I add boiling water and let it sit a couple of minutes, or will the hounds prefer it dry?"

"Mix three or four cups with an equal amount of milk, but make the pots big, so they don't splash it all over the floor," Dewey said. "They had oatmeal with some of the Cayl hounds on Farling Four and Krey says they can't stop talking about it."

Two minutes later, Bill stepped around the happily slurping hounds and put a hand on Dewey's shoulder. "Why are you sitting at the counter alone?" he asked the artificial person.

"I was waiting for you to approach and ask me that," Dewey replied. He removed a wrapped package from his shoulder bag and offered it to Bill. "Belle asked me to bring you this for the café opening."

"Thanks. I've been wondering how she's doing on the Miklat and whether she's settled in and making friends."

"It's hard for Gem, maybe even harder than for artificial people given the universal bias against cloning, but I think she's doing well. "Aren't you going to open it?"

Bill carefully undid the ribbon, neatly removed the wrapping folded without tape as all the advanced species did it, and opened the box to reveal what looked like an over-engineered vegetable peeler made from the finest steel.

"This is neat," he said. "But it's funny because I don't remember Belle being a big vegetable fan."

"She likes almost everything she can digest after being brought up on the Gem's factory nutrition drink, but it's not a vegetable peeler. It's a chocolate shaver."

"Ah, that makes more sense."

"And this," Dewey said, producing something short and heavy wrapped in a silk handkerchief, "is from G32FX. You can give it to Jorb or Captain Pyun, either of them will know what to do with it."

Bill unwrapped the handkerchief. "It looks like a used railroad spike."

"That, and a stolen Drazen historical artifact recovered from a human thief who fled to Farling space. It's better for everyone to deal with these interspecies issues on an informal basis." The artificial person slid off the stool, navigated past the hounds, and went over to where the big aliens were still sitting on their custom chairs, though Razood, Avisia, Jorb, and Forgath had all moved over to join the humans for Rinka's performance. Krey had taken the Horten's seat and was nursing a large mug of the tea Fandaz had prepared.

"So, is this going to be the new hotspot?" Dewey asked.

"It's close to the library, my clinic, and Human Empire headquarters," M793qK rubbed out on his speaking legs. "I think it was a better choice than the food court, but it took a bit of doing."

Dewey nodded. "The plate glass windows on the corridor surprised me. I know how sensitive Flower can be about making structural changes."

"I was talking about getting the print-on-demand publishers to move on," the Farling doctor said. "In the end, I had to buy the machine from them and call in a favor with the Galactic Free Press."

"You called in a favor with them?" Lume demanded. "Chastity doubled up on us. I made the same deal for Flower."

Brynlan let out a rumbling laugh and the Grenouthian director drummed his belly in mirth.

"It's not funny," Flower joined in through an overhead speaker. "I had to commit to double my advertising budget."

"Do you make money as a result of the ads?" Krey asked.

"That's not the point."

"It looks like the Humans are making progress even without our pushing," M793qK observed. "Now, if we can just get Samuel to..."

From the Author

The next EarthCent book will be the seventh entry in the EarthCent Auxiliaries series. If you're new to the EarthCent books, you can start back at the beginning with **Union Station 1, 2, 3**, a discounted three-book bundle.

I also post new releases to facebook.com/E.M.Foner/ and respond to all temperate e-mail sent to e_foner@yahoo.com

Readers have asked me to include the complete timeline of the EarthCent Universe in order so here it is:

Destiny: Union Station
Date Night on Union Station
Alien Night on Union Station
High Priest on Union Station
Spy Night on Union Station
Carnival on Union Station
Wanderers on Union Station
Vacation on Union Station
Guest Night on Union Station
Word Night on Union Station
Party Night on Union Station
Review Night on Union Station
Family Night on Union Station
Book Night on Union Station
LARP Night on Union Station
Career Night on Union Station
Last Night on Union Station
Independent Living
Soup Night on Union Station
Assisted Living

Freelance on the Galactic Tunnel Network
Con Living
Empire Night on Union Station
Space Living
Traders on the Galactic Tunnel Network
Orphans on the Galactic Tunnel Network
Swap Night on Union Station
Slow Living
Artists on the Galactic Tunnel Network
History Night on Union Station
Bits of Anarchy
Double Living
Bits of Flower
Synergy on the Galactic Tunnel Network
Substitutes on Union Station
Bits of Catalyst
Elder Living
Royals on the Galactic Tunnel Network
Deal Night on Union Station
Intellectual Property
Bits of Business

Made in United States
Orlando, FL
03 June 2025